The Sin City Bounty

Markus Matthews

Tellwell Talent
www.tellwell.ca

ISBN
978-0-2288-4867-7 (Hardcover)
978-0-2288-4866-0 (Paperback)
978-0-2288-4868-4 (eBook)

To John, who I first met at a 7-Eleven in the
wee hours of the morning playing video games,
and we've been friends ever since...

Author's note – As the Rose assassin in the story is a shapechanger, I decided to use 'they' as the pronoun.

To John, who I first met at a 7-Eleven in the
wee hours of the morning playing video games,
and we've been friends ever since…

Author's note – As the Rose assassin in the story is a shapechanger, I decided to use 'they' as the pronoun.

Chapter 1

Tuesday, June 19

The sight of the black suit of armor in the mirror brought a smile to my face. I looked pretty badass in it. My monochrome appearance, other than the gold visor and the gold *H.H.* logo on chest of the armor, was intimidating as hell.

I glanced at the mirror and in my best RoboCop voice, I couldn't resist saying, "Your move, creep!"

I felt powerful in the full body armor and it was reassuring to know that I was bullet, claw, and fang resistant. My neck tingled at the thought of fangs, as if reminding me why I got this suit in the first place.

Less than a month ago, a rogue vampire's fangs had torn out a good chunk of my neck in what should have been a mortal wound. If it weren't for my teammates' quick actions, I wouldn't be standing here today.

Stella in her monstrous Hyde form had pulled the vampire off me. Olivia used her vampire speed to get to me and apply pressure to the wound while simultaneously pouring her own blood down my throat to aid in my healing. Blue's shadow travelling ability had transported me from that alley to Marion's apartment in less than a minute. Marion had used every ounce of her healing gift to save me. Even then I still needed a couple of pints of human blood to replace what I'd lost in the attack in order to survive. I'd been lucky that one stupid mistake on my part hadn't cost me my life.

Sharing Liv's blood had side effects. I was now marked as her property to other vampires. I'd also gained a newfound appreciation for designer shoes. That second one might just have been my paranoia kicking in, though.

The day after that attack, my teammates authorized the purchase of this armor.

I moved my arms and legs around, still getting used to the feeling of being encased in armor. The light weight of the armor and my mobility within it was impressive. This was one of the reasons Grundy's was the premier supplier of monster hunting gear to heroes and law enforcement.

The only downside to the armor was it was warm. Sweat was already starting to pour off me even though I was inside my air-conditioned house. Grundy's made a powered version of this suit which had climate control, power assisted servos that increased the speed and strength of the wearer, and several other wonderful features, but that had been way out of our price range. This suit was over a hundred grand; the powered version added another zero to the number.

The only powered feature in the suit was the bulletproof visor. It had GPS, night vision, doubled as a smartphone, and had a camera in the back, which showed me whatever was behind me via a mini display within the helmet. It also worked as a communicator. The suit also had a Taser internally mounted in each arm. They weren't for offense but instead could be used to recharge my Air and Electricity powers. I popped the hatch on my left forearm and looked longingly at that red button that would activate the Taser. It was tempting to test it, but I'd been warned that to get replacement cartridges I'd need to fill out an incident report, which Grundy's would then submit to the RCMP–Canada's federal law enforcement agency. This restriction was due to my retired hero status, which only allowed me to buy defensive gear. Tasers were classed as offensive weapons and the incident report was the compromise Grundy's had worked out so I could get the Tasers in the suit.

The restriction on the Tasers was probably a good thing. It would be my luck that I'd develop an addiction to them. A dark vision of me months from now appeared in my head; I was in a back alley giving hand jobs or worse to support my dozen-Taser-a-day habit. I shuddered and hastily closed the hatch.

When the armor was delivered that morning, I was happy that I had the house to myself, so I could surprise my teammates. Blue and Stella were at our secret lab in London, working on a mysterious project. Liv, Bree, and Alteea were sleeping. Well, Bree and Alteea were sleeping. Liv, my sunlight-sensitive teammate, was in a death-trance until the sun came up.

I kicked around the idea of waking up Bree to show her the armor but decided that was a bad idea. She'd be annoyed that I disturbed her beauty sleep. Also, her being a Werepanther, food would be the only thing she would care about once she woke up.

I popped the faceplate and enjoyed the cool air. I headed back downstairs to put away the armor for now.

I'd just removed my helmet when I heard Stella and Blue's voices in the living room. I grinned and reconnected the helmet and went to greet my teammates. We entered the kitchen at the same time. Stella's eyes went wide and a moment later she transformed from her harmless ten-year-old-looking human form into her monstrous Hyde form. Blue's purple eyes locked on to me a moment later, and her tail went straight down in alert. Before I could blink, Blue drew her sword and ignited it.

Oh shit! My teammates didn't know it was me in the black armor.

"Stella! Blue! It's me!" I cried as I fumbled for the faceplate release on the helmet while they both charged towards me.

Blue was closing on my right, but Stella was just behind her on my left. I hit the button for the faceplate and frantically pulled it back as Blue swung her Keetiyatomi blade at my head. Blue jerked the sword to a halt less than two inches from my neck. I could feel the heat of the flames on the right side of my face before she extinguished it. Stella grunted as she pulled back to swing at me and then her bulbous right eye widened in recognition. She lowered the fist that would have turned me into paste.

I breathed a sigh of relief. I'd also been a spilt second away from my bladder testing how watertight the suit was.

In the blink of an eye, the Hyde creature transformed back into Stella's normal human form.

She glared at me and said, "For someone with years of experience with Enhanceds, you can do some bloody foolish things at times!"

In hindsight, surprising an alien warrior who had almost instantaneous reflexes and a girl who could instantly transform into a raging monster probably wasn't the best plan. My excitement about my new armor had overridden my common sense. I lowered my eyes in embarrassment and nodded my head.

"Your armor came in," said Blue with an excited glee in her purple eyes. "We shall have to test it in some training exercises. Get you used to moving and fighting while being more confined by it. We'll also test its durability with Olivia's sword, and my 9mm pistol can test how bulletproof it is too!"

I groaned at the thought of doing one of Blue's forced marches in this portable furnace I was wearing. There was also no way I was letting Liv hack away at me or Blue shoot at me.

Blue's tail was swishing happily behind her as she was probably excited to use me for target practice. I was about to tell her that the sword and gun thing weren't happening when Stella spoke.

"Never mind that. We have more important things to deal with. I just got a text that the Rose killed a judge in Chicago less than ten minutes ago."

I instantly perked up at that. The Rose was a shapechanging assassin who had been on the UN bounty list for over a decade. The bounty was currently set at $5 million US. The Rose had been a pet project of Stella's since we all started working together. Stella felt that we were ideally suited to take the Rose down due to Blue's shadow-traveling abilities and my ability to see auras around Enhanced Individuals. Blue could take us anywhere in the world in seconds via the shadows. My ability should allow me to spot the Rose no matter what form they were in. I didn't know exactly what the Rose's aura would look like but as Enhanced Individuals were rare, chances were if I spotted an unknown aura it would be the Rose.

Stella had set up programs that searched the web nonstop for any mention of the Rose in the hopes that we could get a shot at them.

Stella continued, "Law enforcement are locking down the courthouse, but I'm guessing the Rose had a plan for that and probably will manage to get out of the building if they haven't already. I think our best bet is to send you to the courthouse or near it and have you fly in concentric circles around it to see if you can spot the Rose."

I nodded. "I guess I get to field test this armor sooner than I expected. Blue, open a portal." Blue opened a portal and then stepped back, which confused me. "You two aren't coming?"

Blue shook her head, "No. It would be more efficient for us to remain here. I will monitor the courthouse from the shadows and search for the Rose. I'll also use the shadows to eavesdrop on the law enforcement on scene in case they have a lead on where the Rose went. Call us and keep a channel open. If you spot the Rose, we will use a nearby shadow to join you."

Since neither of them could fly, Blue was right that I would be able to cover more ground without them. I couldn't fault their plan.

I was about to step into the shadows when Blue added, "I'm putting you on the roof of the U.S. Postal Service. There is a taller building beside it, so a part of the roof is shaded. As soon as you step out, the building directly in front of you will be the courthouse."

I lowered my faceplate and stepped through.

Chapter 2

Tuesday, June 19

The courthouse building was right in front of me like Blue had promised. It was a huge building and so were all the buildings around us. I'd never been to Chicago before and was stunned at the sheer size and scale of the city. As far as the eye could see there were buildings and urban sprawl. My excitement about catching the Rose instantly diminished; finding them in an area like this would be a challenge. It almost felt like I was playing a lottery—I didn't have much chance of winning, but if I did, there was a five-million-dollar jackpot.

Wailing sirens that approached the courthouse from every direction pulled my attention back to the job at hand. I called on my powers and launched myself into the air. I was pleased that the armor didn't hamper my ability to fly. I did a slow lap around the building, searching for an aura that I didn't recognize.

Two SUVs with flashing lights in their grilles screeched to a stop in front of courthouse and six heavily armed people got out. The tactical gear they wore had *FBI* in bright white letters on the front and back. Two of the agents had auras. The first agent, a woman, had an aura that was a large section of blue with a smaller section of brown and two small slices of red and yellow. The colors meant she was a mage with Ice and Water as her primary spellcasting ability and Earth as a secondary. The other agent's aura was purple with a brown and silver outline, which meant Werewolf. They rushed into the building.

I remembered that I was supposed to call Blue and Stella and hoped Blue was now wearing her goggles.

I activated my visor and opened a channel to Blue.

A moment later, an unexpected voice asked, *"Did you find anything?"*

"Stella?"

"Yes, I'm wearing Blue's goggles so she can focus on searching the shadows."

"Oh, okay. I was just opening a connection so we can stay in touch. I'm doing my first flight around the building but haven't seen anything yet."

"Roger, keep us informed."

There were more police and FBI vehicles around back of the building but no auras around anyone. As I completed my lap, I debated what to do. The buildings surrounding the courthouse were all massive, so I had two choices: fly higher than the buildings and start doing widening circles in hopes of spotting the Rose or keep between the buildings at my current height of about fifty feet up. If I went high enough to clear all the buildings, people below would be ant sized and I doubted I'd even be able to spot an aura from that far up. I decided to stay at this altitude.

I hovered over an intersection by the courthouse and tried to figure out which way to go. To the east, I could see the dark waters of Lake Michigan in the distance. I doubted the Rose would flee that way. I guess it was possible that they had a boat waiting to get away, but if I was the Rose, I'd want to get as far as away as fast as possible, which meant heading to the airport.

I used the Internet on the visor to bring up the locations of the nearest airports. Midway International Airport was southwest of my current position. O'Hare was northwest of here. Midway was closer but O'Hare was bigger. I argued with myself about which one the Rose would choose. I reasoned that O'Hare, being much busier, would make it harder for authorities to locate the Rose and went with O'Hare.

I headed north and passed the PNC bank building.

Holy crap this city is huge! I thought as I frantically searched for auras among the people below me.

I was also a tad disappointed. As Chicago was known as the 'Windy City' and as I was an Air elemental, it was a city I had on my bucket list to visit. Today, though, I must have caught it on an off day as it was dead still and muggy. I was starting to bake in this damn suit.

I turned west as I flew and kept searching. A few people below me were looking up at me and pointing and a couple of them were snapping pictures on their smartphones.

I wasn't exactly sure what the Rose's aura would look like, as I'd never come across a shapechanger before; well technically Weres were shapechangers but could only change between their human and animal forms. This shapechanger could take on the appearance of any humanoid form. I was leaning towards them being a member of either the Super class or the Beast class. If they were a Super, the aura would have an orange core and an unfamiliar combination of colors around the outside of it. If they were in the Beast class, like Weres who were also shapechangers, the core would be purple with an unknown combination of colors surrounding it.

As I continued doing loops around the blocks of the city between the courthouse and O'Hare, I kept getting traces of a warm fuzzy feeling, which meant there were other Air elementals nearby. I idly wondered if Chicago was called the Windy City for more than just natural wind. There might be an Air elemental clan living here.

With each passing minute, the Rose was potentially getting farther and farther away. I started questioning my deduction that O'Hare was the Rose's destination. They might have gone with Midway, figuring that the authorities would be focused more on O'Hare as the bigger of the two. Heck, the Rose might not even attempt to fly out of either of the Chicago airports and might just hop a bus or train to Milwaukee, St. Louis, Indianapolis, or Detroit and fly out from there instead. At those airports, the authorities wouldn't be nearly as alert as here.

"Stella, I'm not having much luck here. You guys find anything interesting at the courthouse?"

"No, the police and FBI have locked it down and they're searching floor by floor for the Rose but so far nothing. Blue's gone over everywhere accessible by shadows in the building twice and hasn't caught or seen anything that might be the Rose."

"Roger that. I'll keep searching, but this city is huge. I'm pretty sure you could hide the Goodyear blimp here and it would be hard to find…"

I'd barely finished speaking when I spotted a purple aura disappear into an alleyway in the distance. I rushed to get a better look. The owner of the purple aura lifted a sewer grate and started climbing down. I now could clearly see the small grey and brown outline around it, which meant it was a Wererat. I cursed to myself and continued searching.

A few minutes later, I was on the western edge of my search area and spotted not one but two orange auras up ahead. As I flew closer, my excitement grew, as both auras were combinations I hadn't seen before.

The closer one had a tan and pink checker pattern around it. The only time I'd seen pink in an aura was for an empath. I'd also only seen tan once before too; it had been one of the colors of Hexadecimal's aura. Hexadecimal was an Acolyte who could clone herself. I tried to puzzle out how the ability to sense emotions and cloning worked together and figured maybe this person could copy or experience someone's emotions. The aura belonged to a homeless guy who was slowly pushing a shopping cart. A homeless person was a decent disguise; most people didn't pay attention to them or avoided them, so it was a good way to stay under the radar. The problem was he was heading south, back towards the courthouse. Also, the aura didn't feel right to me for a shapechanger.

The second was a black and white checker pattern but every few seconds the colors reversed places. This felt more like a shapechanger's aura. Maybe the colors of the aura shifted the way the shapechanger did. The aura was also moving away from the courthouse. But the aura was around a Chicago policeman. If I fried him with lightning and this wasn't the Rose, I was in for a world of trouble. Being disguised as a police officer though would have let the Rose walk out of a locked down courthouse—no one would stop a police officer in pursuit of a suspect.

I flew past the police officer. I stopped and hovered about twenty feet up and in front of him and loudly said, "Rose, your days of murdering the helpless are over! Surrender or I will be forced to use lethal force!"

The officer and some of the crowd below stopped and looked up. Others in the crowd, kept walking, oblivious to anything due to their earbuds and their fixation on their phones. The officer glanced around as if in a panic which made me feel that I'd guessed right—this was the Rose. I started calling on my lightning powers when the Rose pushed a guy in a business suit talking on his Bluetooth earpiece out into traffic. The Rose then bolted and disappeared into the subway station on their left.

The businessman fell right in front of an oncoming bus. The bus driver slammed on her brakes, but it wouldn't be in time. With barely a thought, I switched to my Air power and hastily sent a huge blast of air under the helpless civilian. He shot into the air like a rocket and missed the top edge of the bus by just inches, screaming as he flew up.

I adjusted the air under me and flew upwards to intercept the helpless man. I caught him a few seconds later. The look of sheer terror he gave me had me concerned. It hit me that my new suit might be the reason for his fear. Well that, and the fact we were a hundred feet up being held up by nothing but air. Maybe I needed to rethink the color of my suit and change it to something that looked less intimidating than black. A big red and white Canadian flag or at least a brighter color might help.

"Relax," I said in a calm and hopefully reassuring tone. "I have you and you're going to be fine. Are you hurt?"

The man seemed to get a handle on his fear and shook his head in answer to my question.

A few moments later, we landed gently on the sidewalk just in front of the subway station the Rose had fled into. I kept a firm hand on the guy's arm to make sure he had his legs under him and asked, "Are you okay?"

"Yes-s-s," he said. "Thank you."

Satisfied that he was okay, I let my hand drop.

"Stella, use GPS to track my location," I said over the comm as I dashed into the subway station. "The Rose is disguised as a male police officer. Dark hair, six feet tall, lean build and looks to be in their late twenties or early thirties. They are on foot and just ran into the Division subway station. I'm in pursuit but they have a lead on me."

I ran down the stairs into the station. I approached a turnstile a few moments later and a heavier-set Transit Authority guard became alert as I headed right for him.

I hit a button on the side of my arm and a panel exposing my hero ID popped open. I held it up and said, "Hero business, did a cop just come through here?"

The guard nodded and said, "Yeah, he ran towards the blue line. Said something about a possible terrorist threat as he went by."

I used my Air power to leap over the barricade and thanked him as I flew past him. I stayed airborne and had just enough room between the ceiling and the mass of people below me, but it allowed me to travel quicker.

I came around a corner and spotted the Rose still in their police uniform pushing through the crowd about a hundred feet ahead. I closed on them rapidly, but at fifty feet away, the Rose glanced over their shoulder and spotted me. A look of concern flashed across their face, and they pulled something out of their pocket and tossed it back towards me.

Green, noxious-looking smoke emerged from the device about ten feet in front of me. The people around the gas collapsed instantly to the floor. Most of them went limp, but a few looked to be having seizures.

The gas instantly caused pandemonium within the crowd below. The mass of people panicked and fled. I worried that more people would be hurt by getting trampled, but there wasn't much I could do about that now. I also wanted to continue chasing the Rose, but I had no idea what that green gas was and needed to deal with it.

"Stella, the Rose is fleeing on foot towards the blue line platform. They are still dressed as the same police officer I described earlier. I'm breaking off pursuit to deal with a gas canister he tossed at me and into a crowd."

"*Roger,*" replied Blue.

I figured Blue must have taken her glasses back and that Stella was probably in her Hyde form now. I landed a few feet from the growing cloud of gas and started creating a small swirling vortex of wind. In seconds, the tiny funnel of wind I'd created started pulling in the green gas.

I spared a quick glance at the six people lying prone on the floor around me. The two that had been having seizures had gone still. I worried that was a bad sign but was relieved to see that all six people seemed to be breathing. The problem was I still didn't know what this gas was or what it did. It could just be a knockout gas and the two that had the seizures may have just had a reaction to it. Or it could be a poison gas or nerve agent and while all six were currently breathing, that might not be the case for long. Whatever the gas was, I couldn't risk any more of it getting loose in the subway and focused on keeping up the vortex.

The wind funnel was doing a great job sucking in all the gas, but the damn canister continued pumping more and more of it out into the air. The running and flying also had me short of breath, and I was sweating like a pig in this suit. I would have killed for a bottle of water at that moment. I made a mental note to add a water bladder with a tube to the inside the suit for next time.

After what seemed like forever but was probably less than a minute, the canister sputtered a couple of times and then stopped releasing gas. A few seconds after that, I had all the gas inside the vortex, but now I need to do something with it.

I used my Air power to extract a small amount of the gas from the swirling funnel. Once it was out, I sent a strong blast of air behind it to disperse it farther down the tunnel. I hoped by sending tiny amounts of the gas down the corridor that it would be diluted enough to be harmless. It was tricky maintaining the vortex and doing the dispersion at the same time. I did this again and again, but the effort was starting to take a toll on my powers.

I'd probably dispersed about half the gas when a voice yelled, "Police! Get on your knees and put your hands on your head or we will shoot!"

I activated the rear camera built into my helmet and spotted a full SWAT team pointing a crap load of automatic weapons at me. If this went south, I'd get to test how bulletproof this suit was. Even if it was fully bulletproof, the impacts from the shots would cause me to lose control of the vortex and the gas would be released.

I slowly moved my right arm out to expose my hero ID and said, "I'm a registered hero. The Rose tossed a gas canister into the crowd and this vortex I've created is the only thing that is stopping it from spreading. I'm trying to harmlessly disperse it, but I need another five minutes. After that, I will surrender, okay?"

There was a long pause and then the voice answered, "Continue what you are doing but no sudden moves!"

"Will do. Can you pull these civilians back and get them medical help?"

"Copy that."

The cop pointed at two other officers who shouldered their weapons and started running towards me. I noticed they kept to the outside edges of the tunnel so not to impair the other officers' line of fire on me.

I ignored them and continued dealing with the gas.

It was probably a bit longer than five minutes, but I got all the gas safely dispersed. The two officers had also gotten all six people back down the hall and hopefully they were all on their way to the hospital.

Once I was done with the gas, I said softly, *"Blue, I'm about to be arrested or taken into custody. Don't try and find me as you'll get caught up in this mess too. Zack out."*

I closed the channel before Blue could answer. I hoped they had luck finding the Rose.

I carefully got on my knees. I slowly brought my hands up and, after popping open the faceplate on the helmet, put them on my head.

The corridor echoed with the sounds of heavy, booted feet running towards me.

Moments later, I was surrounded by the entire SWAT team who were all still pointing weapons at me. They were more pissed once they got a closer look at my hero ID and saw that I was listed as retired/inactive and I confessed that I was here bounty hunting.

A few minutes later, I showed them how to remove the suit's gauntlets and helmet. Once they were off, they slapped a power blocking collar and spelled cuffs on me. I hated being cut off from my power, as it felt like losing one of my senses. They hauled me to my feet and the SWAT sergeant started reading me my rights.

I asked what I was being arrested for, and once he was done with the Miranda warning, he said, "Assaulting a police officer, accessory to murder of a federal judge, and committing a terrorist act."

Well shit! This day really wasn't turning out how I'd pictured it when I got up this morning.

Chapter 3

Tuesday, June 19

Eight long hours later, I hadn't made any friends with the Chicago PD or the FBI, but I was home. In my defense, they'd been total dicks to me. The Chicago police, after I was arrested, locked me in a stuffy interrogation room for over two hours before they even talked to me. So, when they eventually did come by, I told them to get bent and that I'd only talk to the FBI. As two of the three charges were federal crimes, and were the most serious of the three, it made sense to deal with the FBI directly.

The FBI agent assigned to me was a total hard-ass and was convinced I was working with the Rose. It was only once they retrieved my helmet and I played the recording I'd initiated while chasing the Rose that the agent reluctantly dropped the charges.

While I was being questioned by the FBI agent, a member of her team came by and said that the fingerprints on the letter opener used to the kill the judge belonged to the former president of the United States. That team member joked about issuing an arrest warrant for the ex-president and left. I probed about this and the agent shared that during the investigations of the two previous Rose murders, they'd found prints that belonged to the Pope and the current Queen of England respectively.

That information cost me. To get it, I had to share my secret about being able to see auras around Enhanced Individuals, as the agent had been curious about how I knew the police officer that I'd confronted was the Rose.

The series of illustrious fingerprints did explain why the Rose had a $5 million bounty on their head. To get those fingerprints, it meant the Rose had to have gotten close enough to shake their hands or make physical contact. If the Rose had gotten that close to three of the most protected people in the world, they could get to anyone.

Once the FBI was finished with me, I thought I was done and could leave. It turned out that ATF and ICE also wanted to have a chat with me. The ATF in the United States was responsible for reviewing superpowers and determining whether excessive force was used or not. I'd used my powers to fly, save the businessman, and to create the vortex I'd used to deal with the gas. They were satisfied that all three were well within reasonable limits and elected not to charge or fine me.

However, ICE wanted to charge me with illegally entering the country. This situation was a bit stickier. Heroes are exempt from the typical rules about crossing borders. The exemption had been long established, as in the past, villains and criminals used to flee across a border to escape and heroes were permitted to pursue them. My problem was that bounty hunters weren't exempt. I argued that as I saved the businessman from getting killed by a bus and used my powers to contain and disperse the gas safely that I was acting as a hero most of the time I was in Chicago. They countered with that I'd entered the country to pursue a bounty on the Rose. After a long debate, they issued me a warning and I was free to go.

The sun was down by the time I got home, which meant everyone was up. All I wanted was to have some dinner and beer, but both of those things were put on hold the moment my sensitive-nosed friends caught a whiff of me.

Bree's face bunched up and she gagged slightly. "Dude, you smell like a hockey bag."

An unpleasant expression appeared on Liv's face as she sipped her pint mug of blood. She used her free hand to pinch her nose closed.

Even Stella and Blue, who just had a normal sense of smell, looked uncomfortable as I stood there.

I rolled my eyes, thinking they were all messing with me. I then lowered my chin, took a sniff, and coughed.

Yeah, I was just a bit ripe at the moment.

I sighed and headed upstairs. I was starving but getting out of this damn armor did appeal. I took a quick shower and got changed. I filled the bathtub, added some dish soap to it, and dumped the entire suit of armor in. I was smart enough to remove the visor and rear camera in the helmet first. I was impressed that the helmet had been designed so that it was easy to pop them all out for cleaning.

Thirty minutes later, I finally got dinner. The whole team was gathered around the kitchen table with me. Stella and Blue had already eaten so they just had tea. Bree, our always hungry Werepanther, had eaten with them too, but elected to have dinner again with me. Liv sat there sipping on another pint mug of blood. She had poured a small amount into a shot glass for our pixie companion, Alteea.

Between bites of burger, I updated the team on what had happened.

Stella said, "Sorry we had no luck catching the Rose. We used the shadows to portal to one of the subway platforms and then split up to look for the Rose in their police disguise but didn't have any luck. I don't understand how we missed them. We were there only seconds after you called about the gas."

I swallowed and said, "I forgot to mention, the FBI agent shared that the Chicago PD found a male commuter knocked out and stripped to his underwear in one of the subway restrooms. There was a police uniform stuffed into the trash in that same bathroom. They think the Rose knocked the guy out and then took his clothes and used his appearance to escape."

"That would explain why we did not spot the false police officer in our search," said Blue.

Bree paused eating and said, "You guys should have woken me to help."

Stella shrugged. "I thought about it but assumed that the three of us would be more than enough to deal with the Rose if Zack spotted them. When he broke off pursuit to deal with the gas, I felt it was more important to get to the platforms quickly than to lose the time getting you out of bed."

I couldn't fault Stella's reasoning. Shapechangers aren't much stronger than normal humans and can't duplicate powers. Stella in her Hyde form would be more than a match for them, same with Blue or me.

Liv piped up and said, "It sucks that you were that close to scoring $5 million..."

I finished a fry and said, "Yeah, instead of nailing the Rose, I got to sweat my ass off and annoy local and federal authorities in what turned out to be a total waste of a day."

Blue shook her head. "I do not consider the day a waste. You spotted the Rose and now know their aura pattern, so if we do get another shot at them, they will be easier for you spot. You also won't have to give a verbal warning to confirm their identity like you did today. You field-tested your new armor and found out its strengths and limitations. Any time you gain knowledge of your opponent or your equipment is a win."

There were nods around the table at that. I had to admit that Blue's comments did make me feel a bit better about our efforts today. Sure, we missed out on collecting the bounty but learning what the Rose's aura looked like was an important gain. Other than learning that the armor was uncomfortably hot, I wasn't sure how good that field test was. I will admit though that knowing I was bulletproof did make things less stressful when I had that whole SWAT team pointing way too many guns at me. I also found out I could easily use my powers while in the suit. I'd still have to test it to see how well my electrical power worked but flying and manipulating the air around me worked great, so lightning shouldn't be an issue.

I noticed Stella was deep in thought and asked what she was thinking about.

"I was pondering your suit. The heat issue is a problem. Your idea about adding a water bladder and a tube to help with dehydration is a good idea but really only fixes a symptom and not the problem."

"Yeah, earlier today I kicked around the idea of getting Grundy's to add small holes to the suit to let it breathe and hopefully lessen the heat, but I was concerned that might affect the integrity of the suit."

Stella shook her head, "The holes are a bad idea. The whole idea of the suit is to protect you, if you weaken that protection, it undermines the entire purpose. No, I was thinking about designs for a thin, battery-powered cooling system. I can probably create something that only weighs a few pounds but should drop the temperate in the suit by a fair amount."

Stella wasn't a Mad Scientist, but she did invent some useful things. The water cannon she created for Liv was pivotal in dealing with the demon we'd battled during our first case together. The tracker she designed when Bree was kidnapped by the Acolytes let us find their hideout and take them down. The new modular training building she and Blue had created last month was much better than our old training stuff. I had to admit I was excited at the idea of her figuring out a cooling system for the suit. A little extra weight for cooling was a trade-off I'd be happy to make. "That would be awesome. How long would the batteries last?"

Stella was about to answer when Blue cut her off, "While lessening the heat in your new armor is a worthy goal, maybe you and Stella can discuss that later between yourselves. I think now we should review how we dealt with the Rose and what we can do better next time."

We spent a good hour going over everything and refining what we'd do next time. By the end of it, I was feeling pretty good about our chances of taking down the Rose if we got another shot at them. My main concern was whether we would get a second chance at the Rose. Most times when they struck, the victim was discovered hours later, and they were long gone by then. Today was the exception to that and I doubted we'd get that lucky again soon. I brought up my concerns with the team.

"I have been monitoring hit contracts on the dark web," said Stella.

During her pause, I couldn't resist making a shot, "Liv's annoying but I doubt anyone is going to put another contract on her."

Olivia was sipping her pint of blood and rolled her eyes at my comment. Bree snickered and the rest of the table grinned.

Stella shook her head. "Not that. When I brought up the Rose while we were picking our first bounty case, you turned it down at the time as you felt it was too ambitious."

Bree laughed and said, "Yeah, thankfully we went with an easy one like a full-blown demon instead."

There had been nothing easy about that demon. In hindsight, the Rose probably would have been the better bounty to pursue.

"As I was saying, at the time I asked you how you would go about chasing the Rose. Your first suggestion was an alert system that monitored social media, news sites, and the rest of the Internet for any mention of the Rose. Hopefully, we'd get an alert as we did today and could shadow portal out immediately and try and catch them. Your other suggestion was to watch for large hit contracts and then observe the target and hope to catch the Rose in the act. I have been checking for the right contract since then…"

"Are there any that look promising?" I asked.

Stella's excited expression fell, "Not at this moment. The point is, if one does show up, I think we should shadow the victim and hope that the Rose shows up."

I scratched my chin and thought about it. That probably was the best shot at nailing the Rose. That $5 million bounty was tempting.

The downside was that we'd have to drop whatever bounties we were working on at the time to shadow the victim full-time, and there was no guarantee either that the Rose would be the one to take the contract. On the other hand, a lot of the professional assassins were Enhanced so even if it wasn't the Rose, we might still walk into a bounty. The more I thought about it, the more I was in favor of the idea.

"Okay, should we vote on this?" I asked and got nods around the table.

The vote was short and sweet—everyone was in favor of giving this approach a shot. With that settled, that pretty much wrapped up our discussion on the Rose. I was beat and said, "I'm off to bed."

Blue shook her head. "No, it is still early enough that we can get in some training."

"Oh, c'mon. I'm wiped. I just spent the whole day sweating my ass off and you want to train?"

Blue's purple eyes focused on me and narrowed. "That's why you should be training now. The people and creatures we hunt won't care if you are exhausted. Also, if you were in better shape, today wouldn't have been as taxing for you."

The lecture continued and I groaned to myself, as I knew I wasn't getting out of this.

Five minutes later, I was strapping a fifty-pound pack to my back. Blue opened a portal and we stepped out into a dark, hot, and humid jungle. I used my Electrical power to zap the bugs that descended on me like someone had just rung a dinner bell. Blue began berating us as we started trudging down what could barely be called a trail.

I swear somedays it was just not worth getting out of bed.

Chapter 4

Sunday, July 28

When I woke up, I knew it was going to be another hot one. I could feel the heat and humidity even with air conditioning. Thankfully, it was Sunday, and we were between cases at the moment, so I planned on having a nice lazy day building model planes in the frosty-cool basement.

I got dressed and headed downstairs to grab some coffee and breakfast. I'd barely entered the kitchen when Stella said, "Great news! A hit contract was posted last night, and it fits the profile for one the Rose might take."

I realized my plan of wasting the day on model airplanes was going down faster than a B-17 with three engines shot out.

It had been five weeks since we'd missed our shot at the Rose in Chicago. We'd spent a good chunk of that time researching the Rose in more depth. While looking over the Rose's infamous ten-year career, Blue and Stella had noticed a pattern of sorts. The Rose never took another contract until at least a month had passed since their previous job. The longest time between jobs was eight weeks. That meant their next job could take place any time now.

"What are the details on the contract?" I asked while I started making myself a much-needed coffee.

"The contract is on a Max Schnell aka the 'Merchant of Death,' four million US, contract must be completed before this Friday at six in the evening Pacific time."

With a name like the 'Merchant of Death,' this Max guy sounded sweet—not. I wondered if letting the Rose finish the contract before we took them down would be doing the world a favor. On the other hand, it was also possible that the moniker was meant ironically like a big guy being called 'Tiny' as a nickname. I finished making my mug of caffeine and joined an excited Stella and Blue at the kitchen table.

"Who is Max Schnell and what did he do to gain such a pleasant nickname?" I asked.

"Max Schnell is the largest independent arms dealer in the US. If there is war or conflict going on in the world, one side or both sides are probably using weapons he provided."

Well that explained the nickname. "What do we know about Max and do we know where he is currently?"

"At this moment, he is staying in a Cloud Suite at the Aloha Resort and Casino in Las Vegas. There is an arms convention happening in town this week. He flew in last night."

Now I knew why Stella and Blue were excited. I'm sure part of it was us getting a chance to get the Rose, but both of them loved Las Vegas. I knew they'd stayed at several hotels in Vegas but couldn't remember if the Aloha was one and asked, "Have you and Blue stayed there before?"

Stella shook her head. "No. We've been sticking to the older hotels first. The Aloha only opened five years ago, so it is way down on our list, but we did do a quick walkthrough of it last time we were in Vegas. As you probably guessed, the Aloha is a Hawaiian themed resort. It has lovely bright tropical flowers throughout. The wonderful aromas of those plants are just amazing. The centerpiece of the hotel is a massive indoor waterfall which is surrounded by water jets and laser lights. That sounds garish, but when you see it, you'll be in awe of it, I promise."

An indoor waterfall was pretty cool, but I doubted I'd be in awe of it. On the other hand, Stella didn't impress easily, so I should probably reserve judgement.

I pushed my thoughts aside as Stella continued, "Max is forty-one, single, never married. Got an MBA from Stanford and worked on Wall Street with a large investment firm after leaving school. He stayed with the firm for three years until the 2008 financial crisis hit. He left and joined his uncle's import/export business, which was a front for arms smuggling. The uncle died in an arms deal gone wrong in the Middle East in May of 2010. Max took over the business and lifted it to a whole new level. He used shell and offshore companies to move weapons legally. Set up warehouses and distribution networks all over the world. Estimated net worth is hundreds of millions, possibly more."

I frowned and asked, "So this guy sells weapons that are used in conflicts all over the globe and it's all legal; how is that possible?"

Blue answered this one, "By using a long buyer/seller supply chain. For example, say rebels in Syria want American assault rifles. If you tried to ship from the US to Syria, the shipment would be intercepted by the US government due to an arms embargo they have on Syria. Max instead would ship the weapons to Ecuador, where they are bought by a shell company he owns there. From there, they would be shipped to Yemen as Ecuador also has an arms embargo on Syria. Once again, the weapons are purchased by another shell company Max owns there. It is still illegal to ship new weapons from Yemen to Syria. The rifles are all unpacked, fired once, and then cleaned. Once the rifles have been fired, they become classed as used. There are no restrictions in Yemen on selling used firearms. They are packaged up again and shipped to Syria."

Clever. He was using different countries' laws to get around any embargos or restrictions like large corporation use different countries' tax laws to get out of paying taxes. By keeping it legal, it probably also made the business more profitable, as he wouldn't have to worry about a shipment getting seized and confiscated like he would have to worry about if he were smuggling them illegally. He also wouldn't have to worry about the Feds kicking his front door in and arresting him either.

"The timeline on the hit seems very specific, any ideas on why it must be by Friday at six?" I asked.

Blue nodded. "I have been monitoring Max and his security team from the shadows. The Minister of Defense for Iraq is in town for the show and on Friday at six he will be accepting bids on a new arms deal to reequip police and military forces. The contract is said to be worth close to half a billion dollars."

I whistled at the amount. It looked like someone didn't want Max to bid. I had no idea how the arms industry worked but I doubted they worked on low margins. If the contract was worth half a billion, then the profit was probably in the range of $100 to $250 million for whoever won it. That was more than enough to cover the cost of the $4 million dollar contract.

Part of Blue's statement twigged another question for me, "You mentioned a security team. How well protected is he?"

"Max has eight full-time bodyguards around him. All of them seem to be ex-military or ex-law enforcement. The head guard is Kurt Schmidt and he's Max's right-hand man. They have rented nine suites on three adjacent floors. The rooms are all located directly at the end of the halls. On each floor they have rented two rooms on the right and one on the left."

I visualized the setup in my head and asked, "So Max is living in one protected by suites they have rented above, below, and beside it?"

That one made the most sense as the rooms above, below, before, and across from him would be empty, so he'd be protected on all sides.

Blue smiled and shook her head, "That's what you would think, but he is currently on one of the outside ones on the top floor. They have a body double living in the one you guessed. They have a guard posted at the end of each hall on all three floors."

Despite his nickname and occupation, a part of me admired Max. The security arrangements, just like the way he modernized his uncle's business, were clever. There was a good chance that his double would be the more likely target if anyone attacked them at the hotel. The problem was while Max and his team were good, the Rose was better. The Rose had taken down much higher profile and better protected targets than that in the last ten years. I suspected that Max's crafty security arrangements wouldn't stop them.

"Are you able to monitor Max and his double from the shadows at the same time?"

Blue rolled her purple eyes at this question. "Child's play."

I finished my mouthful of coffee and said, "Sorry, still waking up. Are any of the guards Enhanced?"

"I suspect Kurt is. The amount he ate for breakfast and the way he is always eating reminds me of Bree."

"So, you're thinking he's a Were?" Blue nodded and I continued, "The high-calorie diet probably means you're right but there are other Enhanceds that require lots of food so keep an eye on Kurt and see if there are any other clues to what he might be."

With that, I drained my coffee and got up to get another one.

As I was making a second coffee, Stella said, "I don't think our original plan of shadowing the target will work here…"

The plan we'd came up with for this scenario was to have Blue monitor the target from the shadows during the day with Stella. If the Rose struck during this period, Blue and Stella would pop out of the shadows and take them down. At night, Bree, Liv, Alteea and I would monitor the target's home from an adjacent building while Blue and Stella rested. I didn't see why that plan wouldn't work.

"…you've never been to Las Vegas, have you?"

I shook my head as I poured my coffee. "No, why?"

"The hotels are all massive. You really can't imagine the size of them. Due to that size, there is a good chance that if the Rose strikes, they will be able to get away. You were probably thinking that we could rent rooms on the same floor and hallway to monitor Max at night, right?"

That had been exactly what I was thinking. I nodded and Stella continued, "You could have a room on the same floor and hallway and still be more than 300 feet away. You also assume that the Rose will take the elevator up and walk by your door. They could just as easily use the staircase at the end of the hall by Max's room. If they did that, they could sneak in, kill Max, and be gone without us being any wiser. They could also kill a person in a closer room and take over that room during the day when we aren't monitoring the hallways."

I grabbed my coffee and joined them at the table again. "Both are possible. What do you suggest we do instead?"

By the way they both grinned I knew I wasn't going to like this…

Chapter 5

Sunday, July 28

At 11:30 p.m. that night, our whole team was geared up and ready to go. The sun had set in Las Vegas less than ten minutes before. I still wasn't a fan of Stella's and Blue's plan but agreed that it was our best shot at catching the Rose.

Liv drew her silver edge katana and looked at Blue for the signal. I was directly behind her and called on my powers to thicken the air in front of me in case this thing went sideways, and so I could produce showy-looking intimidating blue sparks around my hands. I was also in my armor and surprisingly cool thanks to Stella's cooling system version three. I was nervously sniffing the air for smoke but so far so good.

The first version of Stella's cooling system had worked, but it barely made a difference and only dropped the temperature inside my suit by a couple of degrees. Version two of the system worked well, as it dropped the temperature inside the suit by a huge amount. The problem was, not ten minutes after I turned it on, the batteries that powered the system caught fire. Thankfully, they were in the lower back area outside of the suit. Blue, moments after they caught fire, used her sword to cut the batteries away from me so no real harm was done, but the memory lingered. Stella refined her design and assured me that there would be no fire this time, but we'd only tested this version a few days ago. It had passed the tests with flying colors, but a part of me worried about the batteries catching fire again or worse—exploding.

Bree was right behind me in her standing Werepanther form, and Stella was in her massive Hyde form on Bree's heels. Alteea was at the back of the group.

Normally we'd go heavy formation with Stella's Hyde in the lead to soak up damage, but for tonight speed was key, hence why Stella was at the back of the group.

Blue opened a portal and said, "Go!" and Liv sped forward with her vampire speed and disappeared into the shadows. I charged through right after her and came out into Max's opulent suite in Las Vegas. Liv was already behind Kurt and had the sharp edge of her sword against his exposed neck. I used my powers to silence the air around the couch Max and Kurt were sitting on. Bree ran by and in seconds had her claws on Max's neck, pinning him in place. Stella lumbered by me and proceeded to block the double doored entrance to the suite. Blue and Alteea arrived next. Alteea had her glamor up, and I watched her aura circle around the room, investigating things.

I walked around the couch so I was in front of Max and Kurt, while Blue ignited her sword and moved beside Liv. I was briefly distracted by the spectacular view of the Las Vegas lights shimmering in the darkness through the floor-to-ceiling windows to my right that ran the length of the suite. I tore my gaze away and forced myself to focus on the job.

In less than five seconds, we had the room secured. "No one moves—" I spied Kurt's large Werewolf aura, and amended, "—or changes form, and nobody gets hurt."

Kurt's piercing blue eyes widened at my comment about changing. The slight glow in those same eyes faded, meaning his beast was being put back in its mental cage. Kurt's large, impressive frame didn't come as a surprise to me; he looked like an NFL linebacker in the prime of his career. He looked about thirty but by the notable seven-inch purple, brown, and silver aura around him, he was probably twice that age. Weres aged slowly thanks to their remarkable healing abilities. He was alert and gave off an aura of danger and menace. The way he ignored the silver blade against his neck and just focused on everything in the room was also a remarkable testament to his discipline. He was about what I'd expected from a professional bodyguard.

Max Schnell took me a bit off guard, though. The so-called Merchant of Death looked tiny compared to Kurt on the opposite end of the couch. He had short blonde hair with quite a bit of grey creeping in at the edges and blue eyes that peered out at me from behind wireframed glasses. He was average and unassuming. I wouldn't have given him a second glance if he passed me in public and probably would forget him almost instantly. The only thing that did jump out at me was the expensive-looking tailored suit and high-end Italian dress shoes he was wearing. I'd bet that his current outfit was worth more than my entire wardrobe combined, not counting this armor, of course.

Max's mouth opened and closed for a few moments, but no sound came out.

"I'm going to drop the barrier of silence I placed around you. Do not call out to the guards outside. They can't help you, and it will just lead to them getting hurt, understand?"

They both nodded, so I cut off my power, and the air around them returned to normal.

"I'm assuming you're here because of that $4 million contract that was posted last night?" asked Max in a defiant tone.

I smiled and said, "Yes, but not in the way you are expecting. We have no plans to hurt you or any of your men. We believe the Rose will be interested in your contract, and we wish to take them down."

Max blinked in surprise at that. "So, you're not here to kill me?" I shook my head and he continued, "Then you are here to protect me?"

"Indirectly. As I said, we are here to take down the Rose. We believe our best shot at that is by staying close to you."

He frowned at that and went silent for a bit as if considering my words.

He still had Bree's claws around his neck and Kurt still had a silver sword at his throat. "If I can get both your words that we can have a reasonable discussion about all of this, I will have my companions remove their claws and blades."

I got a "Yes" from Max and a "*Ja*" from Kurt and gave Liv and Bree a nod. Bree removed her hands from Max's neck and stepped back. Liv lifted her sword but kept it out and stayed standing with Blue behind the couch.

Kurt immediately turned his head towards Bree. His eyes glowed as his beast rose to the surface to challenge Bree. Bree growled softly and matched his gaze. These dominance contests between Weres used to freak me out, but after being around Bree and many other Weres over the past six months, I'd gotten used to them. Any time two Weres met for the first time, dominance had to be established. It wasn't much different than businesspeople shaking hands or dogs sniffing each other—it was protocol.

This one though, as the long silence dragged out, was starting to concern me a bit. After a good thirty seconds, Kurt finally lowered his gaze. Bree growled softly in muted triumph.

Max's voice pulled my attention back to him. "Since you're not here to kill me, please take a seat and let's discuss what you have in mind."

He gestured at the couch across from them. We'd made our point and I didn't expect either of them to do anything stupid—if we'd wanted them dead, they would be, and both knew it. I figured I might as well be comfortable. I sat down and popped the front visor on my helmet to expose my face. I used to be much more concerned about protecting my identity, but after our adventure with the Acolytes months ago, which caused my identity to be exposed in the national media, there wasn't much point in hiding it anymore. Even if Max didn't know who I was, and he probably didn't. The gold *H.H.* on my chest and two seconds of Google kung fu and he would find out that I was Zack Stevens, the former hero known as the Hamilton Hurricane.

I introduced myself and my team. Max was surprised when Alteea dropped her glamor, buzzed by him, and gave a playful wave. Kurt wasn't shocked at Alteea's sudden appearance. I had no doubt that his enhanced hearing and smell had long since detected her.

"I'm still not entirely sure at what you are proposing, Mr. Stevens," said Max.

"Please, call me Zack." He nodded and I continued, "We were originally going to watch you from the shadows or from a nearby room. Our goal is to take down the bounty on the Rose. Your bodyguards could impede us in doing that. If they interfered with us, that might give the Rose enough time to either complete their assassination or get away. We thought it best if we introduced ourselves so that your guards wouldn't attack us if we suddenly appeared and went after the Rose."

"I see. So, you aren't concerned about whether I live or die, just in capturing the Rose."

"Blunt, but accurate. We will try to stop the Rose before they strike, but our main goal is taking down the Rose."

Max rubbed his chin for a moment and said, "I'll give you $2 million in cash if you can keep me alive until Friday."

Liv gasped at that and blurted out, "Oh, that will buy so many pretty shoes!"

I rolled my eyes and sighed—*so much for us coming across as professionals.*

Kurt also turned his head sharply towards Max and was about to say something when Max held up a hand and cut him off, "Relax, my friend. I'm not questioning your ability to protect me. We knew this week would be tricky when that contract came out last night. These people will beef up our protection considerably with their abilities. That amount of money is going to bring out some powerful players. This is just extra insurance that we make it through the week."

Kurt nodded abruptly but stayed quiet.

$2 million was a nice chunk of change. However, accepting it changed our priorities considerably. Keeping Max alive would become goal number one and catching the Rose would fall to a distant second. This meant that we'd have to deal with everyone who wanted a shot at that contract and not just the Rose. On the other hand, we were just guessing that the Rose would go after Max, and if we were wrong, we'd not see a penny of bounty money. If we took Max's deal, we were guaranteed $2 million, if we kept him alive of course. There was also a chance at bonus bounty money if we took down any Enhanceds that pursued the contract.

The biggest problem I had with his offer was that we were bounty hunters, not bodyguards. Sure, in my Hurricane days, I'd protected civilians from villains and criminals during my encounters with them. We'd also indirectly acted as bodyguards for Liv when she had a contract on her from the French Vampire Court, but it wasn't what we specialized in.

It dawned on me that if we were just interested in the $2 million and didn't care about the Rose, this could be easy money. We could hide Max and Kurt in our secret lab in London until the meeting on Friday. Once Friday came, we could shadow portal them directly into the meeting room with the defense minister so they could submit their proposal and we'd be done.

I mentioned this to Max, and he said, "That would keep me alive, but it doesn't work for me. I have numerous meetings I must attend this week. This convention is by far my biggest week of the year. The bid at the end of the week is the largest of the deals, but the multitude of side deals actually will surpass that amount. A large part of being successful in this business is trust, reliability, and face time. If I cower away in some hideout, I might as well not be in business. My competitors will scoop up my clients, and I can't let that happen."

So much for that plan. I kicked around bringing the clients via shadow portals to Max, but if I was a shady arms buyer, there was no way I would go to a meeting at an unknown location. As I pondered whether we should take this job or not, Blue glared at me. It hit me that I was making this decision and that wasn't something I should be doing alone. I was the leader of this team during combat, but outside of that we were all equal partners, which meant I needed their input.

"Sorry, Max. I'll need input from my team before we accept or decline your offer."

"Of course, do you want to use one of the bedrooms to discuss this in private?"

I pondered that and said, "Not necessary. I just need a quick show of hands from my team." I looked around the room and said, "All in favor of taking Max's offer?"

Liv, Bree, and Blue all raised their hands. I turned to look at Stella and she shook her large, misshapen head at me. Alteea had her hand up too but she wasn't a voting partner. That made it three in favor and one opposed which took the decision out of my hands, as even if I sided with Stella, my vote would only make it three to two. I wondered why Stella was opposed and then realized that catching the Rose had become her mission. If we took Max's deal, the Rose came in second after keeping Max alive.

I also wondered why my other three teammates were so gung-ho on taking Max's offer. Liv and Blue were the most materialistic and mercenary of the group respectively. Their decision to go with the surer thing money-wise wasn't a huge surprise. Bree's motivation puzzled me though. She probably had the kindest heart out of all of us and keeping Max alive would be something that she'd want to do. She was also the most optimistic of us as well. I was betting she figured we could easily do both the bounty and protection and walk away with $7 million in our pocket.

I figured we had at best a fifty-fifty shot at keeping Max alive and collecting his reward. For collecting the Rose bounty, I put the odds of them showing up at forty-sixty, and now with Max being the main priority of this mission, we'd have to get exceptionally lucky to take the Rose down while keeping Max breathing.

I turned to Max and with a half-hearted smile said, "Looks like we have a deal."

"Excellent," answered Max, who added, "Now, let's work out the details."

Chapter 6

Monday, July 29

Thirty minutes later, Max and I shook on the deal we'd hashed out; we'd keep him alive until the Friday deadline and get $2 million for our services. The part I really didn't like was he had final say, which meant he could override anything security related if it interfered with his business dealings.

Bree during this time had disappeared off to the bathroom, changed back to her human form, and now was hanging out in her sweats. Stella too had changed back to her harmless ten-year-old looking human form. Blue and Stella had taken Kurt to the dining area of the suite and I assumed the three of them were working out the logistics of how our two teams would work together. Liv and Alteea had both been buzzing around the suite like hummingbirds on crack, checking the place out and generally making a nuisance of themselves.

The second I ended the handshake with Max, Liv blurred up and said, "Zack, you seriously need to get fashion advice from this man. I almost died when I saw the labels on the suits and shoes in his closet."

A delighted laugh escaped from Max's lips. "I wish I could take credit for that, but I have a fashion consultant who picks out my outfits for me." He turned to me and added, "If you desire his services, I can give you Pierre's contact information. His rates are very reasonable, and as your vampire companion has noticed, his taste is exquisite…"

"Thank you for the kind offer but I'm a jeans and T-shirt kind of guy. Being a fashion plate isn't something that helps in my business."

Liv sighed and cuffed me lightly off the back of my head. "And you wonder why you are still single…"

I'm still single because I happen to be dating an on-again-off-again crazy vampire whose moods change on a dime. Trying to figure where our relationship stood was a full-time affair. I did, however, change my mind and gave Max my e-mail address so he could forward me Pierre's information. I might not need to be fashionable for bounty hunting, but if it helped with my pathetic social life, maybe spending a few bucks on some nicer clothes might be worth it.

Max cleared his throat and said, "Before you arrived, I was just about to order a late dinner from room service for myself and Kurt. Would you and your companions like to join us?"

Bree perked up instantly and nodded her head rapidly. Kurt immediately mirrored Bree's motions at the mention of food. I briefly thought about making a wager with Max on which of the two Weres would eat more, but as Kurt had almost a foot of height and a good hundred pounds on Bree, decided that would probably be a losing bet. The rest of us declined the late dinner.

"Do you mind if I borrow one of the bedrooms to talk with my team?"

"Help yourself, but before you go, let Kurt take your pictures so he can update his team on our new arrangement."

We gathered around and Kurt snapped pictures on his smartphone of us. After the first few shots, Blue engaged her hologram disguise on her wrist which instantly changed her appearance to a tall, heavyset old man who kind of looked like Albert Einstein. Stella changed into her Hyde form. Bree asked if she needed to change but Kurt said that Werepanthers weren't that common so it wouldn't be necessary.

Kurt left to brief his team on this latest development and we disappeared into one of the suite's two bedrooms. The bedroom was as impressive as the rest of the place. I felt like I was in a palace rather than a hotel room. The room was probably twice the size of my master bedroom at home. A king-sized bed was the centerpiece of the room and looked like it could sleep a family of six. It was tastefully decorated with muted soft colors that blended together, giving the room a soothing tone.

Las Vegas wasn't what I'd pictured. I'd always imagined Vegas would be plastic Elvis's and flamingos—cheap, trashy things. Max's suite, however, was shattering those illusions quickly. If the rest of the town was anything like this, I'd gotten things very wrong.

I focused back on the task at hand, which was to discuss our new priorities now that the job had changed. "From now to Friday we are going to stick to Max like glue. During the day, Blue and Stella will be on guard. At night, it will be Liv and Alteea. Bree will be a floater between the teams depending on the schedule each day. I will join

Stella and Blue during the later parts of their shift and then Liv and Alteea during the early part of theirs. Max mentioned to me that he does most of his business in the late afternoon and into the night."

Blue raised a purple eyebrow at me and asked, "You can spot the Rose by their aura, but how are the rest of us supposed to identify the Rose when you're not around?"

This was the one flaw in my plan, as I couldn't be there 100 percent of the time. Thankfully the one constant to all the Rose's kills was that they were all up close and personal. The ice pick they killed the judge with was one example, but they had also strangled, injected their victim with poison, stabbed them, and snapped a victim's neck, but they had never killed at range or used a gun to kill a target. That meant we just needed to keep anyone from getting close to Max.

"You can't. I will talk to Max, but no one other than Kurt is to get within six feet of Max. If room service comes by, Stella will take Max off to the side so that the person doesn't get near him. If one of his security detail comes by to make a report or something, allow them to make the report, but once again, no closer to Max than six feet, and I want Stella standing between them and Max. I also want Blue right beside any person who enters the suite. Stella, if you have the slightest doubt about the situation, go full Hyde and get Max behind you. Blue, take down the stranger hard, okay?"

Liv asked, "What about when we are on duty?"

"In the early part of the evening Bree and I will be with you; you shadow whoever is visiting and Bree will be right at Max's side."

Alteea's tiny high-pitched voice broke the short silence. "What about me, Master?"

I scratched my chin as I pondered Alteea's role. While Alteea had wickedly sharp claws and fangs, not to mention the ability to cast tiny fireballs, her small size always had me worried about her safety. Pixies were Fae, and Fae were tough but there were limits on how much a six-inch tall being could take. Also, Liv loved Alteea to death and would kill me if anything happened to her. I smiled as I found an important role for her. "You are to supervise Liv and make sure she stays focused on whatever person is visiting the suite, okay?"

Alteea nodded her small head and smiled. Liv frowned for a moment, but then gave me a wink as she figured out that my main plan was to keep Alteea safe and near Liv.

"When I'm around, I will always be close to Max. I'll keep the air thickened around both of us to stop anyone taking a shot at him when a new visitor is in the suite. Bree and Stella, during those times, you are to shadow whoever has entered the suite. Our code word for an active threat is 'Lincoln.' If you hear that word, take down everyone around us and I'll shield Max."

The team and I spent the next twenty minutes hashing out ideas and coming up with the best ways to keep Max alive in different scenarios.

Once we were done, we rejoined Max in the main area of the suite. He looked up from his laptop as we entered and asked, "Everything okay?"

"Yeah, we were just working out your protection details. To be honest, this whole bodyguard thing is new to us and we're still figuring things out. I will talk to Kurt when he gets back about what we have come up with and get his thoughts."

Max laughed and said, "Good luck with that. Kurt is a man of few words, but he'll at least give you a yes or no about what you have planned."

I nodded and joined him on the couch. He mentioned that the food would be here soon. I was a bit surprised that Kurt wasn't back yet, but the security team was spread over three floors and nine rooms, so I figured that's what was taking the extra time. I went over some of our ideas with Max and he approved of them. I worried he might have had issue with the 'no one within six feet of him' part but he understood.

"Before the food gets here, can we take a minute to go over your schedule for tomorrow?"

Max nodded and clicked something on his laptop. "I have a three o'clock client meeting in one of the hotel boardrooms for an hour. A six o'clock dinner reservation at the tapas restaurant here in the hotel that is also a client meeting. Then a client seminar in the same boardroom at ten that will go to midnight."

I frowned at the client seminar, as it seemed kind of odd to be having it that late. I reasoned that Max's clients were from all over the world and different time zones so maybe this was a better time for them. It was also Las Vegas, which was the city that never slept.

Of the three, the restaurant meeting was the one I was concerned about the most. If the restaurant was busy, it would make it difficult to keep an eye on everything. I'd join Max at his table, and I'd place the rest of my team at the adjacent tables which would provide more protection. Thankfully, it would also be a Monday night, so I hoped that would mean the restaurant would be quiet.

I turned to Stella and said, "Call the tapas place and change the reservation to add me to the table. Have them give us a secluded table and reserve the two tables right by it, okay?"

Max shook his head. "That won't work—the client I'm having dinner with is a touch paranoid. He always insists we meet in a public place and he will freak out at you being at the table. I've dealt with him for years and he's still is nervous with even Kurt joining us."

I really didn't like this, but Max was the boss, and we'd have to play by his rules. I hoped the two tables nearby were really close. It was the best we could do.

Stella nodded and walked over to the phone.

I shifted back toward Max and asked, "When do you have access to the boardroom?"

"I have it rented for the entire week starting tomorrow morning, why?"

"I'd like to get in there before the meeting and have my team make sure it is secure."

"Kurt will be doing the same thing; you and your team can join him when he does his inspection."

Max and I were discussing security concerns when there was a knock at the door. The guard outside the door poked his head in and announced room service was here.

"Send them in," ordered Max.

He started to get up from the couch, but I put a hand on his leg and shook my head. Max frowned at this, but then shrugged and sat back down. I thickened the air around us as a precaution.

A man in an Aloha uniform came in pushing a cart stacked with stainless steel covered dishes. I spotted *Crisanto* on his nametag, as I quickly gave him a once over—mid-thirties, average height and build. There was noticeable perspiration along his dark hairline and his eyes were darting all over the place. His nervousness had me concerned. The uniform was formfitting enough that there was no way he had a gun hidden on him. On the other hand, the cloth-covered cart was somewhere you could have hidden an assault rifle without issue.

Bree's attention instantly locked onto the food and I mentally cursed her for getting distracted. Stella positioned herself between us and the server but stayed in her little girl form. Blue and Liv though both shadowed the man closely.

"Will you be dining at the table?" asked Crisanto, turning his attention to Max and me on the couch.

Max nodded and Crisanto pushed the cart to the four-seater table in the dining area. He reached under the cart and I started calling on my Electrical power. I relaxed when he just pulled out a white tablecloth, shook it out, and laid it on the table. He started setting the table with utensils and unloading the food from the cart.

A minute later, the table was set for four and he placed the extra three meals in the center. He pulled the bill in a leather folder from his belt, and Blue held out her hand. Crisanto seemed surprised that Blue in her elderly man disguise was the one doing the signing but didn't say anything. Blue signed for the food and handed the folder back. Crisanto checked it briefly, smiled, and thanked "Mr. Schnell." He wished all of us a good evening and headed for the door.

The moment the door closed, Bree was already in one of the seats eying the food. As Max and I got up, I asked, "Did he seem nervous to you?"

Max laughed. "Yes, but that is normal. You may or not be aware, but my nickname is the Merchant of Death. Spending so much time in hotels, I have learned that the grapevine and rumor mill among hotel staff is exceptionally efficient. He was probably informed of my moniker and that tends to make staff a touch nervous around me."

Max's explanation made sense and eased my paranoia. I guess if I were serving someone called the Merchant of Death, I'd be a little shaken up too.

Max grabbed a seat and smiled as he gazed at the grilled New York strip in front of him. The loaded baked potato and side vegetable also looked delicious and part of me was wishing I hadn't declined the late dinner. I took the empty seat across from him.

I was impressed that Bree hadn't started eating and was waiting for Max to start—at home her table manners were nowhere near as good. Max picked up his knife and fork and was about to eat when Bree suddenly reached across and yanked the entire plate away from him.

So much for table manners, I thought.

"Bree!" I yelled, "Give the nice man back his food. He ordered you three dinners, so there is plenty of food."

Bree shook her head. "It smells wrong. All the food smells wrong…"

I blinked at her answer. "Wrong how?"

"Every dish smells like almonds but even the almond smell isn't quite right either."

Stella rushed over with an expression of deep concern etched on her young features. "Could it be bitter almond?"

Bree shrugged. "I guess. It certainly isn't a sweet smell, why?"

"In a number of the murder mysteries I read, a bitter almond scent indicates cyanide."

My eyes went wide. "You think the food has been poisoned?"

The door to the suite opened and Kurt walked in.

"Poison?" asked Kurt as he approached the table, concern on his features.

For a brief second, I wondered how Kurt heard the comment about poison from outside the suite, but then I remembered how impressive Were hearing was.

Max brought him up to speed. Kurt closed his eyes and inhaled. He nodded and in a strong German accent said, "*Ja*, everything smells like bitter almonds."

We all got up and stepped away from the table.

No wonder Crisanto was so nervous. The bastard was willing to kill three people just to get Max. It was a crude attempt as there was no guarantee that Max was one of the people who'd be eating the food. Also, if someone had eaten the food first and suddenly dropped dead, I doubted Max would have taken a bite at that point. $4 million made people do stupid things.

Max took command. "Kurt, get hotel security on the phone and tell them what happened."

Kurt nodded and picked up the phone on the bar.

As Kurt was yelling at hotel security, Max sighed and said, "What a waste of a lovely steak."

Chapter 7

Monday, July 29

Three hours later, all of us, including Max and Kurt, were in our secret underground lab in London. Bree, Max, and Kurt were enjoying a much-delayed meal from the Food-O-Tron.

It had taken that long for hotel security and then the LVPD to process the scene, get our statements, and bag the food for evidence. Aloha security swept the hotel for Crisanto, but he was gone. They did find him on the surveillance footage where he was shown leaving from the employee entrance not five minutes after he dropped off the food. His shift wasn't supposed to end for another three hours.

The LVPD put out an arrest warrant for Crisanto on four counts of attempted murder. The head of security also assured Max that Crisanto would not step foot on this property again. If he did, he would instantly be detained and held for arrest.

"This, what did you call it, Food-O-Tron?" I nodded and Max continued, "It can replicate any meal added to it?"

"Yup," I said.

"And it was built in the 1900s?" I bobbed my head and Max said, "Remarkable. Truly remarkable. This filet is perfect and more than makes up for the loss of that poor steak earlier. Is this dish also from 1900s?"

"No, I cooked that dish and added it to the Food-O-Tron. The shepherd's pie Kurt is currently eating is one of the original recipes."

Max glanced over at Kurt's plate and raised his fork in a questioning manner. Kurt growled, but then shook his head and said, "Sorry," and made a hand motion for Max to try some.

Kurt's growl made me smile; it was nice to know our Were wasn't the only one protective of their food and had table manners that took second place to that priority.

Max took a small bite under Kurt's watchful eye and smiled. "That is really good. Hard to believe that food was cooked over a century ago.

I'd have expected it to taste different too, but it's pretty much the same as modern equivalents I've tried. Can the machine replicate anything?"

I shook my head. "Unfortunately, no. Just organic items. So, no making a fortune in diamonds or gold. It also can't replicate living things. We tried replicating a live mouse as an experiment. It copied the mouse perfectly, but the replicated mouse was dead."

Max was about to say something but paused as Liv dropped off another meal for Bree and Kurt. "Pity. It still does save you a ton in keeping your lovely Were fed. I swear Kurt costs me more in food even though I pay him a substantial salary."

Kurt laughed but didn't pause in inhaling his food.

Max glanced around the lab, his eyes fixating on the two sparking Tesla coils across the room for a moment before continuing, "This lab is also quite charming with all the polished hardwood and brass and feels like a preserved slice of history. You mentioned it is located underground in London?" I nodded and he added, "Prime location then. Any chance you would be willing to sell it? I would make you a very generous offer..."

"It isn't mine to sell," I said and gestured at Stella.

Stella shook her head. "I have no doubt that your offer would be quite impressive, but I'm afraid I will have to decline. I have an attachment to this place, and it would be quite useless to you." Max raised an eyebrow and Stella explained, "We are at least 500 feet underground, probably deeper. The three exits to the surface have long been blocked and filled in. The three entrances are also boobytrapped and I don't have the codes for them. The only way in or out is via Blue's shadow travelling ability."

Max and Kurt suddenly looked a bit nervous and both glanced at Blue as if to reassure themselves that she was in good health and not going anywhere.

I laughed and said, "Yeah, I felt the same way when I was first brought here. If anything happened to Blue, we'd be trapped here for a long time. I reassured myself by knowing there is unlimited water, air, and food, so we'd be able to survive easily. There are enough tools around this place that I'm sure, given enough time and effort, we could dig our way out if we had to."

They both relaxed and went back to eating.

After giving Max and Kurt a quick tour of the lab, Blue shadow travelled all of us back to Max's suite at the Aloha.

Max allowed us to use the suite across the hall to sleep in. As he wasn't expecting any guests for the rest of the night, and he and Kurt were turning in shortly, we decided that Liv and Alteea would be the only ones guarding him for the rest of the night.

After Max and Kurt each retired to the two bedrooms in the suite, I turned to Liv on the couch and said, "No one comes into the suite until dawn. Blue and Stella will relieve you just before sunrise and shadow travel you back home. You have your communication goggles so if anything odd happens, sound the alert and we'll all come running."

"Uh-huh," said Liv only paying me half-attention as she browsed through the movies available on the screen.

I swear it would be a miracle if we kept Max alive until Friday. Under Liv's 'watchful' eye, I'm sure a whole team of assassins could get to Max without her noticing as long as they didn't block her view of the TV. I debated having Bree stay as well, but tomorrow was going to be a long day, and I wanted her rested. I was probably being overly paranoid, as there was also a guard stationed just outside the suite, so Max should be fine. I was also willing to bet that at the slightest disturbance, Kurt would be out of his room in short order.

Blue opened a portal in the shadows and the four of us stepped through and ended up back at the house. We quickly packed up overnight bags with a change of clothes and all the toiletries we needed.

Ten minutes later, we stepped out of the shadows into the suite across the hall from Max's. This suite was laid out and decorated exactly like Max's; it had a bathroom in the main hall, a living room, a combined dining area and bar, and two bedrooms at either end of the suite.

Bree and I were going to share one of the bedrooms and Blue and Stella would take the other one. They wished us a goodnight and we headed for our room.

Bree groaned as soon as we entered the room. I followed her line of sight and realized what she was unhappy about—the room only had one bed. The bed was a king, and I didn't think us sharing it would be that big of a deal, but I couldn't resist teasing her, "One bed? I know it will be hard, but I need to get some sleep, so keep your hands to yourself and try to resist throwing yourself at my hot body…"

Bree rolled her eyes. "Yeah, that's the problem."

I winced at the amount of sarcasm in her tone. "Look, I know it's not ideal, but the bed is easily big enough for both of us. I will behave myself. We are both adults, and I'm sure we can handle this..."

Bree just kept staring at the bed and didn't say anything.

I sighed. "I can sleep on one of the couches in the living room, if you are that uncomfortable about it."

She slowly shook her head. "No, I can't make you sleep on the couch. You're right, I'm just being silly. We'll share it. I'm going to get ready for bed."

Bree, after grabbing a small bag from her overnight bag, entered the en suite bathroom. She closed the double doors behind her. I started taking off my armor. I put the helmet on the nightstand beside the bed and plugged in the recharging cable. I set the visor to broadcast any alerts in case Liv ran into trouble. I disconnected Stella's cooling system from the back of the armor which I realized had worked perfectly the whole time and plugged it in to recharge it as well.

I carefully laid out the armor on a plush chair near the bed so I could put it back on quickly if I needed to.

I was also pleased the shorts and T-shirt I had been wearing under the armor weren't soaked in sweat. Before Stella's cooling system, I always came out of the armor a bit ripe to say the least; this was a pleasant change.

Just as I was wrapping up, Bree came out of the bathroom. She was carrying a bra and underwear in her hand but was still wearing the same plain grey sweatpants and matching T-shirt. "I was hoping for something sexier, perhaps with a bit more lace..."

"You are supposed to behaving yourself, remember?" said Bree as she dumped her undergarments in the open overnight bag without looking at me.

"You're no fun," I said as I grabbed my bag of toiletries.

"And you are lucky not to be on the couch."

We passed by each other and I entered the bathroom and stopped dead. This place was huge. Marble everything. There was a good-sized hot tub in the center of the room. On my right was a full-length vanity mirror with two sinks. Bree had her stuff by one of them, so I'd take the other. On the opposite wall there was a massive closet. On the far wall on the right side was a large, frosted glass shower. Beside the shower, in the corner, was a toilet in its own little frosted glass enclosed space.

I raised my voice and said, "Bree, you seem a bit tense. We could have a wonderful little soak together in the hot tub; that might help you relax…"

"Good night, Zack," said Bree coldly.

I was going to make another smart-ass comment but figured that would have me riding the couch, so I kept my mouth shut. I closed the connecting doors and got ready for bed.

A few minutes later, I returned to the bedroom. The lights were out, and Bree was already under the covers and looked to be sleeping. I quietly walked around the bed to my side, shucked off my T-shirt, and climbed in.

Sleep didn't come quickly, as my mind was busy going over the day and what the rest of the week might have in store. Thanks to Bree's sensitive nose, we'd stopped one attempt on Max's life, but I knew there'd be more. The problem with this whole protection gig was the opposition just had to get lucky once whereas we had to be perfect.

On the upside, I was currently in a luxury suite, sleeping in a comfortable bed with a beautiful woman—I'd certainly had worse bounty cases than this. With a smile, I kicked around the idea of renting one of these suites for Liv and me once this case was done. With the three-hour time difference between Hamilton and Vegas, we could hang out in Hamilton first and then once the sun went down in Vegas, we could have Blue shadow travel us here. I'd get extra time with her due to that time difference and I'm sure she'd like spending time in the hot tub too. Happy images of that filled my mind and I drifted off.

Chapter 8

Monday, July 29

The next morning, I awoke spooned around something lovely and warm. My right hand was cupped over an ample cotton-covered breast. Another part of me was already awake and standing at full attention. It was currently snuggled up against a pair of warm buns. I blinked opened my eyes with a lazy smile on my face.

Oh shit! Was my first thought when I realized where I was and who I was currently up against. I froze and didn't dare to even breathe. I must have rolled over during the night. *I was so screwed.* Bree was going to kill me for this. Hell, once Bree was done with me, Liv would probably torture whatever was left of me.

I sighed to myself at the unfairness of it all. Liv and I were dating but we weren't a couple. Her choice, not mine. I'd bugged her about us becoming exclusive and her answer was that "It didn't fit the vampire lifestyle," whatever the hell that was supposed to mean. I knew she went out clubbing with Bree on a regular basis and had no doubt she was meeting guys, but I didn't say anything. Yet, she'd be pissed at me if she found out about me accidently snuggling up against Bree. That was my life with my crazy vampire.

I pushed thoughts of Liv aside and focused on the here and now problem. I honestly would have preferred waking curled up with an angry rattlesnake than being against Bree like this. The rattlesnake might only bite me, which, compared to what an enraged Were could do, was a pleasant alternative.

Think, Zack, think! I just needed to carefully lift my hand off her chest and then slowly roll away from her and pray I didn't wake her while doing that. If I could just do that, then she wouldn't be the wiser and no blood would be spilled.

"That better be your phone that is pressing up against my ass…"

I'm dead, so dead.

"I'm sorry. I just woke up and found us like this. I didn't do this on purpose, I swear."

Bree laughed and I just blinked stupidly, as that certainly wasn't the response I'd been imagining.

"I know. I trust you, and Liv would kill both of us if anything had happened. That said, you can remove your hand now…"

"Sorry," I said as I quickly lifted my hand and rolled away from her.

Bree turned over and had a twinkle in her ice blue eyes. "Since you spent the whole night feeling me up, the least you can do is buy me breakfast."

"Sure, no problem."

She cocked an eye at me and added in a firm tone, "That breakfast isn't going to order itself."

I scrambled out of bed and awkwardly dashed for the living room. Just as I reached the connecting door, Bree said, "Oh, Zack…"

"Yeah?"

"You might want to skip ordering yourself a coffee."

"Why's that?"

"I think you are perked *up* enough already…"

I realized she was taking a shot at my badly tenting shorts. Heat filled my cheeks as I was chased from the room by the echoes of Bree's laugher. Thankfully, the gods were smiling on me and Blue and Stella weren't waiting for me in the living room. The sun was up, so I assumed they must already be on duty protecting Max.

I picked up the room service menu and gave it a quick once over. I staggered at the prices on the menu—we'd need to keep Max alive just to cover the cost of the food for the week. Heck, for the money they wanted for a coffee, I expected Juan Valdez to deliver it and personally roast the beans in front of me. I wondered if we or Max would be picking up the cost of the food. The rooms were under his name, so he'd get the bill, but whether that was covered by him as expense or we'd have to reimburse him wasn't something we discussed. I made a mental note to discuss it with him.

Despite the high prices, I owed Bree for not killing me this morning, so I called room service and ordered one of everything on the breakfast menu for Bree and an extra order of pancakes for me.

After a quick call via my helmet comm to Blue and Stella to make sure everything was okay, I grabbed a quick shower in Blue and Stella's bathroom since Bree was still occupying ours.

We were both showered and dressed when room service showed up and laid out a buffet for Bree on the dining table.

I had to admit my pancakes were pretty damn good, enough so that they almost justified their exorbitant price. Judging by the lack of conversation and multitude of happy moans from Bree, the rest of the food was that good too. The view of sunny Las Vegas out of the floor-to-ceiling windows was stunning. I'd only seen comparable views when I was flying using my Air powers.

After I finished my pancakes, a quick glance at my phone showed it was coming up on 11 a.m. "We have about three hours before we need to join Kurt in scoping out the boardroom for Max's three o'clock meeting. I want you there for that, as your nose will be handy in checking the place out." Bree kept eating but nodded. "You're free to use that time to get more sleep or do some exploring around town. I'll leave you to the rest of your breakfast. I'm going down to the main level to check it out. I also want to get a look at the tapas restaurant to get a better idea of what we are in for."

I left Bree and the long walk to the elevators started to give me a better idea of the scale of this place. If that walk didn't drive home the scale, the number of floors listed on the elevator control panel certainly did.

I exited the elevator and a short walk brought me out to the casino floor. This place was massive. After a five-minute walk around the outside edge of the casino area, I'd completely lost my bearings. It took me another half an hour of walking around to get a better idea of the layout of this place. I found the waterfall and just stopped and stared in awe.

Stella was right—it's amazing. It had to be at least forty stories tall and the water came down in a huge rush. There were laser lights that changed patterns and colors behind it and all along the outside edges of the pool of water at the base of the falls were waterspouts that shot perfect arcs of tight tubes of water in a timed pattern. I wondered at how they managed to keep the water so neatly in the arcs. More impressive was the massive amount of water that displayed in a city in the middle of a desert. As remarkable as the waterfall was, whatever system they had to drain and push all that water back up to the top of the falls was equally impressive. Odin only knew how much power was needed to do that.

On the other hand, the system might not be mechanical at all. There very well could be a spell doing it. It would be brutally expensive, but it wasn't as if the casino lacked money.

During my explorations, I'd also located the tapas place and inwardly groaned when I saw it.

The restaurant only had a half-height wall to separate it from the main casino floor area. That was nice from a design perspective, as it made the place seem larger and more open, but it sucked from a protection standpoint.

I grabbed a seat in front of a slot machine to rest for a second and studied the restaurant and surrounding area. I'd noticed there was a ton of uniformed Aloha security on my walk, only outnumbered by the dark plexiglass bubbles of surveillance cameras in the ceiling. With the money that must flow through this place on a daily basis, you needed that level of security. Under the watchful eye of human security and electronic cameras, I felt better about our chances. Anyone pulling out a weapon in this place would be spotted in seconds. I doubted anyone would be brazen enough to take a shot at Max from out on the casino floor.

The back of the restaurant had a full wall. I'd talk with Stella when I got back to make sure our three tables were against or near the wall. With the wall behind us, that only left three directions we'd have to watch from.

I resumed my wandering. Stella was also correct that the tropical flowers all over the place looked and smelled great. I'd never been to Hawaii, but after being here, I really was getting an urge to check it out one day for myself. Maybe after this case was done, I'd have Blue take us out there on a day trip. Considering Blue could travel anywhere in the world instantly, we really hadn't taken advantage of that enough.

Something about this place put me at ease, which, considering we were currently trying to save a guy called the Merchant of Death from a $4 million hit contract, was surprising. I inhaled deeply and just took everything in for a moment before regaining my focus and got back to scoping the place out.

I found there was a whole second floor above this one with shops and restaurants and I figured I might as well check them out too.

***

At just after two that afternoon, I was back at Max's suite in my armor. I was surprised to find that Alteea had stayed in Vegas rather than returning home to sleep the day away with Liv. I asked her about this.

"The chance to observe humans on vacation wasn't something I was going to pass up, Master."

I nodded. Alteea was odd for a pixie, as most of them lived to eat and fornicate and not necessarily in that order. Alteea though was fascinated by human behavior and our technology, which probably made her the biggest pixie nerd on the planet. Thankfully that passion worked out for us. A normal pixie would have been miserable being away from their swarm and lacking the intimacy that went with it. Alteea though always seemed happy, like this was the great adventure she'd always craved.

Kurt was ready to go down to check out the boardroom, but I hadn't figured out which of the team was going with us. I wanted Blue, as she could shadow travel us directly into the boardroom and get us back to the suite in seconds if anything happened. Alteea would enjoy exploring so I added her to my list. This left me with Bree and Stella. I decided to take Bree with us for her nose. Between her and Kurt, they would be able to sniff out anything odd in the room. That left Stella behind to protect Max. Her Hyde form would be able to easily handle anything that attacked this place and shield Max long enough for us to return.

Blue opened a portal and we stepped out behind a large screen that had been set up in the front of the room. I froze at the size of the room. Max had called this place a boardroom, so I'd expected one long table in a room large enough to fit it. Conference room would have been a better description of what I was currently looking at. There were ten round tables in the large room. Each table had eight chairs around it, which meant this room could seat eighty people.

The meeting this afternoon was a client meeting and this room seemed a bit much for that, but Max referred to tonight's meeting as a seminar. I'd assumed that would be sixteen people around the same boardroom table that I'd pictured in my head. By the size of this room, I suspected the seminar was going to be much bigger than that. That made it much more challenging to keep Max safe.

"Zack?" said Bree.

"Sorry, the place was larger than I expected. Look around and make sure the room is safe, okay?"

Blue and Bree nodded and slowly started searching the place. Kurt was already way ahead of them. Alteea had also gone by this point, and I watched her aura darting around the room at high speed, checking everything out. She had her glamor up, as there were Aloha staff around the area setting things up.

With its high-definition projector and sixteen-foot screen at the front, the meeting room was impressive from a technology standpoint. There were also four eighty-inch flat screen televisions, two mounted to the walls on either side. Currently all five displays were showing a rotating version of the Aloha's palm logo on them. There were also three rows of flushed mounted speakers in the ceiling for the sound system. Between the multitude of display and speakers, every seat in the house would have a great view of the presentation.

The tables and chairs weren't anything special, but each table did have a nice centerpiece of brightly colored tropical flowers.

My first task was checking access to the room. There were three entrances to the room—a double door main entrance at the back, an emergency exit at the front, and a side serving entrance to my left. The emergency door only opened outwards, so after a quick check to make sure it was locked, we wouldn't have to worry about it. That left two entrances to deal with. I'd position Stella at the serving entrance and Bree at the main doors for the afternoon meeting. That would leave Blue and me to hang out near Max. I could keep the air thickened around him, and if things went sideways, then Blue could grab Max and disappear to safety in the shadows.

The side serving area had two long tables along the wall. One of the tables had a coffee machine and there were also pitchers of water and juice laid out. The other table had a selection of pastries on it, which Alteea had already found. I cleared my throat, which got me a look from the Aloha employee currently stocking the area, but I spotted Alteea's aura shoot off back into the main room. I apologized and said that I just had a dry throat. The employee nodded and went back to work. Clearing Alteea out turned out to be a waste of time as Kurt and Bree showed up a moment later and went to town on the desserts.

I caught the employee's attention again and said, "You may want to get another tray or two ready; these ones aren't going to last long…"

The guy looked at me like I was crazy but then a look of understanding appeared as he watched the two Weres going to town on them. He fled the room shortly after that. I assumed to get more.

"Did you two find anything out of the ordinary?"

Kurt and Bree paused long enough to shake their heads and went back to their mission of making sure every pastry was safe to eat. I left them to it.

A few minutes later, Blue and I were at the front of the room discussing the best ways to cover the room for the upcoming meeting. Blue was pretty much in line with my thoughts earlier about having Bree and Stella cover the two doors while the two of us stayed with Max.

We had just about finished when Alteea popped up from under the head table I'd been leaning against and dropped her glamor. I glanced around in concern but was pleased to see that there were no Aloha staff in the main room.

"This place has everything. Those TVs are amazing—why isn't our one at home that size, Master?" Before I could even answer her question, my excited little fairy added, "The sound system is cool; the pastries were really tasty... though they could have used more sugar. They even have a clock under the table."

I was about to answer her first question when the last part of her ramble hit me. I froze and asked, "Which table has the clock?"

Alteea smiled and said, "This one, Master. None of the other tables have clocks."

With the utmost care I stepped away from the table, being careful not to shake it in the slightest.

Blue cocked an eyebrow and simply asked, "Lincoln?"

For a split second I was confused, and then I remembered that was our code word that things had gone south and nodded.

Alteea's smile disappeared. Blue made a gesture and opened a small portal in the shadows nearby and said, "Alteea, go!"

The pixie disappeared.

"Go get Kurt and Bree and bring them up to speed," I said as I started lowering myself to the floor.

"What are you going to do?"

"I'm checking to see if what we think is under the table is really there or not."

"Be careful." And with that, Blue headed for the service area.

I thickened the air around me and with a slightly shaking hand slowly lifted the white tablecloth. I turned on the camera recording feature of my helmet as my worst fears were realized. Directly under the center of the table was a bomb. The display was counting down from thirty-three minutes. I checked the clock on my helmet display and figured out this thing was to go off at quarter past three. The device was a large brick of what looked like grey Plasticine with a crap load of wires running from it to the clock. I had no idea how big a bang a brick of plastic explosive would be, but I was willing to bet that anyone in this room would have a really bad day when it went off.

I lowered the tablecloth I was holding, slow enough that a turtle would be annoyed at the pace, and then got to my feet and fled to the far side of the room where Bree, Kurt, and Blue were waiting. I kept the air thickened between us and the bomb in case it went off.

"Call Security?" asked Kurt.

I pondered that. "Yeah, let them know what is going on, but Blue and I will deal with this."

Bree placed her hand on her hips and asked, "Zack, are you nuts? Let the bomb squad deal with this."

"No time. There is only thirty minutes left on the timer, and it will probably take them that long to get here. You and Kurt get out of the room and stop anyone from coming in, okay?"

Bree wanted to argue but after a moment, nodded and pointed Kurt towards the main entrance while she headed for the service one.

"I know nothing about how to disarm a bomb," said Blue calmly.

"We aren't going to disarm it...I have a plan."

Blue's tail twitched in an unhappy manner as I told her my idea.

A few minutes later, we'd pulled the two tables to the right of the center table back and out of the way. That cleared the space for my grand idea, which I hated more with every passing second. Blue was in position and gave me a nod that she was ready to go.

I took a deep breath and prayed to Odin I wasn't about to make a very big mistake here. I started calling on my Electrical power and hoped this worked. This was the part I was most nervous about; a stray spark and bad things could happen. I kept the air thickened around me and Blue and raised my hand. I aimed a powerful blast of lightning at the bank of fluorescent lights over the cleared area. They exploded in a blast of sparks and glass and that area of the room went dark, giving us a huge shadow.

No giant *kaboom*. I let out the deep breath of air I'd been holding.

Blue made a motion with her hands and said, "Portal is open. Go!"

I nodded and called on my Air power to gently lift the table from the floor. I then pushed a gentle blast of air at it and watched as it slowly hovered towards the open portal.

C'mon, c'mon, I thought as it floated closer and closer to the shadow portal. I was tempted to give it one good hard push to shoot it through but kept it slow and steady. The edge of the table disappeared into the large portal, and a few seconds later, the rest of the table went through.

"Portal's closed. We're clear," said Blue.

I exhaled deeply and lowered my shaking hand. "Where did that portal lead to?"

Blue grinned a mouthful of pointy teeth and said, "Human's First headquarters…"

My eyes went wide at that. Human's First were an anti-Enhanced group that believed anyone with powers should be killed or imprisoned in reservations. "You didn't."

Blue shook her head and laughed. "No, it ended up in a remote part of the Canadian Arctic where it will only disturb a polar bear or maybe a seal when it explodes."

Chapter 9

Monday, July 29

The meeting got moved to Max's suite. Bree, Stella, Alteea, and I stood guard there while Blue stayed to deal with hotel security and LVPD. I'd forwarded the video I made of the bomb to Blue's phone so she could show them the footage.

Max's clients were the CEO, CFO, and a bodyguard from Black Horse Inc. Black Horse was a private military contractor and longtime client of Max's. All of them were sharply dressed. At the sight of telltale bulges at the chest area of their suits, I went on alert. Kurt noticed my tension and gave me a slight shake of his head as they entered the suite.

The upside was, while they were armed, none of them had auras, which meant they were just regular people. Regular people though who had extensive military training and who I had no doubt were more than competent with the weapons they carried. It dawned on me that my nervousness was due to a culture difference. In Canada, police and armored car guards were the only people who carried guns. Here in the US, a lot more people carried them. I assumed this was why Kurt was so casual about letting three people who were armed into the suite when his boss had a $4 million contract on his head.

I forced myself to sit back and reexamine the whole situation. It would take any of the Black Horse people time to draw the weapons they were carrying if they had ill intent. In that time, I could thicken the air around Max to protect him. Stella could change into her Hyde form and place herself between Max and any threat. Kurt and Bree, even though they were in their human forms, were much stronger and faster than any human and would be all over them before they could get a shot off. Even Alteea would be able to serious mess one of them up, as she was invisible and could blind them with her claws or distract or injure them with her mini fireballs. I realized this was why Kurt was so unconcerned about them being armed.

All three of the Black Horse people eyed me with curiosity as they passed but didn't say anything. Maybe they thought my armor was a new product line Max was offering. All stopped dead at the sight of Stella's young form standing by one of the couches with Bree. The CEO turned to Max, "Max, I wasn't aware you had a daughter."

Max laughed. "I don't. This is a member of my protection team."

To my surprise, the CEO didn't immediately laugh but instead took another look at Stella. As the CEO studied Stella, I found myself studying him. Besides his bearing, which would have me guessing military or law enforcement, it was his eyes that told me this man had seen some dark things in his life. The CFO and the bodyguard both had the same qualities to them as well.

The CEO's shoulders slumped. "Alright, Max, you got me. She is too young to be a Were, Super, or mage. It's daylight, so she isn't a member of the undead class, so what I am I missing?"

Max smiled and said, "Stella, if you'd be kind enough to show Dan your other form."

In the blink of an eye, Stella's harmless young form was replaced by her monstrous misshapen Hyde form. My respect for the Black Horse people instantly went up a few levels as not a single one of them flinched at Stella's imposing new form.

"Fascinating. A Hyde. It looks like our Enhanced research department will have to update their files, as they were listed as extinct."

The CEO's comment tweaked my curiosity. "Why do you have an Enhanced research department?"

He turned to me and asked, "And you are?"

Max jumped in and said, "Sorry, allow me to introduce Zack Stevens, former hero turned bounty hunter. He and his team have joined my protection team for the rest of the week due to a sizeable hit contract that has been put out on me."

The CEO grinned. "I saw that $4 million contract. I felt it was insulting to you—you are worth at least three times that. I assumed it was one of your minor competitors trying to crudely level the playfield." Max gave a slight bow and Dan turned his full attention to me, "We have one because it is not uncommon for our adversaries to employ Enhanced Individuals against us in the field. At Black Horse, we also have an entire squad made up of Enhanced Individuals called Angel Squad. We keep them on standby in case one of our regular companies runs into Enhanceds or we send them in when one of our teams gets in the deep stuff."

A squad of Enhanceds with military training and experience. I shuddered to myself, as that would be one group I wouldn't want to go up against. I knew various governments had special forces teams made up of Enhanced Individuals but was surprised a private company had one. Black Horse Inc. though was huge and one of the primary military contractors for the US government, so this shouldn't have been such a shock.

Stella returned to her human form and Max suggested they start the meeting.

The Black Horse people took one of the couches and Stella and Bree stood behind them. Max, Kurt, and I took the opposite couch with Max in the middle. The CFO and Max did most of the talking during the meeting.

I don't know what I was expecting, but I thought it'd be more interesting than logistics and supply chains. I could see big box stores or large beverage companies having this type of discussion. Most of their conversation was over my head, but I gleaned that the bulk of it was about arranging supplies to be delivered to key areas Black Horse had current and upcoming commitments in.

The meeting ended without incident and just shortly after it, the LVPD arrived at the suite with Blue in tow to discuss the attempted bombing. Thankfully, due to Blue's time with them and the video from my helmet, that meeting as well went quickly. LVPD detectives just wanted to ask the rest of us a couple of questions to confirm what Blue had told them.

They did let us know that they had found the suspect on the hotel's video surveillance. The man had been dressed as an electrical contractor. Average height and, unfortunately, with the thick beard, mustache, glasses, and cap he was wearing, none of the shots gave them a good picture of his face. The guy was also smart in that he came in from the second floor entrance and didn't approach the casino or the cage area of the casino, which allowed him to avoid being questioned by hotel security. After planting the bomb, he left the same way he'd come.

The detectives mentioned that the Aloha security team was hiring additional staff for the rest of the week and would have someone stationed on the second floor area to prevent something like this from happening again.

"I'm a bit surprised that after an attempted poisoning and bombing that the Aloha isn't asking you to leave," I told Max after the detectives had left.

Max shrugged. "This is the third year in a row we've stayed here. Between the nine suites and the conference room rental for the week, they are making more than $50,000 a day from me."

I blinked at that. No wonder the hotel was willing to put up with a bit a risk if they were making that sort of coin. It would be interesting to see how much they were willing to put up with before they'd had enough.

Chapter 10

Monday, July 29

The dinner meeting at the tapas restaurant was going smoothly, other than us confusing the staff. Bree and I showed up and were seated at a table by the hostess. A minute later, Max, Kurt, two of Max's security people, Stella, and Blue in her old man disguise suddenly appeared out of the shadows at the back of the place. Stella, Blue, and the two security personnel took the first table. Max and Kurt took the table behind them. Bree and I were also in front of Max and Kurt's table. Max was sitting to my right and was close enough that I could easily thicken the air in front of him to keep him safe. Anyone who wanted to get at Max would have to get past our two tables.

Alteea was currently sleeping back at Max's suite. As the menu didn't have blood on it or many sugary items, she had no interest in tagging along.

The hostess frowned at seeing two tables that had been reserved and empty unexpectedly filled with people. I watched her almost run to the manager, who then proceeded to come over and find out what was going on.

Max handled all of it with poise. The manager after finding out that all the people who were seated were the ones who had reserved the tables in the first place was happy. The only one happier was Bree when she heard that the food bills for all three tables were to come to Max.

I really hoped the client Max was meeting with was a big spender as between Bree and Kurt the tab tonight was going to be huge.

The interior of the tapas restaurant was helping calm my frayed nerves. I hated being in the open like this with a man who had a price tag on this head—it made it seem like we were trying to tempt fate. My paranoia should have been working overtime, but the airy open concept design, the bright colors tastefully accenting the interior, the calming scent of the tropical flowers, the mouth-watering aromas coming from the kitchen area, the lovely polished hardwood of the tables, and the remarkably comfortable red leather chairs were all having a positive influence on me. I actually found myself looking forward to dinner.

The client showed up with a bodyguard a couple of minutes later. The client seemed nervous as he approached the table. His eyes were darting all over the place and he looked like he was about to jump out of his skin. He was a shorter man, with short dark hair and glasses. The only thing that stood out about him was his suit and the gold watch on his wrist. The suit was tailored to perfection, and if Olivia were here, I'm sure she would have guessed the designer. The large gold watch on his wrist was probably a high-end brand and worth a small fortune.

The bodyguard was built like a sumo wrestler and was easily one of the largest people I'd seen in my life. Despite the man's massive size, he moved with impressive grace and agility. That combination of strength and speed would make him a very dangerous opponent. His suit hung loosely off him and I had no doubt that was by design so it wouldn't restrict his movements, and under it, he could be carrying a freaking rocket launcher and no one would be the wiser.

That bodyguard made me more nervous than the client did, but I took a deep breath and told myself that despite the man's size and prowess he was still just human, which meant that Kurt would be more than a match for him. I'd leave him to Kurt, and I'd worry about external threats.

Max and Kurt stood up as the client and his mountain of a bodyguard approached the table. After the hostess had left, the four of them exchanged bows and took their seats. I was in awe as Max said something in what sounded like fluent Japanese. The client smiled and replied in his native language. Max said a few more words in Japanese, and the client nodded but then switched back to English.

The restaurant was less than a quarter full and the nearest diners were three tables away. They were an older couple who seemed to be having a good time. It seemed unlikely the two of them were a pair of international assassins. I continued scanning the restaurant, but it seemed like a mix of tourists and businesspeople and nothing twigged my radar as a threat, especially as none of them had an aura.

The continuing conversation going on beside me at the main table was surprisingly mundane. Max was asking his client about his flight, his family, and the weather. The conversation ended when the waiter showed up to take their order. The server barely lifted an eyebrow as

Max listed off ten or so items from the menu and commented, "We'll see how that works as a starter."

He approached our table next. I was embarrassed, as I hadn't even glanced at the menu. Bree though gently put her hand on my arm to stop me from sending him away and rapidly ordered four items off the menu.

I hoped that I would like whatever Bree had ordered but didn't overly worry about it. Bree would happily finish anything I didn't like. I also got the impression that this place was like a sushi joint in that you just kept ordering items until you were full, so if I didn't like what Bree had ordered, there would be many more times for me to order something I would enjoy.

The waiter returned ten minutes later and dropped off the starters to Max's table and my attention was pulled to them. Each food dish was on a long flat rectangular white plate with four identical portions. Every dish was almost a work of art and looked amazing.

Our food arrived next. It had barely hit the table before Bree helped herself to the beef dish. I went for the same one. The beef was tenderloin, thinly sliced and cooked medium rare. It was served on a lightly toasted slice of baguette, topped with blue cheese, walnut, and a clear thick amber liquid. The liquid turned out to be honey and the whole combination was to die for. Bree let out a soft, almost orgasmic, moan as she tried hers too. I eyed the dish longingly when I finished my one portion, but Bree gave me a look that warned I would lose an appendage if I even considered going for either one of the two remaining pieces.

I turned my attention to another of the dishes while Bree devoured the rest of the tasty beef one. This one was calamari that was served on a thinly sliced roasted potato and topped with caramelized onions and a citrus aioli.

By Odin's beard! I thought as all the flavors of it melded in my mouth, this might be better than the beef dish. There was a tanginess to it from the citrus, but there was also something with a bit of heat to it as well. I was really starting to love this place.

I did manage to lift my attention away from the food for a minute as I remembered I wasn't here to have a leisurely dinner. I scanned the restaurant which was now about half full. At first, I wasn't overly concerned, as it was just more tourists and businesspeople, but as I scanned the place, a couple caught my eye. They were both well-dressed and in their early forties. They looked like an executive couple out for a late business dinner, except for the three-inch aura surrounding the lady.

The aura meant she was Enhanced and had an orange core, which meant Super class. It was surrounded by a pale green ring, then a grey one, and a thick dark black one. The black outer ring was what really caught my attention, as that usually meant demon possession or someone exceptionally evil. My instincts leaned towards the latter; I didn't see someone who was possessed by a demon having a casual dinner. That black outline instantly pinged my threat meter to its highest setting. I also didn't like that I'd never seen an aura of this combination before. Pale green usually meant telepath, but I had no idea what the outer grey band represented. The only positive was that a three-inch sized aura meant she wasn't particularly powerful.

She had also been looking over in this direction, but quickly turned back to her companion when she saw that I was glancing her way. I called on my powers and thickened the air between her and Max.

"Bree. Don't look but we have an unknown Enhanced at my two o'clock. She is a brunette, in her forties, with a male companion, both in business wear. She has some sort of telepathic ability and a nasty black outline around her aura. Let Blue know."

Bree nodded. She casually knocked her fork on the floor towards Blue and leaned over and brought her up to speed. Blue instantly went on alert and leaned towards Stella to spread the word I assumed. The two bodyguards at their table also perked up. I'd noticed that Kurt paused in his eating long enough to do a quick scan of the restaurant.

You've got to love Were hearing, I thought to myself with a smile.

The waiter chose that moment to stop by and check how everyone was enjoying the food. We all smiled and nodded that it was great, and he went on his way.

This was a public venue and hotel security would be here in less than a minute at the slightest disturbance, so that should limit what she could do. I also wanted to keep things low profile, as I worried another incident involving us and Max would have the hotel asking us to leave. Currently, the suspicious couple was busy ordering food, so I continued eating and kept an eye on them. The latest dish was a shrimp one, it too was delicious, but I really wasn't giving it the attention it deserved.

The waiter finished taking their order, collected their menus, and left. The lady's attention turned back to our tables. To my surprise, she was looking at Stella and Blue's table and ignoring Max's, which had me relieved until her eyes started to glow. The guard on Blue's right suddenly went rigid and began reaching inside his suit jacket.

"Blue! Lincoln, right!" I whispered loudly while I shifted the thickened air so it was between Max's table and Blue's. Bree relayed my warning to Blue.

The guard mechanically pulled his 9mm pistol from his shoulder holster and began raising it towards Max.

Not good! I thought as I realized this lady had mind control powers.

Blue instantly reacted. She jammed her finger behind the trigger and proceeded to efficiently disarm the entranced bodyguard. In an attempt to keep this low profile, I used my air powers to silence the whole area over the table in case the gun went off. The gun fell to the floor and thankfully didn't go off. The guard tried to retrieve the gun, but Blue yanked his hand towards her and under the table. She casually picked up a steak knife in her other hand and drove it into the guard's hand, pinning it to the underside of the table.

Ouch! That had to sting.

The guard let out a silent scream, which probably would have been heard on the other side of the casino if I hadn't silenced the air around them. The pain also seemed to snap the guard out of his trance. Blue placed her hand firmly over the guard's mouth and tried to explain to him what had happened, but no sound came out. Trusting Blue to keep him quiet, I dropped the cloud of silence I'd placed over the table.

The lady shook her head and an angry snarl appeared on her lips at being thwarted. I doubted she'd stop at this one attempt and I needed to take her down. I started calling on my Electrical powers but remembered I needed to keep this low profile. I quickly changed tactics and went to my Air powers instead. I played with the air around her, but this attack would take time to kick in.

My fear grew as she turned her attention to Max's table. She focused on Kurt and her eyes started to glow again. I let out a deep breath of relief as Kurt was the best target from my perspective that she could have picked. Weres, due to their dual personalities, were quite resistant to mind control or mental probes. Now it was a race between my attack on her and her attack on Kurt. He continued eating like nothing was happening, which I took as a good sign.

A puzzled look suddenly appeared on my opponent's face as she tried to breathe. I'd removed the oxygen from the air around her. Her face went red and then started turning a pale blue shade. Just before she would have passed out, I returned the air around her to normal.

She sucked in air but the panicked expression on her face remained. Once she had caught her breath, she turned to her companion, frantic. He pulled out his wallet and dropped a stack of money on the table and they both got up and fled.

My attention was pulled to Blue's table as the guard with his hand pinned to the table got up enough to move back the chair he was sitting on and awkwardly climbed under the table. He stuffed a cloth napkin in his mouth and gave Blue a nod. She yanked the knife free and immediately opened a shadow portal directly under the guard. He disappeared. Once he was gone, she closed the portal and opened another one and casually tossed the bloody knife into it. Blue extended her foot and slid the gun that had fallen under Bree's chair into the portal and then closed it.

"Bree, tell Blue to use the shadows to track the attackers. We'll deal with them later."

Bree leaned over and whispered to Blue, who immediately tilted a menu up to create a small shadow and went almost into a trance as she stared into it. There was nowhere the two would-be assassins could hide now; their freedom was just an illusion.

Remarkably, the client and the bodyguard who had their backs to us were blissfully unaware of everything that just happened. Kurt gave me a small nod and went back to his eating competition with the big dude across the table.

The rest of the dinner was uneventful. At the very end of the meal, the client reached into his jacket, which instantly had me thickening the air between him and Max. He pulled out a neatly folded piece of paper. I dropped the air barrier between them as he handed it to Max. Max quietly studied the document.

After a long pause, Max simply said, "Forty-seven. Delivery September first," and placed the letter in his inner pocket.

The client nodded, extended his hand, and they shook on it. The client and bodyguard got up. Max and Kurt got to their feet as well.

They exchanged brief bows and the client and his large shadow left. Max and Kurt sat back down.

Max made a finger motion for me to take one of the empty seats. I joined him and Kurt at the table.

"Care to explain why one of your team pinned Brian's hand to the table like it was a butterfly on display?"

I was confused at the name for a moment and then realized Brian was the poor guard Blue skewered. I spent the next couple of minutes going over the attack.

"Where did Blue send Brian?"

I shrugged, turned to Blue, and asked her the same thing.

Blue broke from her trance-like state and said, "He is currently being treated at a nearby hospital."

She immediately went back to staring at the shadows again.

Max nodded. "It was a shame that Brian had to be injured, but your companion's response was appropriate under the circumstances. I also must congratulate you on doing all of this so discreetly. If my client had gotten wind of what had happened, it would have cost me a great deal of money."

The waiter came over and dropped off the bill to Max.

He left to give Max time to examine the bill. Max barely glanced at it and pulled out a shiny black credit card and placed it on top of the leather folder.

One thing was bugging me, so I asked, "At the end of the meal when you were speaking to your client, what did you mean by 'forty-seven'?"

"The price," Max smiled and added, "And to answer your next question—million."

Holy shit, one dinner and he made a deal worth $47 million. No wonder he was pleased we didn't spook the client. I also didn't feel as bad about the massive food bill Bree and I well, mostly Bree, must have racked up.

Max added, "I told you there was a reason I couldn't hide away for the week. This was just one of those reasons..."

***

Thirty minutes later, we had Max tucked back in his suite and had an hour before we needed to head down to sweep the boardroom for the seminar. The sun was down, and Blue had retrieved our favorite vampire, which gave us a full team. Blue had also tracked the two would-be assassins to rooms at Caesar's and it was time for some payback.

I'd been pondering what to do about our two attackers. The woman had attempted to murder Max, but the problem was I couldn't prove it. By the black outline around her aura, I had no doubt that she'd killed this way many times before. The implications of that slammed home. If she had succeeded, Brian would have been arrested for murder and she and her companion would have gone scot-free. I wondered how many of her victims were currently serving lengthy prison terms for crimes they physically committed but weren't mentally in control of their own actions for.

As our first responsibility was to keep Max safe, my initial thought had been to track them down, threaten them, and to force them to leave town. If they left town that would end the threat towards Max, but the idea of letting a serial murderer walk didn't sit well with me. They would kill again in the future, and if I just let them go, that would be on me.

The practical solution of just Blue and me paying her a visit and taking her out was my next thought. I knew Blue wouldn't have an issue with this, as in the world she came from a response like that was expected. That would end the threat to Max and prevent her from killing anyone else in the future. I dismissed it almost instantly; I had enough deaths on my conscience and didn't want to add another one if I could avoid it, no matter how much she probably deserved it.

I smiled as the perfect solution popped into my head. We could do a snatch and grab and drop her off at EIRT headquarters in Toronto. As she was Enhanced and was suspected of a crime, EIRT would be allowed to bring in a telepath to scan her mind. If the telepath found evidence of a crime, then she would be arrested. She may not have committed any crimes in Canada, but they would find out where she had done her previous killings and hand her over to the UN for trial. This approach was perfect, as it ended the threat against Max, she would wind up in prison for the rest of her life, and lastly, it would hopefully clear any innocents she'd used to commit her killings.

I made a call and was overjoyed that Sergeant Bobby Knight was on duty this evening and was currently at EIRT headquarters. I told him not to go anywhere and that we'd be there shortly. He wanted to know what this was all about, but I asked him to trust me and told him that he was better off not knowing. He groaned at that but said he'd wait for us.

I'd kept him in the dark on purpose, as EIRT had no jurisdiction in Las Vegas and technically he couldn't sanction us doing what we were about to do. If we just appeared in Toronto with an Enhanced Individual, he'd be duty bound to investigate her crimes and everything was good.

I brought everyone up to speed on my plan and had Bree go change into her standing Werepanther form, which would make her completely resistant to any mental attack. I was going to bring Liv as well, as vampires had a strong resistance to mental compulsion. Elementals also had high resistance, so I was covered. The only one of our party that was vulnerable was Blue. We knew this from Liv testing all of us before our confrontation with Gisele, the former Master of the French Vampire Court. The problem was we needed Blue's shadow abilities to do this. I wasn't overly concerned because Liv or Bree on their own would be more than enough to take down the target so we should be fine. Just to be extra safe, I also donned my armor.

Stella and Alteea would remain behind to protect Max while we were gone.

The four of us found a darkened corner in the suite and Blue opened a portal. Once again, speed was key here, so Liv was going first. She pulled out her katana and Blue nodded that it was time to go. Liv blurred through the portal and Bree dashed after her. I sprinted through, hard on her heels.

We came out in a large luxury bathroom. It wasn't as large as the ones in Max's suites, but it wasn't far off. It too had lovely marble floors, and I thought that whoever was importing high-end marble in this city must be making a small fortune. Bree was already out the door, so I focused back on the mission.

I entered the main room and found our brunette assassin with her hand extended towards the bed, but Liv's blade on her throat had stopped her dead in her tracks. Bree slipped in behind the killer and placed the claws of her right paw firmly on the back of her neck.

"Resist or attempt to mentally control one of us and you die," I announced as I walked closer to the bed.

"Who are you people?"

I realized that as Liv hadn't been with us at the restaurant, Blue had been in her old man disguise, Bree had been her human form, and my identity was obscured by my armor, so as far as our assassin was concerned, we were all strangers. I ignored her question for the moment and moved closer to the bed. I flipped up the pillow closest to her and found a loaded 9mm pistol. I picked it up and handed it to Blue. She opened a portal in a small shadow and the gun was gone.

I turned to our captive and popped the latch on the faceplate of the armor.

"You!" said the brunette.

I shifted my attention to Blue, "Go open another portal. We'll be right behind you."

Once Blue had left the room, I told Bree and Liv to take our prisoner to the bathroom. I followed behind them, and in almost no time, all of us disappeared into the shadows again.

This time we emerged at EIRT headquarters and Bobby's team was right there waiting for us in full tactical gear.

I said, "Arrest this one for attempted murder and get some power blocking cuffs and a collar on her. She is Enhanced and has the ability to mentally control people."

One of Bobby's team slapped the cuffs on her and another added the power blocking collar on her a few moments later. They led her away.

"You want to tell me what the heck is going on?" asked Bobby.

I filled him in and then we all had to give statements except for Liv who hadn't witnessed the hit attempt at the restaurant. Blue and I answered all his questions. With Bree he had to ask a series of yes or no type questions to get her statement and she nodded or shook her furry head in response.

Bobby asked why we didn't grab the accomplice as well. I explained that the man with her had no aura so if we grabbed him, he couldn't legally be mentally scanned as he was human. Enhanced Individuals didn't have those same protections, so when they were charged with a crime, a telepath could be brought in to scan their thoughts and find out if they were guilty or not. I figured that if this guy was an accomplice and had been there for a number of her killings, it would come up when she was scanned. She'd probably turn on him and agree to testify against him as a way to get a slight reduction in her sentence.

In the end, Bobby said, "It will be interesting to find out how many poor people ended up in prison or on death row because of her. Hopefully in the case of the latter, they haven't been executed yet."

Chapter 11

Monday, July 29

We made it back with ten minutes to spare before we had to go sweep the boardroom. This gave us just enough time for Bree to change back and chow down on some food.

We ended up in the same boardroom as we'd been in this afternoon. I was impressed that the lights I'd blown out earlier had been replaced. The Aloha staff had also swapped in another table to fill in for the one we warped out to explode in the arctic.

This time the sweep was uneventful and none of the tables had clocks that go boom under them. The event turned out to be a full house with most of the sixty-four seats filled. The attendees were from a wide range of cultures and backgrounds. All were nicely dressed, and by the gold rings, watches, and state-of-the-art laptops they carried, they weren't hurting for money.

Despite the nice attire, I had no doubt that almost every person here was a killer. The look and the way they carried themselves had my threat radar pinging off the scale. It didn't help that just about all of them had the telltale bulge of a shoulder holster, which meant they were armed. I spent the entire hour of Max's presentation thickening the air around him in case someone took a shot at him. There were a few tense moments when attendees reached inside their suit jackets, but they just pulled out a pen, a phone, or eyeglasses, and not a firearm.

The presentation was a disappointment, as most of it was about superior supply chains and logistics and their on-demand ordering system, which put Max's organization above their competitors. I'd been expecting cool pictures of the latest and greatest in modern weaponry, but a dentistry conference would have been more exciting than what Max was pitching. To be fair, everyone in the room seemed to be enthralled and Max got an enthusiastic round of applause when he finished.

I got even more anxious once the presentation was finished, as Max and an assistant insisted on visiting each of the tables to collect orders.

67

Blue and I shadowed them closely the whole time and watched each group they sat down with like hawks. Kurt also sat at each table beside Max and was on alert.

It was just past midnight by the time the whole thing wrapped up. Max had a happy smile on his face and an armful of orders, so I assumed everything went as planned. I was shocked that we got through the whole thing incident free.

The satisfaction of that and the calmness that came with it lasted about five minutes. We shadow travelled Max and Kurt and our entire group back to Max's suite. I was sorting out the protection detail to watch the suite for the night when the guard stationed in front of the suite poked his head in and said, "I have four guys out here who wish to speak with Zack Stevens and Olivia Dick. They are here on behalf of the West Coast Master."

Max raised an eyebrow at me, and I just shrugged as I had no idea what the Master vampire for the west coast of the United States would want with us. I did have a feeling that whatever it was, it wouldn't be good.

"Thanks, Jake. Tell them they'll be out in a moment."

I tried remembering everything I could about the West Coast Vampire Court. They were the newest of the vampire courts and had only been established in the 1920s. If I recalled correctly, they were a faction of the East Coast Vampire Court that had broken away due to some sort of falling out. The current Master was also the youngest Master vampire in the world at just over 300 years old. His name escaped me at the moment. Peter, or something with a *p*, and an Italian-sounding last name. They had also grown remarkably in power in the last hundred years, as the population on the west coast had exploded with rise of the tech industry out here.

"Stella, Blue, what do we know about the West Coast Court? And any idea why they'd be asking for me and Liv?"

Stella shrugged. "I have no idea why Pietro Inzarillo wants to see you. Blue and I in our roles with the English Court have not had much exposure to him or his court. We've only seen him briefly during the annual Master/Alpha Were summits but have never talked with him before. Generally, the only thing the US West Coast Court is concerned with is the US East Coast Court and vice versa—there is a lot of bad blood between the two of them."

We'd never had dealings with the East Coast one before either or anything to do with that rivalry, so that couldn't be the reason they wanted to see us. I also wondered how they even knew we were in town. On the other hand, all vampire courts had massive resources and all of them prized knowledge, so I shouldn't have been that shocked they knew we were in Vegas.

Stella dragged me from my thoughts as she continued, "Both courts are young compared to other courts in the world, but due to the economic power of the US, they are as powerful as any of the European or Asian courts. Both courts also have strong Sicilian backgrounds, and they are related through blood, and the West Coast family is a cadet branch of the East Coast ruling family. They are also tied heavily into the mafia. It has been speculated that all mob activity is run by both courts from behind the scenes and they are the true power behind them."

That also wasn't surprising; most major criminal organizations are usually tied in some ways to the vampire courts. They were first to do organized crime in a big way and those old habits were still around. Though in recent years, all vampire courts had invested heavily in legitimate enterprises, but I had no doubt they also kept their hands in the not-so-above-board stuff.

"So, do we decline the invitation and thank them for stopping by?" I asked.

Stella shook her head. "No. We are in his territory. It is his right to ask any vampire in his domain to make an appearance. If we decline, we will have to leave immediately and never return, or at a minimum, send Liv home and be without her services for the duration of this contract."

Shit, that is what I was afraid of, I thought. The idea of losing Liv for the rest of this protection detail didn't sit well with me. That meant we had no choice but to go meet Pietro and see what he wanted. "I guess we have no choice. Here's how we are going to do this..."

***

The four vampires outside of Max's suite looked like they had all come from the casting call for a mafia movie. All four were big, tall, and had no necks. I'd never met a group that suited the word 'goon' more in my life. The pit in my stomach was getting bigger by the second.

The one vampire who I sensed was in charge gave a small nod of approval at the formal tux I was wearing and the elegant emerald green lace dress Liv was wearing. Before stepping out the door for this meeting, I had Blue transport us via the shadows to our underground lab so we could change first. I'd made the mistake of appearing underdressed once to a vampire court and wasn't about to make that mistake again.

"Mister Inzarillo would like a word with you. We have a car waiting downstairs," said the lead goon in a deep unwavering voice.

He made an 'after you' gesture as two of his companions started walking down the hall towards the elevators. Liv and I followed them, and we were trailed by the lead goon and another no-neck.

The whole trip down the hall, elevator, and through the main level of the hotel, none of them said a word. I was tempted to make a smartass comment or two to get a reaction but wisely decided to use the time to study them instead. Their auras were the standard vampire one with a blood red colored core and a black outline. Size-wise their auras were all between five and seven inches, which meant they'd been vampires for at least fifty years or closer to hundred years for the seven-inch ones.

Due to their physical size, they would be dangerous as humans. Add in vampire speed and strength and the four of them made a very lethal group.

I also didn't like the fact that I had no idea what the West Coast Master wanted with us. At best, he was aware of our connection to the English Vampire Court and this was some sort of courtesy gesture on his part. He also might want information on the English Vampire Court or think that we were spies for the English Court. I worried too that this might just be an attempt to split our team so they could make an attempt on Max's life for the contract. I dismissed that last thought due to the contract only being $4 million—to most people that was a ton of cash, but to the Vampire Courts that money would barely qualify as pocket change.

Holy Mother of Thor! I thought as we exited the hotel and the heat hit us. It felt like we'd just walked into a blast furnace. It was coming up on one in the morning and it was as hot as home got during the height of summer. Dry heat or not, I instantly began sweating in the full tux I was in.

Thankfully, it was a short trip from the door to the air-conditioned black stretch limo that was waiting for us. We all piled in. I was on one side with a vampire on either side of me and Liv was seated across from me in an arrangement that mirrored my own.

In a short time, we left the bright lights of the main strip behind us and were on an expressway. I recalled stories of the early days of Vegas where mobsters would take people out to the desert and they were never heard from again. I prayed that wasn't the case here.

Five minutes later, we pulled off the expressway and ended up in a commercial industrial area that was far different from the glitter and lights I'd seen so far. This place wouldn't have been out of place in Hamilton's industrial north end. The car slowed down and made a left onto a street with a row of worn looking warehouses. I was starting to doubt that this meeting was the courtesy visit I'd been hoping for.

We stopped in front of a warehouse that had two black full-sized SUVs with tinted windows parked out front. There were another couple of large vampires waiting for us as we exited the limo. All six boxed us in and led us inside. The lighting inside the warehouse was dim and there were large wooden crates and boxes arranged in rows. Most of the shipping information was in Chinese and I had no clue what was inside them.

We walked deeper into the warehouse between the rows until we reached an open area in the center. A vampire with a two-foot aura sat in a chair behind a plain empty metal desk. The aura instantly tipped me off that this was Pietro Inzarillo, Master of the West Coast Court. While his aura was impressive, physically he wasn't much to look at; small, wiry, dark greased back hair, beady brown eyes, a large nose, and thin lips. A nicely tailored dark suit, red tie and pink dress shirt made him stand out from his men. He extended his right hand and pointed to the two vacant chairs in front of the desk, motioning that we should take a seat. There was a huge gold watch on his wrist and three oversized gold rings on his fingers.

There were also another six vampires, all male and with the same massive builds as the ones we'd met so far, standing alertly behind him. I was starting to wonder if Pietro had some sort of vampire goon cloning factory.

I took a seat in the cool metal chair and Liv did the same. Our escorts fanned out behind us, which put us in a circle of a dozen linebacker-sized vampires. Those were not good odds. Liv would be hard-pressed to take down one of them, and I probably wouldn't manage much better than that either. If I had the time to get airborne, I might be able to make this interesting, but with their vamp speed, I doubted I'd get that lucky.

A gravelly voice cut the air, "Thank you for accepting my invitation, Mr. Stevens. We have much to discuss."

Liv frowned at being ignored but didn't say anything.

I was tempted to say that we didn't have a choice, but so far he was being polite, so I decided to respond in kind, "Always an honor to meet a powerful master. How can we help you, Mr. Inzarillo?"

He gave a small smile which didn't reach his eyes and said, "I require information. There was a sizable contract put on your companion by the French Court. Shortly after that, the Master of the French Court died under mysterious circumstances, and a new Master came to power and the contract was rescinded. I want to know why."

Shit! This wasn't good. He was talking about us killing Giselle, the previous Master of the French Court. We'd been forced to, as it was the only way for us to get the hit contract that Giselle had put out on Olivia lifted. If he found out the truth, there was a good chance that he'd kill us for daring to harm another master. Elizabeth, the Master of the English Court knew about it, but she had been informed ahead of time and sanctioned it, as she viewed Giselle as a threat. She had also ordered us to never tell anyone about what happened.

Liv was about to say something, so I cut her off. "You'll have to ask Elizabeth about that. She has ordered us never to discuss what happened."

He frowned at my answer. Another thought occurred to me, so I asked, "May I ask why you wish to know? France and England are a long way from here and I would think you'd be more concerned about things closer to home."

He was quiet for a moment and then shrugged. "You may or may not be aware, but I'm the youngest master in the world. My court is also the newest. That should make us the weakest, but we are able to hold our own with any court on the planet. The reason for that parity is information. Silicon Valley, Seattle, and all the other thriving tech centers on the west coast are mine. Their information is my information. Anything typed into a browser or a phone, I know about. I use that information to keep other courts focused on things other than us. I like knowing everything and it troubles me when a major event, like when a new Master of the French Court comes unexpectedly to power, and I don't know why this happened. As the contract on your companion was lifted after the previous Master of the French Court died, I suspect you know the answer and you will share it with me."

I really didn't like where this was heading but took a deep breath and said, "As I said earlier, you will have to ask Elizabeth as we are not allowed to discuss the events in question."

"Very well, we'll do this another way then." He gave a small nod and before I could blink, his goons were on us.

Less than a minute later, Liv and I were bound securely to our chairs. A nameless goon dragged my chair back from the desk by a few feet and the lead goon who picked us up at the hotel stepped into the space my chair had just occupied. He cracked his knuckles and gave me a half smile as he towered above me.

This was going to suck, I thought before he punched me in the gut hard enough to push me and the chair back another six inches. I gasped for breath and it felt like I'd been hit by a crowbar. A sharp crack filled the air as he broke my nose with his next hit and the entire world went black for a moment and I saw stars.

"Stop!" screamed Olivia to my left.

"Tell us what happened and this ends," said Pietro, looking at Liv.

"Don't say a fucking—" was all I managed to get out before another hammer blow nailed me in the chest. I may have screamed a bit as I felt a couple of my ribs crack.

Only three hits and I felt like I'd been run over by a freight train.

"Zack?" cried Liv.

"I'm fine. Reminds me of Blue's training, only gentler..." I laughed, but the effect was spoiled as I coughed and gasped for breath again.

I caught the goon winding up for another blow and tried to brace myself.

The blow didn't come and instead Blue's stern voice pieced the air, "Let them go or everyone dies!"

The cavalry had arrived. I looked over to my right and spotted Stella in her Hyde form, Bree in her standing Werepanther form, and Blue holding a large anti-tank missile on her shoulder.

"Is that a rocket launcher?" asked Pietro in astonishment.

Liv giggled. "No. A rocket launcher wouldn't do enough damage. That is a Javelin Anti-Tank Missile."

Memories of the last time Blue had one of those came flooding back and I suddenly was more scared of her at this moment than I had been during this whole brutal integration. "Um, Blue, we've discussed this. What is my policy about you using stolen military-grade hardware?"

"Silence, Zack," was Blue's reply.

"You'll kill your friends if you fire that," Pietro said with a smirk.

"You'd have killed them anyways if this continued. This will be less painful for them and I will rest easy knowing that I avenged them."

The smirk disappeared and he mumbled, "Crazy bitch!" under his breath.

Understatement of the year there, I thought with a grin to myself. Blue might be bloodthirsty at times but at least she was on my side. Though another part of me knew she would pull that trigger if she had to.

"Cut them free and everyone walks out of here in one piece," ordered Blue.

The vampires all looked at Pietro who sat motionless for a moment. He sighed and said, "Cut them loose."

The lead goon reached into his suit and slowly pulled out a switchblade. He flicked it open and cut the ropes on my chair first and then Liv's. I struggled to get to my feet, but Liv blurred up to me and put her arm around me to help. She led us away but kept us out of the direct line of fire between Blue and Pietro.

"This isn't over!" warned Pietro.

In a low voice, I asked Liv to stop. She did. I called on my power and manipulated the air around us. I turned my head towards the Master and said, "Yes, it is. Your word that this ends now and that you won't bother us again or I'll have Blue pull the trigger."

"You're bluffing."

"I have thickened the air in front of us and that should be enough for us to survive the blast. I'm going to count to five. Your word or we'll see if your vampire speed can outrun a missile. One…"

As I continued my count, I was a touch worried that Pietro would have enough speed to escape the blast if Blue did launch the missile. The only thing that was probably keeping him in check was that this was probably his warehouse full of inventory. The warehouse and its contents were undoubtedly insured, but I was willing to bet there was probably a small fortune of illicit goodies stashed in here too, and those wouldn't be covered. I was also betting that he wouldn't want the attention that would come from having a large explosion happen here.

At four, Pietro yelled out, "Enough. You have my word that I will leave you and your companions alone."

I let out the deep breath that I'd been holding. I nodded and Liv and I continued walking towards Blue. The moment we reached her, she made a gesture with her free hand and pointed at the shadows. Bree got on the other side of me and all three of us went through the portal together and left the warehouse behind.

We came out of shadows and into the living room back at our house in Hamilton. Stella's Hyde form emerged from the shadows and instantly transformed back into her harmless little girl form. I silently urged Blue to appear, as a few long seconds went by without her appearing. I gave a silent prayer of thanks when she finally stepped out of the shadows. My concern went back into overdrive when I noticed she wasn't carrying the missile launcher anymore.

My expression must have telegraphed my thoughts as Blue looked at me and said, "Calm yourself. I stopped by the underground lab first to put my toy away." She moved closer to me and took over Liv's position in supporting me. She opened another portal and said, "Liv, Bree, go back and keep an eye on Max. Stella and I will get Zack the help he needs."

Once Liv and Bree disappeared into the shadows, Blue closed the portal. I heard Stella apologizing on the phone to Marion about waking her and asking if we could stop by to get me healed. Stella once again said sorry about calling so early and added that I was badly in need of her help.

It was probably close to two in the morning Las Vegas time, which meant it was 5 a.m. here in Hamilton. No wonder Marion wasn't happy. Thankfully, her sense of duty overcame her surliness at been awakened so early and a few minutes later we were at her apartment door.

Marion opened the door in a pink bathrobe and bunny slippers. Her long silver hair was all over the place. She also looked every one of her seventy-two years at this moment. It bothered me to see age catching up with her. Marion had always been in my life. She'd been my mother's healer too. She was probably the closest thing I had to family other than my team.

The unhappy look on her face instantly changed to one of concern as she looked at me. My right eye had swollen shut and I was sure I had two black eyes to go with the broken nose. Add in the cracked ribs and possible internal injuries as well, and I probably looked like total shit.

"Damn! Someone got a good piece of you."

"It was mutual. I'm sure my face and ribs messed up his hand real good."

Marion rolled her eyes. "Get in here and I'll get you patched up."

Blue helped me across the threshold and walked us across the apartment to the couch. I winced as she helped me sit down.

Marion offered Stella and Blue tea, but both declined. I noticed Stella cover her mouth as she yawned.

"You two can go. Get some sleep. I'll fly back to the house after this and sleep at home for the night. I'll call you when I'm up."

"You sure?" asked Stella with concern.

"Yeah. Bree will be happy that we won't have to share a bed."

The two of them left and Marion began looking me over. "So, what did this to you?"

"Vampire mobsters wanted to have a chat about a prior adventure my team and I had. They didn't like my lack of answers."

"Where the hell did you run into vampire mobsters?" asked Marion as she numbed the nerves around my face.

"Las Vegas."

"I'd ask, but it is too darn early in the morning for this crap, so we'll just enjoy some quiet time as I fix you up."

Thirty minutes later, Marion had done her magic and I was pain free and more or less in one piece. I thanked her for her work.

"You'll be less thankful when you get my bill. I'm charging you double rate for disturbing my beauty sleep."

"Ah, so that is your secret to staying so young and lovely."

Marion shook her head at me but there was a smile creeping in at the corners of her mouth. "Get out of here. And stay out of trouble."

I left Marion's and headed for the roof of her building. I stepped out and saw the sun was just starting to come up over the horizon. I called on my Air powers, lifted off the roof and flew towards home.

We'd gotten through our first full day of protecting Max. We'd almost been blown up, had an Enhanced try and shoot Max via one of his bodyguards, and been worked over by vampire mobsters, and we had four more days of this shit to go. At least I'd get to sleep in my own bed tonight, err, this morning—this time zone thing was annoying.

Chapter 12

Tuesday, July 30

I was stunned that I didn't drag my sorry ass out of bed until after three that afternoon. But I shouldn't have been surprised about my long sleep. Marion had healed me enough that I knew this was a side effect. Her magic sped up the healing but that came at a price, as my body needed lots of rest and food to offset that. I smiled as my stomach predictably rumbled on time and decided food was my first priority.

I sighed at the sight of the bloodstained tux and dress shirt lying on the floor where I'd dumped them last night in my haste to get some sleep. I wondered if the Aloha's dry-cleaning service would be able to save them or not.

As I headed downstairs to the kitchen, I panicked for a moment as I remembered that Max had another three o'clock client meeting, which meant I wasn't there to protect him. I calmed down as I remembered that Vegas was three hours behind us and it was only noon there.

After enjoying a hearty breakfast, I needed a quick shower and shave. I examined my face in the mirror as I shaved and was pleased that there was no visible bruising around my eyes, my nose seemed back to normal, and a quick glance at my ribcage also showed no damage. Marion had done good work.

It also dawned on me that even though there were five of us on the team, the majority of the time it was I who needed healing. Last night was a classic example. The vampire goon could have just as easily smacked around Liv instead of me. Liv would have been a better choice to beat on, as with her vampire healing, she could have taken a lot more abuse than I could have. A part of me though was grateful he worked me over, as watching that happen to Liv would have been much harder to take than the beating I received.

I studied my plain face in the mirror and wondered what made it so punchable. Maybe it was my not-so-sparkling personality that made people want to hit me. Either way, it was a bit annoying that I kept ending up on Marion's doorstep at all hours of the day.

As I showered, I remembered why I was the one who always needed healing—I was the only one of us who didn't have supernatural healing abilities. Liv just needed fresh blood to repair any damage she took. Bree had her incredible Were healing. Stella was healed each time she changed between forms. Blue could put herself in a healing trance. Alteea was the only one other than me who couldn't rapidly heal, but due to her small size, we usually found roles for her away from any direct combat.

By one that afternoon Vegas time, I was back in Max's suite and going over his schedule with him for the day. The meeting at three wasn't a client meeting but an employee seminar. Max liked to have his people from around the world come in for a meeting so that they were all ready to go for the orders he would be picking up from this week. I relaxed when I heard the attendees were Max's employees. That should make things easier from a protection standpoint.

Whatever ease I got from the employee seminar went out the window when Max brought up his next and last meeting for the day. He was meeting with one of his larger clients at a private club for dinner at nine that night. I hated the idea of someone else picking the venue. We'd have no control of it, and we'd be on someone else's home turf. The club was called the Blind Tiger and was located in the basement of one of the original hotels on Fremont Street. The news got worse when Max added that we were only allowed to bring four people.

"That is annoying, but four of my team should be able to keep you safe."

Max shook his head. "No, four people total. I will be bringing Kurt which means it will be you and one member of your team."

This just keeps getting worse.

We had to go to a venue of someone else's choosing, and to top things off, I had to leave more than half my team behind. That pretty much meant it would be Blue and me going as we'd need her powers to travel there directly rather than risking going out in public on the trips there and back. On the upside, if we were attacked with Blue there, I'd just have to keep the attackers busy long enough for Blue to get Max to safety. She could just duck under the table and shadow portal out of there with him. I still didn't like it, but Max was the boss, and it was his neck on the line. I decided to find out more about tonight. "Does the hotel own the club?"

Max shrugged. "No idea. I have been there a couple of times. Manny always likes to meet there. The food is first rate."

Kurt nodded in agreement and a small smile appeared on his usually neutral face.

"Blue, Stella, see what you can find out about this club." Blue disappeared into a bathroom and I assumed would be using the shadows to spy on the club. Stella moved to the dining room table and opened her laptop.

"What can you tell me about Manny?"

"Manny is a vampire. He supplies most of the vampire courts with weapons and equipment for their daytime security forces. We've been doing business for years and he is one of my larger clients."

There were a dozen or so vampire courts and each one probably had a hundred or so security people that worked at them. Supplying weapons to 1,200 people didn't seem like it would be that large an order compared to full nations and other large groups Max dealt with and I asked about that.

"Quality over quantity. The vampire courts only want the best on the market. An AK-47 goes for around $600 and up. For most of my clients that is all they need. The average price for an assault rifle that the vampire courts buy is close to $25,000."

"Why such a price difference?"

"They usually kit the guns out with custom everything and just about every accessory you could imagine. They are also fanatical about going with the latest and greatest and upgrade their inventories much more frequently than anyone else on the planet. Add in that they are also buying silver or wood composite rounds and that they live-fire train more than any other group and the numbers add up pretty quickly."

That made sense. It was kind of like buying a Rolls-Royce versus a Honda Civic—you had to sell a heck of a lot of Civics for the same price as a single Rolls.

Max and I chatted for a few more minutes about other details. I asked about tomorrow's first appointment and Max informed me that his first appointment was a client meeting in the boardroom downstairs at three. Max's cell rang, and after he checked the display, said he had to take the call. I got up from the couch to find out what Stella had found on the club.

"Nothing. I have been searching for the Blind Tiger in Las Vegas, but there isn't a single mention of it online," said Stella as she kept clicking away.

I frowned at that. "You must be losing your touch. Max said he'd met Manny there a couple of times, which means the club has been open at least three years. There has to be something about it."

Stella exhaled deeply in frustration. "You'd think, but I have been searching the whole time and not found even a hint or a mention that this club exists."

I was puzzled. It was a private club, but this was the Internet. There was no way an exclusive private club doesn't get mentioned or leaked to the Net.

Blue appeared shortly after that and said, "The club is closed at this moment and there is no one there. The place is decorated like a 1920s speakeasy. It has a long bar running the length of it and no more than a dozen tables. The tables are all eight seaters and spaced far enough apart from each other that privacy is not an issue. The kitchen area in back is modern and clean. The only thing of note was the sign above the bar proclaiming that the Blind Tiger is Neutral Ground, and that neutrality was enforced by the West Coast Vampire Court, the West Coast Mages' Council, and the Las Vegas Pack."

I heard rumors about neutral meeting places for different members and races of Enhanceds but had never come across one before. This also explained why the Internet was coming up blank, as either Pietro's tech connections had wiped it clean, or the Mages' Council had used a spell to erase any information about the club.

I had mixed feelings about this neutral ground. On the one hand, any assassin who took a shot at Max while he was there was screwed, as they'd be hunted down by three powerful groups. The problem was one of those groups probably wasn't happy with me at this moment. I doubted Pietro would be dumb enough to take a run at us in a club under his protection. He would have to deal with the Mages' Council and Vegas Pack if he did. He'd also given his word to leave us alone, though that word might have just covered us leaving his warehouse in one piece. Just to be safe I wanted some more insurance. "Stella, call Sarah and tell her what happened last night with Pietro. See if she or Elizabeth can send Pietro a strongly worded statement to leave us alone."

Stella stopped typing instantly. "You sure that is a good idea? If they do this, we will be in their debt…"

Blue didn't say anything, but her tail was making quick unhappy movements behind her which pretty much told me where she stood on this idea.

"I'm sure it is a bad idea but it is better than Pietro coming after us again. We have enough on our plate trying to stop everyone out there trying to collect on this contract. If Pietro is harboring a grudge about his interrogation being interrupted and turns his full attention to us, we are going to get overwhelmed very quickly. I'd prefer to take my chances that whatever task the English Court wants down the road won't be too onerous."

Stella nodded and headed into one of the suite's bedrooms to make a call.

I knew I was playing a dangerous game by involving the English Vampire Court in our mess but hoped it would be worth the cost. My doubts grew about this plan as minutes ticked by and Stella hadn't emerged from the bedroom.

To my surprise, Stella came out of the bedroom with a big smile on her face which was one of the last things I was expecting.

"Sarah has sent a strongly worded statement to Pietro on behalf of Elizabeth stating that we are 'Friends of the English Vampire Court and are to be treated accordingly.' Elizabeth is also demanding an apology from Pietro for the breach of protocol."

I was shocked by the first part of Stella's statement. 'Friends of the Court' meant we were under the protection of the English Court and they would avenge us if anything happened. That would make Pietro think twice before attacking us. The second part of the statement had me confused. "Huh? What breach of protocol?"

Stella's eyes twinkled and she said, "Once you told him that Elizabeth had ordered you to not discuss what happened with Giselle, he should have stopped the interrogation and contacted Elizabeth. Since he continued to question you, the English Vampire Court takes that as a slap in the face to their authority; Sarah and Elizabeth were quite angry."

You have to love Vampire politics, I thought to myself with a smile. "Do we owe them for this then?"

Stella shook her head. "No. They are doing this as a courtesy due to you being assaulted by Pietro when you were just upholding Elizabeth's order." Stella paused for a moment and all joy left her face. "We got lucky here. When I first asked Sarah for a favor, she was very concerned that we were about to get in over our heads with the English Court and she begged me to reconsider. If it hadn't been for Pietro violating protocol, we would have owed the English Court deeply. Sarah always warned me that once Elizabeth gets her claws into someone, very few have broken free of that grasp."

I nodded somberly at that. She was right, and I'd probably underestimated what that favor would have cost us. The English Vampire Court treated us very well, but they were still a vampire court, and there was a reason vampire courts were feared throughout the Enhanced world. For now, it was a win and I'd take it.

***

An hour or so later, all of us except for Stella, who was back at the suite guarding Max, and Liv, who was in her daytime slumber back at the house, were doing a sweep of the boardroom in advance of the employee seminar.

Thankfully the search was uneventful, and we didn't find anything out of the ordinary. Of the eight tables, seven were in use. The head table had a Management sign on it. The other six tables were divided up by region—North America, South America, Europe, Asia, Africa, and the Middle East. Europe, and South America only had four place settings whereas all the other tables had the full eight. I guessed that meant the two with four settings weren't as busy as the others, which made sense. North America having eight seats puzzled me, but then I remembered Max's meeting with Black Horse and the North American table size made sense. Odin only knew how many private military contractors worked out of the US and supplying them would be some serious coin.

Just before 3 p.m., people started to arrive. Kurt was at the main doors greeting staff as they arrived while I was seated beside Max at the head table. Bree, Stella, Blue, and Alteea were all positioned at strategic places around the room.

The Asia contingent was the first group to arrive and the aura around one of them put me on alert. Red made up the primary part of the woman's aura, with a good-sized chunk of yellow and then slivers of blue and brown. The aura meant she was a mage with Fire as her primary element, Air as her secondary, and the barest amounts of Water and Nature. Thankfully, her aura was barely a couple of inches wide, so she wasn't that powerful. She also looked like she was barely out of her teens. Mages aged slowly though, and she was probably at least in her mid-thirties and possibly in her early forties.

The problem with Mages was that they didn't need a lot of power to be dangerous. Sure, she probably couldn't create a massive fireball that would instantly fry everyone in the room, but what if she could cast a six inch one that originated in the center of Max's chest. That mini one would kill him just as effectively as the huge one.

I used my Air power to gently push Alteea's invisible form over to me and said, "The woman in that group is a mage. Tell Stella, Blue, and Bree."

A high pitched, "Okay, Master," seemed to come out of thin air, and I watched her tiny rainbow aura dart off towards Bree.

The smaller South American group arrived next, but they were just human. Right behind them, the African staff arrived, and I groaned to myself as the tallest man in the group was a Werelion. His purple, red, and gold aura though was a few inches smaller than Kurt's, and the dominance game between them barely lasted a second. The second it was over, Kurt leaned in and whispered something in his ear and then pointed at Bree.

The man nodded and walked directly towards Bree. As he approached, she went rigid and her ice blue eyes glowed briefly as her beast woke up. He stopped a few feet from her, and they locked eyes. Almost instantly he lowered his gaze and then said something and held out his hand. Bree smiled and shook his hand.

Bree winning these dominance battles despite her youth always amused and confused me. I could only speculate that it was willpower and not actual power that was the determining factor, as Bree had more willpower than almost anyone I'd ever met.

I knew that Kurt had purposely pointed out Bree, so she and the newcomer could get their dominance thing out of the way which prevented it from becoming an issue if either was caught by surprise.

I thought about summoning Alteea again and having her tell Blue and Stella about the Werelion, but Stella had watched the whole encounter and would recognize the man was a Were. Blue also would have been keenly aware of what had happened.

I pulled my attention back to the door as another group showed up. They were a diverse group, but I figured as there were eight of them, they either had to be the North American or Middle Eastern group; I leaned towards them being American.

My hunch was confirmed a few minutes later as they sat down at the North American table. A group of four showed up next and they had to be the Europeans. Just behind them was another group of eight, which had to be the Middle Eastern staff. I sighed as I caught a flash of orange aura through the crowd before my view was blocked.

Orange meant the person was a member of the Super class. The Super class had such a wide range of powers that unless I'd seen the same aura, I usually had no clue what their abilities were.

I strained to get another look through the crowd. As the Europeans cleared the doorway, I finally got a better look. I was simultaneously relieved and concerned at the full aura which consisted of an orange core surrounded by a red and white checkered pattern. The good news was I knew that aura; the bad news was he was a Tank. Tanks were immensely strong and could soak up tremendous amounts of damage. Thankfully, his aura was barely two inches wide which meant he wasn't overly powerful. He still wasn't a person I'd like to run into in a dark alley if my power was depleted, but Stella's Hyde form had him drastically outclassed in terms of raw power.

I used my Air power to push Alteea back over to me and told her to spread the news that the man in the green tie was a Tank. This time she didn't say anything and just darted right off towards Stella.

I now had a mage, a Werelion, and a Tank to worry about, and that didn't include Odin-only-knew how many of Max's staff were packing. Out of the three Enhanceds, the mage concerned me the most. To go after Max, the Tank and Werelion would have to get close to him first, and we should be able to prevent that. The mage, however, could strike at range, and that was why she made me the most nervous. Worse, she could have just enspelled an item, so she wouldn't have to chant or make complicated motions with her hands, which would have given us some warning she was up to something. All it would take was for her to point the item at Max and say a single word to activate it. She would be the one I'd be keeping the closest eye on.

At this point, she was smiling and talking with her group and didn't seem to have a care in the world. That made me relax a bit, as I would have thought that if she was planning to assassinate her boss, she'd be quiet, nervous, watchful of Max. So far, she'd barely even looked this way.

I hoped Max's presentation would start by announcing juicy bonuses for all employees, which would deter them from taking a shot at the $4 million.

With the last party seated, Kurt had locked the doors and returned to our table. We also asked the Aloha staff not to disturb the meeting and we'd locked the door to the service entrance after we completed our sweep earlier. The emergency exit was also secured. With the doors locked, that allowed us to have more people standing close by all the tables. We also killed the bank of lights behind the area of the main screen behind us. This would allow Blue to grab Max and disappear into the shadows at the slightest hint of something going amiss.

Max had assured me that his staff was loyal, and none of them would even think about trying to collect the contract on him. I pressed him on that, and he mentioned that some of his better salespeople had cleared that number in commissions in previous years. Bree asked if he was hiring. I hoped she was joking.

He also informed me that all employees had gone through rigorous screening before being hired and that he ran random checks to test that loyalty on an ongoing basis. I was puzzled at how he tested loyalty and he explained that he'd pay an actor to offer a bribe from a competitor to employees, and if someone took the offer they'd be dismissed on the spot.

Once everyone was seated, Max stood up with a remote for the PowerPoint presentation on the main screen and the TV's around the room. The room quieted down, and Max started to talk. I thickened the air around him and focused on the mage, watching for any sign of trouble from her.

Max covered last year's sales number and congratulated a few of the groups and certain individuals for their accomplishments last year. A lady in the North American group was awarded the Golden Gun, which was a trophy for having the highest sales number. Max's assistant walked it over to her and Max thanked the woman for all her hard work. The crowd also politely applauded, but there were one or two individuals around the room whose fake smiles certainly didn't reach their eyes. I guessed they were the second- and third-place finishers.

Max pointed out that a couple of the groups' numbers were down and encouraged them to do better this year. He flipped to the next slide and excitedly unveiled new improvements to their automated inventory and ordering system which would be rolled out next week.

I tuned him out as he went over the features, but his staff clapped or cheered at certain changes. The mage was just listening contently to Max and didn't seem to be doing anything that made me overly nervous.

Thirty minutes later, Max was still going through his presentation and I was feeling pretty good. The mage hadn't done a thing to arouse my suspicion, and I hoped this whole thing was going to end quietly and uneventfully.

Not two seconds after I had that thought, things went to shit.

Bree yelled out, "Ford!" and I watched her dive at the South American table and take two guys down who had their hands inside their tailored suits. The other two at the table were pulling out pistols from their suit jackets.

I briefly puzzled at the "Ford" battle cry but then realized Bree had meant to use "Lincoln," which was our code word for trouble.

Kurt sprang from his seat and hauled Max away. Stella jumped up on the Middle Eastern table and ran across it to close the distance between the two guys with guns out. Bree was pummeling the snot out of the two she'd engaged.

I kept the air thickened between Max's fleeing form and the shooters. I also called on my Electrical power to take them down, but a few people had stood up and blocked my shot.

I watched in horror as one of the shooters turned his gun towards Stella's tiny human form that was barreling towards him at top speed. Just as he brought the gun in line for a shot at her, she morphed into her monstrous Hyde form. Screams erupted and chaos descended. I messed with the air around the shooters' table to silence the noise.

A split second later, the shooter fired two shots at Stella. Smoke and a small flame erupted from the barrel of the pistol, but it was completely silent. Those two shots were all he managed to fire before Stella plowed into him like a freight train. He went down hard. His companion turned his weapon at Stella, but she swung a brutal left hook at him. He flew across the room and crashed into a massive flat-screen TV on the left wall. The screen cracked on impact and a shower of sparks erupted from it. The sound of the impact echoed in the room. I winced at that and wished I'd widened my cloud of silence. Someone outside this room must have heard that. That would bring us attention we didn't need.

Kurt leapt up on the table to my right and was making a beeline for the South American table. I figured that meant he had gotten Max to Blue and she'd gotten him to safety. He reached the table but just stood there sort of dumbfounded for a moment. Bree was getting back to her feet as both of her would-be assassins were down. Stella's first shooter was lying on the floor not moving and the other one was in a heap under the wrecked TV screen. Kurt recovered from his surprise at seeing all the threats down and quickly picked the two discarded guns off the floor.

With the four down and Max safely back at our secret lab, the threat was over. We'd stopped another attempt on his life.

Chapter 13

Tuesday, July 30

I had just started wondering what I should do about the four would-be assassins and the whole room full of attendees when Max's voice calmly and firmly came from behind me, "Everyone take your seats! The excitement is over. Is anyone hurt?"

I turned to see him walking back towards me with Blue right behind him. I shot a glare at Blue and she just shrugged.

Kurt relieved the two unconscious men Bree had taken down of their weapons.

The room went quiet as Max took his original spot back. "Sorry for the disruption and I'm glad no one was hurt. Under the circumstances, I'll be cutting the rest of the presentation short. I will email it out to everyone, and you can read it at your leisure. For now, I ask that you all calmly leave the room by the main exit and enjoy the next few days here in Vegas. Get plenty of rest—the next few weeks and months are going to busy."

The groups all got up and slowly walked to the doors. Max whispered something in his assistant's ear who then dashed off to get to the door ahead of the groups.

Blue closed on me and said, "Sorry, I observed from the shadows what was occurring in the room after we departed. Once I told Max the threats were down, he insisted we return. He said these were his people and he wanted to know what happened."

I nodded. Max was the boss while we worked for him so I couldn't fault Blue for obeying him. The assistant unlocked the doors and the main group streamed out. I spotted an anxious looking Aloha employee trying to peek around the exiting people as if trying to see what had happened in the room. The moment the last person had left, Max's assistant followed, closing the door behind him, and I got a brief glimpse of him leading the Aloha employee away from the room as the door shut.

Max joined Blue and me and said, "Danny will keep the Aloha staff busy for a few minutes, but we don't have much time. I want to know why my whole South American team just tried to kill me."

He didn't wait for my answer and walked over to the three downed men where Kurt, Bree, and Stella stood over them. We followed him over.

Max looked over the three men and then walked over to a nearby table and grabbed a pitcher of ice water. He came back to the two Bree had dispatched and tossed the entire pitcher over both of them. The one didn't react, but the other sputtered and cried out as the icy liquid splashed over him.

The man cried out in Spanish, and then blinked his eyes open. A look of complete fear came over him but then he tried to lunge for Max. Kurt was quicker and drove a foot into the man's chest to keep him pinned to the floor.

Max shook his head and asked, "Why, Mateo, why? Have I not been good to you and your coworkers?"

A crestfallen expression appeared on Mateo's face. "*Si*, you've been very kind. We had no choice. The Binoa Cartel has our families. We were instructed to kill you, or they would torture and kill our loved ones."

Max cursed under his breath. "I should have known that deal would come back to bite me…"

"What deal?"

Max sighed. "About two years ago, the Binoa Cartel contacted me and placed a large order. But they wanted to pay cash on delivery which is something I don't like to do. Normally, we get half the money electronically first and then receive the other half the same way after delivery. I got greedy and took the deal, but a part of me was worried this was a scam, so I hired Black Horse's Angel Squad as insurance in case things went south. They got there ahead of the shipment and were in the hills on overwatch. Sure enough, once the plane landed with the weapons, my agent came out of the plane and insisted on seeing the cash. The cartel personnel showed the cash but then gunned him down as well as the pilot and the two cargo handlers. Angel Squad hit them hard and recovered the weapons and the cash."

Max paused and shook his head. "This was where I made my biggest mistake. I should have taken the cash and left some of the weapons, less the amount I'd need to compensate the families of the four killed. Or even taken both the cash and the weapons. If I'd done that, then they probably would have let things go. Instead, I made some calls and got in touch with the Binoa's main rival cartel. I had them come by and pick up the weapons as I wanted payback for the Binoa Cartel killing my people…"

I liked Max's solution—they tried to screw him over, so he paid them back in kind. "Did that work?"

Max nodded. "Oh yes. The two cartels have been at each other's throats nonstop since. I figured the two of them would eventually wipe each other out and promptly forgot about the whole thing. I'm guessing once that hit contract came on the market the Binoa Cartel saw it as their chance to pay me back for what I'd done and make four million in the process. And now that decision is going to cost these good men their families."

Mateo had tears streaming down his face and all fight had gone out of him.

Max glanced down at him and said, "I'm sorry, Mateo, for getting your families pulled into this mess. If I could, I'd try and get them back."

"Why can't you?" asked Bree.

"Because it would take at least a day for me to get Angel Squad down there and that is assuming they are available and not already on assignment. Once the cartel finds out the attempt failed; they will dispose of the families."

Blue piped up, "Do you know where the families are being held?"

Mateo nodded and said, "*Si*. They are at the main compound of the Binoa Cartel."

"Kurt, let him up." Blue then turned back to Mateo. "Can you show me where that is on a map?"

Mateo bobbed his head and Kurt lifted his foot off Mateo's chest. Mateo was slow to get to his feet and stifled a gasp of pain once he did. He was unsteady on his feet but slowly managed to stagger after Blue. Bree had given him quite a beating. That also made me realize that the remaining three were still unconscious and needed medical help.

"Stella, call Marion and see if she is available to heal these guys."

Stella nodded and grabbed her phone.

A map of Columbia came up on the main projection screen and the three remaining working flat-screens around the room. I knew why Blue was having Mateo show where the Binoa compound was. Once she had the location, she'd be able to spy on it from the shadows and find where the men's families were being held. The next logical step was for us to mount a rescue, but I was struggling with that. Our job for this week was to protect Max, not to leave him unguarded while we risked our necks on a rescue mission. I also didn't want to see innocent women and children killed either, so I was torn on this.

Stella interrupted my thoughts as she ended the call and said, "Marion is waiting for us."

I nodded and turned my attention to Blue. There was a Google satellite map up on the screen now of a large building surround by jungle, which I assumed was the Binoa compound. Blue had also wandered off and was now behind the main screen and was standing there in a trance staring into the shadows. I held my tongue and waited for her to finish.

A few seconds later, Blue blinked her purple eyes and gave a pointy toothed smile. "I've found them. They are being held in two rooms in the basement of the compound. There is an armed guard outside the door to each room. The one room has a closet which is closed; it is dark and large enough for me to create a portal to get us into the room. The other room though is a problem. It is fully lit and the biggest shadow in it is no bigger than a foot wide."

Stella added, "We can pull the same trick we used with the Mint to get into that room?"

The trick Stella was referring to was sending Alteea through the small shadow with an umbrella so she could open it and create a larger shadow that we could use. "Okay, folks; let's pump the brakes. Our job is to keep Max safe not to be traipsing off to Columbia."

Bree jumped in the moment I finished, "But if we don't do anything, innocent people will die…"

Max said, "These are my people; I'll pay you $250,000 to bring them back alive."

I held out my hands and said, "Whoa. Let's hold off on this for the moment. Aloha staff will be coming in here soon and we'll be caught up with them if we don't get out of here soon. Stella, Bree, grab those guys off the floor. Blue open a portal to our lab—we'll all go there and regroup and figure this thing out. We'll also bring Marion there to treat them. Once we are secure, we can figure out what we are going to do, okay?"

I got nods from everyone and Stella changed back into her Hyde form and tossed an unconscious man over each shoulder. Bree carefully lifted the guy who'd smashed into the TV screen. Blue opened a portal and Max, Kurt, and a nervous looking Mateo went through first. I let Bree and Stella go next and followed them and then Blue was the last one through.

***

Fifteen minutes later we were all at our underground secret lab in London. Blue had gone and picked up Marion, who started healing the three injured people moments after she arrived.

In the meantime, I discussed things with Max and worked out that he'd pay us the $250,000 for rescuing his employees' families and he agreed to hide out here in the lab while we did this. That way he'd be safe while we were gone. I also planned on leaving Bree here for extra protection.

We came up with a quick and dirty plan as we had no time to waste; The cartel might start torturing and killing at any time.

As we stood around getting ready, my nervousness at this whole plan began to build. If we screwed this up, the best we could hope for was a quick death. More likely we'd be looking at a slow, painful, and gruesome end. My gut was screaming at me that this was a very bad idea, and I voiced those concerns.

Bree laughed and said, "This can't be any worse than Blue's training exercise last month."

I shuddered as I recalled our ill-fated run through the basement of Russian FSB headquarters. Leading up to that exercise, Blue had been very mysterious. She blacked out the gold *H.H.* on my uniform and insisted Liv wear a mask to hide her identity. She'd opened a shadow portal and handed me a folded piece of paper with the instructions not to open it until I went through. It was a map of where the exit portal would be waiting. We'd barely stepped into the drab and dingy place when the alarm went off. We spent the next fifteen minutes running from Ice elementals, Werebears, and a half-mage half-cyborg thing that all tried their best to kill us.

We made it out by the skin of our teeth. I remember after Marion shaking her head at me and asking how I'd managed to get a severe case of frostbite on my left arm while also getting first degree burns on my right leg. I'd also been on edge for weeks, expecting a Russian hit squad to give us a payback visit for our little incursion.

I'd torn a strip out of Blue after that adventure, and we had a long discussion about limits to her crazy training exercises going forward.

Blue perked up at Bree's comment and in a mock Russian accent said, "What? You survived. Good training exercise, *da*?"

I shook my head at her. "You've been spending way too much time with Dmitri..."

Dmitri was a Russian Werebear who was currently running one of the two GRC13 teams. GRC13 was Canada's federal elite anti-monster squads. Dmitri and Blue had been dating since we'd worked with them to take down a demon at the beginning of the year.

She gave me a pointy toothed smile and then made a motion with her hands. "Portal's open. Go!"

Mateo and I went through the portal first and emerged in a dark closet. I'd brought Mateo along as we didn't speak Spanish and because the hostages knew him and would cooperate quicker with us with him there.

I messed with the air around the room outside the closet to dampen down all sound. The moment I'd done that, I gave Mateo a nod and he opened the door. There were two women and five kids in the room and all of them tried to talk as soon as they saw Mateo, but no sound came out. All of them got dumbfounded looks at the loss of their speaking abilities. Mateo shook his head and put a finger to his lips. He then made hand motions for all of them to come to him.

So far so good. If everything went to plan, we'd snatch the women and children right out from under Binoa Cartel's nose and we'd be long gone before they were even aware of what had happened.

Mateo got them all lined up and we waited. On cue, Stella popped out of the shadows and Mateo began pointing at the shadows and herding the group towards them.

Just as the first child disappeared into the shadows, I watched in horror as the doorknob to the main door started to turn. Either we had bad luck or the complete lack of sound from the room tipped off the guard that something was amiss.

I dropped the cloud of silence and said, "We've got company! Mateo, get these people moving."

Mateo excitedly said something in Spanish and the group surged towards the open shadow portal.

I thickened the air between the door and us and called on my Lightning power. The door opened revealing a surprised looking guard. He pawed frantically for the AK-47 he had hanging off a shoulder strap. Before he could even touch it, I nailed him with a bolt of lightning. The force of the blast knocked him off his feet and out of the doorway.

Not even two seconds after that an alarm blared throughout the compound.

"New plan!" I yelled. "Stella, change and go through that wall and block the door to the other room."

Screams erupted from the women and children as Stella's harmless little girl form was replaced by her massive, monstrous Hyde form. Thankfully, Mateo wasn't fazed and kept pushing, herding the group towards the shadows.

Stella grunted and then charged at the solid wall. There was a huge crash as she went through the cinderblock like it was paper. Screams of fear and pain came from the other room. One of the kids and a woman in that room were hit by the debris.

Before I could assess their damage, another guard appeared at our doorway. He opened up instantly with a burst of gun fire. Thanks to my earlier precautions of putting up an Air shield, a wall of bullets hung suspended about two feet in front of me. I tossed another bolt of lightning and nailed the guard. He continued firing as he fell back, and the remaining rounds stitched a line across the ceiling. Thankfully, the bullets buried themselves into the ceiling and didn't ricochet—if they had, they might have made it over my barrier and people could have been hurt.

To my relief, Mateo had cleared the people from this room, and he dashed through the new doorway Stella had created. There was a woman lying unconscious in a pile of rubble and she had a nasty bloody headwound. It was still bleeding which meant she was alive. Standing over her was a little girl screaming and cradling her left arm which was bleeding and broken at an awkward angle. Both of them had been injured from the debris caused when Stella went through the wall. That bothered me, as it was my fault they had been hurt.

Another goon appeared at the doorway and fired his pistol at me. I raised my hand and directed another blast of lightning his way. Unfortunately, he dove out of the way and I missed.

An uncomfortable sensation came over me and I groaned as I recognized it as an Earth elemental. Earth was the opposite element to Air, and it was always unnerving for people with elemental powers to be in the presence of their opposing element. Worse, with every passing second, the feeling was getting stronger which meant they were heading our way.

"Mateo, pick up the pace!" I yelled.

Mateo said something in Spanish and a woman and three kids, including the little girl with the broken arm, came through the hole and made a beeline for the shadows.

A hand holding a pistol appeared in the doorway and started firing random shots into the room. My Air shield caught the bullets that headed towards us. I aimed and shot another blast of lightning at the doorway. I just grazed the hand, but it was enough that he dropped the pistol and screamed in pain.

I gritted my teeth as the nasty sensation of the Earth elemental got stronger. Either the Earth elemental was moments away or they were super powerful. Neither option was good. Mateo came through the hole in the wall carrying the helpless woman over his shoulder.

There was a loud crash in the other room and Stella's Hyde form flew past the hole and went deeper into the room. A large rocky form chased after her—the Earth elemental had arrived.

I wanted to go help her, but Mateo hadn't quite gotten to the shadows yet. Another guard showed up at the threshold to this room and opened fire with the assault rifle he was carrying. More lead joined the growing wall of what I already had in front of me. I tossed a white-hot bolt of lightning at him. He shook like he was having a seizure and then collapsed to the floor.

A familiar angry grunt echoed loudly from the adjacent room and now it was the Earth elemental's turn to fly. His large form tumbled by the hole in the wall and the entire place shook as he hit the far wall. Stella's lumbering form went after him.

"Stella, NO! Let's get the fuck out of here!"

She came to a halt like an elephant on ice but managed to turn towards me. She came through the hole and I pointed at the shadows. I turned and was just ahead of her. Behind us I could hear the massive rumbling steps of the Earth elemental who was in pursuit.

I prayed the portal was still open because if it wasn't, I would probably knock myself senseless on the back wall of the closet. Worse, with Stella just behind me, if the wall didn't kill me, her impact would. I exhaled with relief as I emerged into the hangar area back at the lab. Stella came through a split second later.

"Close the portal! Close it now!" I screamed as I turned around towards the shadows and called on my Electrical power.

Blue made a sharp gesture with her hand. I built up a massive charge of power and watched the shadows with fear.

After a few seconds, I dismissed the power I'd built up, as Blue had obviously closed the shadow portal in time.

Stella's crisp British accent came from beside me, "That was too bloody close!"

I just nodded mutely in agreement.

We headed to the main area of the lab and I stopped in the doorway in surprise at all the activity going on. We rarely brought people here, so seeing this many people felt odd. Marion had been busy while we were gone, as all three of the unconscious men were awake and back on their feet. She was just finishing up on healing the little girl's arm. The dark-haired girl immediately jumped into her father's waiting arms. The man hugged her and stroked her hair, but his worried gaze was on the unconscious woman with the head wound lying on the table. I assumed the woman was his wife and the little girl's mother. Marion turned her attention to her.

I was feeling a bit nostalgic, as I hadn't done any hostage rescue since my Hamilton Hurricane days. As I listened to the excited Spanish filling the room and watched the other three families exchanging hugs and shedding tears of joy, it brought back that same sense of satisfaction I had from my hero days.

Bree was carrying a couple cast-iron pans from the Food-O-Tron to where Max and Kurt were sitting. I had no doubt she and Kurt were both enjoying early dinners. Weres didn't let little things like rescue operations interrupt fueling their hyper-metabolisms. To be fair, food sounded pretty good to me too.

Max spotted me and gave me a smile and nod of acknowledgement. I tipped my head towards him but kept walking by his table to the back of the room. I called on my Air power and lifted myself between the two arcing Tesla coils. The noise of the room was drowned out by the constant hum and crackle of the powerful blue sparks jumping between the coils. I almost moaned at how good the electricity felt flowing into me. All the power I'd expended earlier was rapidly recharging.

After I was topped up, I opened my eyes and found that most of the room was staring at me. I felt a bit self-conscious and left the space between the coils and landed gently on the floor in front of them. Being back at floor level seemed to break the spell everyone was under and conversations resumed.

A quick check of my phone showed it was just past 5:30 p.m. Las Vegas time. We had the dinner appointment at nine, but I figured that was more than enough time for me to have a light meal and still have an appetite later.

A few minutes later, I joined Max, Kurt, Bree, and Stella at a table and sat down to enjoy some chicken fingers with fries and a Coke.

Stella announced that she needed a tea and got up from the table. She stopped for a moment when she was by me, leaned in, and said, "Max has deposited the $250,000 to our account."

A cheer went up across the room and I glanced over. The woman Marion had been working on was now awake and slowly getting to her feet. Her head wound was healed, and she seemed to be okay as she was embraced by her daughter and husband. I said a silent prayer of thanks to Odin for that. She and the little girl were injured because of my decision to send Stella through the wall and I was relieved they were both going to be alright. I had too many faces haunting my dreams from my hero past where things hadn't turned out as planned, not adding another one to that collection was a blessing.

I asked Max what would happen to them now, and he said he would get them new identities and resettle them in the US. He'd roll them into the North American group, as he was suspending operations in South America for the foreseeable future. He said he put them up in a couple of the empty suites at the Aloha while he waited for their papers to be finished. Max did ask if we could feed them here first.

Bree was just finishing up her meal, so I turned to her and said, "Bree, get the nice people some food."

"Why me?"

I laughed and said, "Because they don't know how to use the Food-O-Tron, and you're the expert."

She rolled her eyes, shoved the last bit of food from her plate into her mouth, and got to her feet.

"Feed Marion first—she's just done a lot of healing and probably needs a good meal."

Bree nodded and turned towards Marion who was packing up her stuff at the far table. Once I'd finished my meal, I got up and joined Bree in serving meals to our guests and soon everyone was eating and happy.

Chapter 14

Tuesday, July 30

Max, Kurt, Blue, and I shadow traveled into the men's room at the Blind Tiger just before nine. If the bathroom was anything to go by, this place was swanky. It was done up in polished dark wood with brass accents and cream-colored marble. The bigger tip-off was the hand towels—they were cloth, which was something you only saw at classy places.

Kurt took the lead and I followed just behind with Max on my tail and Blue covering our backs. Kurt was carrying a fair-sized cooler bag and when I'd asked about it earlier, Max just said its contents were a gift for Manny. My curiosity was piqued but I hadn't pressed him further. I wondered what you got for a weapons-dealing vampire—I guess I'd find out soon enough.

We came out into a hallway where the impressive interior décor of the bathroom continued. We exited the hallway and entered the restaurant itself. In front of us was a lovely polished bar top that ran the length of the restaurant. I instantly got a twenties and thirties vibe from the place as I glanced around. Everything was tastefully done and elegant—the place reeked of old money.

Behind the bar was a vampire with a five-inch aura around him which meant he'd been turned for a good fifty years or more. Physically, he wasn't much to look at, thin and a couple of inches shorter than I was. He had a healthy head of dark hair with a touch of grey creeping in near his temples. The pinstriped dark suit he wore seemed a bit dated but it also fit nicely with the nostalgic feeling of the place.

He spotted us, and with speed that was almost like magic, he pulled a sawed-off shotgun from beneath the bar.

I subtly thickened the air between us and him in case he got trigger happy.

"Private club. What are you doing here?" he snarled.

From behind me, Max spoke up, "We're guests of Manny. Here for our nine o'clock reservation. Please excuse our unorthodox entrance."

"Pierre! Those are my guests!" exclaimed an effeminate sounding vampire who blurred up to the bar.

I blinked at the bright pink suit he was wearing as that wasn't something you saw every day. The psychedelic pink and blue long hair he was sporting was also different. Add in the sparkly white alligator skin boots that were peeking out from under the bottom of the tapered pants and I quickly got the impression that this was a vampire who wasn't timid about bold fashion choices. The outfit was so distracting that his impressive ten-inch blood-red-and-black- outlined aura barely registered with me. An aura that size suggested Manny was at least 150 years old, and I was probably on the low side with that guess.

"My apologies, Manny," said the bartender and as quick as it had appeared, the shotgun was gone again.

Manny fanned his hand towards Pierre and said, "No worries. I can't stay mad at a man who makes the perfect Bloody Mary."

I was a bit surprised that Pierre used Manny's first name as I would have expected him to use a last name instead to show respect. I asked about this later and Max told me Manny didn't have a last name. He was just Manny, like Cher was just Cher.

Manny blurred up to Kurt and greeted him. "Lovely to see my favorite hunk of a wolfman!"

Kurt just gave a brief nod and stepped aside. Manny eyed me over. As I was in full armor, his assessment probably didn't yield much. I popped the face plate on the armor to be polite.

Manny grinned and said, "I've never dined with RoboCop before—this will be delightful."

He held out his hand to me palm down. I wasn't sure if he wanted me to kiss it or shake it. I went with an awkward handshake.

Manny went dead still for a moment as he clasped my gauntleted hand. "Does my nose deceive me, or do I detect a tasty Air elemental here?"

I groaned to myself at his comment. My blood was like catnip to vampires—they couldn't resist it. Vampires coveted Enhanced blood over normal human blood as it usually increased their power or came with desirable side effects. My blood generally tended to give them almost an extreme happiness-like high.

Before I couldn't answer, he frowned and added, "Pity. You've been marked by another. The good ones are always taken!"

He released my hand and I moved to the side. His marked comment threw me for a moment but then I remembered Olivia had made me drink her blood one time to save my life. Her doing that had marked me as hers to other vampires. If she did that again, she'd be able to sense me no matter where I was, and if it happened a third time, I would become her human servant. That was something I was avoiding at all costs—lack of freewill and the possible loss of my powers wasn't something I wanted.

"Maxie!" exclaimed Manny with a sheer look of joy on his face.

He blurred forward and theatrically air kissed both of Max's cheeks. He gave Max a once-over and nodded approvingly. "You've been working out. I'm glad you are taking care of yourself. Humans live such short lives; I do so approve of you doing everything to prolong yours…"

Max smiled. "Allow me to introduce the final member of our party. Manny, this is Blue."

Manny paused for a moment and examined Blue who was currently in her old man disguise. He cocked his head and said, "Something is off with you… your heartbeat is way too slow for a human."

Blue tapped the gold band hidden on her wrist and the illusion disappeared.

Manny clapped his hands excitedly. "Oh, girlfriend! I love that shade of blue on you! It is only surpassed by those gorgeous lavender eyes and…" he paused and dramatically put his hand over his heart before adding, "And that hair—purple is such a tricky color to pull off, but that tint is perfect. You'll have to give me a small lock so my stylist can copy it for me when this has grown out. And a sword! That is a fashion accessory that not many can pull off in this day and age."

Blue preened at this. Manny's treatment of Blue endeared him to me. Most people tended to have initially negative reactions to her appearance.

Blue thanked him and reached for the device on her wrist.

"Don't you dare turn that back on! You are not hiding behind that frumpy, boring old man illusion tonight. Your natural form will be accepted here—all members are Enhanced and sophisticated enough to appreciate your true beauty."

Blue shrugged and let her hand fall away.

With that settled, Manny led us to the table he'd reserved. Only one of the eight tables was occupied. That table had a couple of fairly powerful mages who were in a deep and heated discussion about a rogue wizard in Chicago and barely glanced our way when we passed by. There was a vampire maître d' standing at the entrance who smiled and gave a small nod to Max. Off to the side was another vampire who, judging by his attire, I guessed was our waiter.

The tables were all three-quarter circular leather booths with two chairs at the open end. Manny slid into the booth and shimmied around to the center. Max and I sat at either side of him, with Kurt and Blue bookending us.

The moment we were settled, the waiter appeared. "Will there be any more people joining you this evening?" he asked with a slight French accent.

Manny shook his head. "No, Pierre, this is the entire party for the night."

"Very good. Shall I remove these then?" said Pierre, pointing at the two empty chairs.

"Please."

Pierre busied himself with clearing the chairs and was promptly forgotten when Max took the cooler from Kurt and handed it to Manny.

"Oh, a gift!" exclaimed Manny, beaming.

He opened the bag and pulled out what looked like a chilled bottle of wine. His smiled got bigger as he read the label, "Drow blood. Max, you naughty man! Are you trying to get me drunk?"

An image of Liv stoned out of her gourd after she drained the leader of a group of dark elves that had been hunting us came back to me and made me smile. It was the only time I'd ever seen her drunk as vampires had an insanely high tolerance to alcohol and were almost immune to its effects. The only thing more impressive than how wasted she got was the hangover she had the next day.

Max laughed. "You caught me; anything to get an edge when negotiating with you, Manny."

Manny tucked the bottle back in the cooler. "Well your little ploy has failed. Tonight, I will be sticking to my little glass here of delightful O-positive, but I will enjoy your lovely gift afterwards, thank you."

I glanced at the celery salted rim of Manny's Bloody Mary glass. I realized the color of what I thought was tomato juice was off and that it was blood. Before Liv and rest of my team joined me, having someone drinking a glass of human blood would have made me a touch queasy, but after months of watching Liv do this, it barely registered.

Manny and Max made small talk. We ordered our drinks and dinners. Once again, I just had a Coke as I was working.

The seat I was in had a decent view of the restaurant which let me keep an eye on things. A party of fae walked in and was seated at a nearby table. All six of them were wood elves which had me relaxing a bit. Wood elves were generally aligned to good, but that term was relative as fae in general had an odd moral code. They hadn't paid us the slightest bit of attention when passing our table or since they sat down. By their demeanor, they seemed to be celebrating something and were more concerned about the flow of drinks than anything else. I kept an eye on them, but they barely registered on my threat meter.

During our appetizers, Manny regaled us with tales of his past. I was amused about the story he told about a crazy dinner he'd had with King Alfonso XII of Spain. It seemed the discussion between Manny and the king got so heated, that Manny had to flee for the French border after the king summoned his guards. Manny just made it to the safety of France only minutes before the sun came up. This was the third story Manny had told where he'd pissed off someone important or of noble birth and barely got away.

I was enjoying Manny's company; he had this charm and zest for life that just made you enjoy being around him.

Just before our dinner arrived, two new guests were greeted by the maître d'. I eyed the attractive female vampire in the form-fitting elegant red dress with matching heels as she sauntered by. She was hanging off a man who would have looked at home on a fashion magazine or fitness cover. The man's aura indicated he was Werewolf. The two of them were seated nearby. I assessed their threat value as I watched them out of the corner of my eye and with each passing second lowered it. The two of them were seriously into each other. The only danger they currently posed was crossing the line of good taste with their excessive displays of public affection.

Everyone in the room was Enhanced and technically a threat. At this point, I should have been almost freaking out over Max's safety. I wasn't sure if my calmness was due to Manny's unflappable nature, or because this was neutral ground, or the fact that the food was stunning, but this was probably the most relaxed I'd felt since we'd taken this case.

That abruptly changed about halfway through the main course. Manny had us all laughing about a night out he had in Paris with an incubus, a Wererat with a stutter, and three off-duty policemen at the turn of the nineteenth century. A moment later, my mirth disappeared as four familiar vampires walked in. They were the same four that picked Liv and me up at the hotel last night, including the leader who'd worked me over.

At first, I was hoping things would be fine, as all four of them had smiles and were exchanging pleasant remarks with the host. That hope disappeared the moment the lead goon saw me. His mirth instantly vanished, and he marched over to the table like an enraged bull and his gaze never left mine.

I began calling on my powers as a precaution. The problem was I was between a rock and hard place. If I attacked first, the three groups that protected this place would hunt me down to the ends of the Earth. I could defend myself freely if he attacked first. The downside was that his first attack would probably kill me.

He radiated rage as he towered in front of the table. "You dare to show your face here in my Master's club?"

Shit! I knew Pietro had an interest in this place, as he was one of the three protectors, but I hadn't known he owned it. I kicked myself for my stupidity as the vampire staff should have tipped me off.

"Saul!" barked Manny in a cold tone. He had to repeat himself twice before Saul reluctantly pulled his attention from me to Manny.

To my surprise, a look of shock and fear appeared on Saul's large face as he saw Manny.

"S-s-sorry, Manny, I didn't see you there," stammered Saul.

"Everyone here is my guest. I will also remind you that this is neutral ground, and that Pietro wouldn't be amused if you broke that accord. Now apologize to Zack and be on your way."

Every trace of Manny's normally whimsical tone had disappeared in that previous statement and I quickly was re-evaluating Manny. There was more to him than I'd first assumed. I also wondered what the hell was going on. Saul was one of Pietro's lieutenants; the only thing he should fear was displeasing Pietro, his Master. Anyone who dared lay a finger on him would face the wrath of the entire West Coast

Vampire court, and yet, Manny had just ordered him around like Saul was a newly minted vampire. This whole scene had me questioning everything I knew about the vampire courts.

The look on Saul's face implied that he'd rather chew glass than apologize, but after a long few seconds he said, "Sorry for disturbing your dinner, Mr. Stevens."

He looked back at Manny. He was given a dismissive wave and wandered back to his crew.

Manny's face instantly changed back to the smiling and carefree one I'd grown accustomed to. He started talking about an adventure he'd had in the twenties in New York while the rest of us slowly went back to eating.

I kept an eye on Saul and his party as they were seated at the farthest possible table from us, and not once did they even glance over.

As I half-listened to Manny's tale and went back to eating my dinner, my thoughts churned as I tried to process what had happened just now. Some of the crazier conspiracy sites on the Internet speculated that there was a power behind all the vampire courts—a rumored council of Elders that kept the courts in check and policed the entire vampire community. I could tell from his aura that Manny wasn't old enough to be an Elder, but those same rumors also talked of agents of the council. Those agents acted on behalf of the Elders and were judge, jury, and executioners in the vampire world. Could Manny be one of those agents? The brief transformation of Manny when he dealt with Saul certainly indicated there was something more to Manny than first glance revealed, but was that enough to confirm he was one of those feared council agents?

By the end of dinner, I'd given up on trying to figure out what Manny was. His charm was so disarming that I almost wondered if I'd imagined everything earlier. Vampires gained power as they aged; I wondered if Manny's power included disarming people's concerns.

After Pierre cleared our plates and said he'd return with the dessert menus, Manny pulled a thick envelope from the inside pocket of his jacket and handed it to Max. "Read it later and we can haggle over the price later this week by phone. Let's not sully a lovely evening by discussing business."

Max nodded and casually slipped the documents into his own pocket. The rest of the evening at the restaurant was uneventful.

Chapter 15

Tuesday, July 30

We used the shadows to travel from the men's room at the Blind Tiger back to Max's suite. Liv, Bree, Stella, and Alteea were all there waiting for us. Stella was tugging on her braid, which was her tell that something was wrong. Bree's eyes were red and bloodshot like she'd been crying.

"What happened?"

Stella was the first to speak, "About two hours ago, a hit team struck and killed Max's body double in the suite below us. LVPD detectives want to talk to Max. I suspect that Aloha management will also want a word after the detectives are done."

Max stopped dead. "Peter! How could this happen? What about the two guards that were protecting him?"

I assumed Peter was the name of the double.

Stella shook her head. "I'm sorry, Max. They were both killed as well."

I jumped in and asked, "Why didn't you call us?"

Stella got an annoyed look on her face. "We did, both your and Blue's phone, but each time it went straight to voicemail."

I checked my phone and sure enough, there were four voicemails waiting for me.

"Sorry, Zack," said Max. "That was my fault. The Blind Tiger runs cell jammers. They don't like dinners being interrupted by calls."

That little piece of information would have been nice to have beforehand. If we'd been attacked at the restaurant, I'd planned on using my phone to call in the rest of the team. Thankfully, that hadn't happened, and what was done was done.

Max spoke again and pulled me from my thoughts. "What happened? Peter and both guards had military training and had also been trained by Kurt; they shouldn't have been taken down easily…"

Stella nodded. "The first we knew anything was wrong was when we heard gunfire from the suite below us. After Bree changed into her standing Werepanther form, Bree, Olivia, Alteea, and I left the suite and took the stairs down. The guard that had been stationed outside the room was dead and slumped against the wall. He had two small wounds on his forehead—"

Kurt jumped in, "Double tapped, probably by a silenced twenty-two. Very little noise."

Max nodded and Stella continued, "The door to the suite was partially ajar. We went in and the entire suite had been shot up. Peter and the second guard had been shot multiple times. It looked like both had been reaching for their own weapons when it happened."

Stella paused. "After that, we did a quick search of the suite in case the attackers were still around. Once the suite was secured, Liv called us over and pointed to the street below. The window by the couch had been completely blown out. I assumed that the gunfire had done that, but when we looked out, we saw four men in dark tactical gear frantically rolling up parachutes and then they all jumped into a white van and peeled out. We sent Alteea after them to get a license plate number, but she didn't reach them in time, and they got away. After that, we called the police and waited for them to arrive. We told the detectives about the white van and they said they'd put out an alert, but I have no idea whether they found it or not. They finished questioning us about ten minutes ago and gave us this card so you could call them once you returned."

Stella handed the card to Max. I was surprised that the detectives hadn't held them as suspects and asked about that.

"One of the detectives found a video that was trending online which showed the four attackers parachuting from the hotel. Once they saw that, they stopped treating us as possible suspects. Also, there are two armed officers just outside the door, so I'm guessing they assumed we wouldn't be going anywhere. If they had known about Blue's abilities, I doubt they would have been so easy going."

I visualized the attack. The hit team breeched the suite and took the guard down before he could get his gun. Four automatic rifles versus one pistol; Peter didn't have a chance.

The parachuting had me betting these guys were ex-military. The suite below us was on the thirty-ninth floor and that probably meant we were 400 or so feet up. I had no idea what the minimum altitude to deploy a parachute was, but 400 feet seemed pretty freaking low.

Not a lot of room for error at that height. And yet, despite that, all four managed to land safely. There was no way this was their first time doing something like that.

These guys were pros and executed their plans flawlessly. The only mistake they made was hitting the double instead of Max.

I wondered how they got into the hotel, but it would have been easy enough to get a room say on the thirty-seventh floor with a fake name and credit card. Come into the hotel looking like tourists with luggage. Get to the room and gear up. Once the hall was clear, make a beeline to the stairwell. I doubted many people used the stairs this high up.

I worried that they might try again once they learned they didn't get the real Max. I went over our precautions in my head to see if I could spot any flaws. The first flaw was the guard stationed outside this suite would probably be killed, but I didn't see a way to prevent that from happening. Bree, Kurt, or Liv would hear the silenced pistol and from that point things should go more in our favor. The use of weapons meant the attackers probably weren't Enhanced so even if they hit at night when just Liv and Alteea were on duty, Liv should be more than a match for them, and we'd be there shortly to back her up. If they hit us at any other time, they'd be even worse off.

Max dialed the detectives, which was the start of a very long night.

***

It was after 1:30 a.m. by the time the detectives and Aloha management were done with us. The Aloha had had enough and wanted Max out. Max managed to sweet talk them, well, that, and I'm sure the $100,000 damage deposit added to their account helped to change their minds. They did give us a strong warning though that at the next complaint, incident, or even hiccup, we were all out on the streets. A part of me wished they had kicked us out as then we could stash Max and Kurt at our hidden lab and this assignment would have gotten much easier. A part of me knew that Max wouldn't go for that and we'd just end up at another hotel and that would be worse than staying here. At least with the Aloha, we'd scoped it out and knew the layout. Another hotel would mean we'd be starting from scratch.

The detectives revealed that a white van that matched the description of the getaway vehicle had been spotted. It was currently burning at the edge of the city limits. That meant the assassins had switched to another vehicle they'd had waiting and torched the van to get rid of any evidence. I had no doubt that the four were now long gone and in the wind. A part of me longed to go after them and bring them to justice for what they'd done, but that wasn't the job.

Kurt had made some calls and two more guards were on a red-eye flight and would be here by morning. Max had also made arrangements so that Peter and the two unfortunate guards' families would be taken care of financially for the rest of their lives. It was a nice gesture on Max's part, but it was a poor substitute for a father or husband who would never be coming home.

I tried to talk to Max to find out tomorrow's schedule, but he just said, "Seminar tomorrow at one in the afternoon. The rest we can deal with tomorrow."

After that he opened the bar fridge, grabbed a handful of mini liquor bottles, and disappeared into his room. Kurt just shrugged and went to his room, leaving us to our own devices. Max was taking the deaths of his team members hard and I decided that he was right; we could work out things tomorrow.

My own team seemed down too, and I needed to get them focused.

"Okay, people, we kept Max alive so far, but we still have two and half days to go. Bree, good job today spotting the South Americans as they went for their guns. Though I'll point out the code word is *Lincoln* not *Ford*."

Bree shrugged, "Same difference."

I swear that girl was hanging out with Liv too much. I hoped that Bree's discipline, work ethic, and conscientiousness would rub off on my favorite crazy vampire, but it felt like things were working the other way. Though having our rage-filled Were taking on a slightly more easygoing attitude was a plus. It was probably one of the reasons Bree hadn't killed me the other morning when I woke up draped all over her.

"Also, saving those families today was good work. We added another $250,000 to our accounts, and even better, saved innocent women and children from certain death. That makes today a win no matter what else happened."

I noted their smiles and nods and that each of them stood a little straighter. "Tomorrow is probably going to be another busy day and we need to stay on our toes. Liv, do you mind guarding the suite with Alteea; I would like Bree to get some sleep."

Liv gave Alteea a smile and said, "We got this."

"Good. Blue and Stella will relieve you before sunrise." I turned towards Stella and added, "Once Max is out of bed, call me and I'll be right over. I want to get the rest of the day's schedule from him so we can see what we are in for."

We chatted together for a few more minutes, but after seeing Stella yawn for the fourth time in less than a minute, I suggested we call it a night. Stella, Blue, Bree, and I retired to the suite across the hall.

After getting ready for bed, I joined Bree in our king size accommodations for the night. As she turned off the light, I said, "Remember, missy, keep to your side of the bed… I don't want to wake up tomorrow with you all over me like last time."

I smiled as I imagined her rolling her eyes at that comment, and she asked, "You sure you didn't take any head injuries today because your memory seems a little faulty."

"My memory is just fine. I just wanted to remind you that Liv is your best friend and that she called dibs on me, so please try and resist ravaging my manly form."

Bree snickered and simply said, "Good night, Zack."

Chapter 16

Wednesday, July 31

*S**on of a bitch!* I thought as I woke up spooned right up against Bree again. To make matters worse, this time I'd somehow gotten my hand under her T-shirt and currently had her ample breast cupped in my hand. It also wasn't going anywhere fast as Bree's arm and hand were pinning it in place. I was starting to wonder if my subconscious had some sort of unresolved horny death wish.

I wondered if tonight we should change the sleeping arrangements and I'd share a bed with Blue or Stella. I dismissed those options as quickly as I thought of it. Stella with her history of abuse at the hands of her adopted father would be an even worse choice than sleeping with Bree. If she woke up with me spooning her like this, there'd be nothing left of me but a bloody stain by the time her Hyde form was done with me. Blue was always armed, and if I tried to spoon her, I'd probably impale myself on her sword or one of the many daggers she kept tucked away about her person.

I argued with myself about whether I should try and tug my hand free or just face the fact that I was screwed and wake her. Bree was a light sleeper and I figured if I moved my hand, I would startle her, and as she was about three times stronger than I was and could snap my arm like twig, I decided that would be a bad idea.

I decided to wake her, "Um, Bree?"

"Mmm…I don't want to go to school today…" she mumbled back.

I raised my voice and called her name again.

"What?" she answered back in a grumpy tone, and then her whole body went dead still, "Is your hand where I think it is?"

The humorous part of me was tempted to answer, 'Yeah, but only because I got tired of groping your ass…' but I didn't think she'd find that funny at this moment. Instead, I went with, "Please don't kill me!"

She removed my hand from her chest and said, "I'm not going to kill you… that would be too quick."

I may have whimpered as I rolled away from her and quickly apologized to her.

"Words are nice, but food is better—breakfast now! And this time, get a second order of those yummy cherry pastries."

After a quick, "Yes, ma'am, thank you, ma'am," I jumped from the bed and dashed to the main room like I was on fire. I dialed room service like my life depended on it because quite frankly it did. I ordered one of everything on the breakfast menu again. I added in two extra orders of cherry pastries to be safe and went with a Western omelet for myself. I also begged them to make it quick.

I hung up and yelled, "Food is ordered. Can I run you a bath, iron your clothes, or give you a kidney while we wait for it to arrive?"

"Really? Run me a bath—feeling me up wasn't enough, so now you want to see me naked too? Honestly, Zack, I really need to have a talk with Liv about how you aren't good boyfriend material for her..."

I rubbed my temples. *This is going to be a very long day...*

***

After a tense breakfast with Bree, I left her to her own devices and joined Blue and Stella in Max's suite. Max and Kurt were just finishing up their own breakfast when I arrived. I was anxious to go over the day's schedule but waited until he was done eating. Max also looked a little worse for wear today and I suspected he was nursing a nasty hangover. I didn't think it was possible to get drunk off bar miniatures, but if you drink enough of them...

Once he was done, he gingerly made his way to the couch and I joined him. "So, what's today's agenda?"

Max winced a little at the sound of my voice. "Just to survive it." He paused to rub his temples before adding, "Seminar at one in the boardroom downstairs. A group of Scottish buyers. Probably four to five people total."

Four to five people was more than manageable, and I figured it should be pretty easy to keep an eye on that small of a group. That was assuming they weren't Enhanced, but if they were, we'd cross that bridge when we came to it.

I nodded and Max added, "At four o'clock we have another seminar in the boardroom. A group of Taiwanese clients, probably six to eight of them. Should take about an hour."

This group was bigger but still should be easy to manage. I was starting to feel pretty good about today.

Max continued, "After that, the next meeting isn't until ten this evening. One client, a Saudi Arabian sheikh, and his entourage. I booked a table at the Silver Tassel Gentleman's Club for the meeting."

I instantly hated that the meeting was offsite but blinked dumbfoundedly as my mind finally processed that 'gentleman's club' meant 'strip club.'

"Please tell me you're joking."

He shook his head and then groaned at the motion. "The sheikh likes pretty women and insists on being entertained. He is a major client, so I'm willing to do whatever makes him happy. If it helps, I'm good friends with Johnny, the owner of the Silver Tassel, and he'll be willing to do whatever I ask."

Great, Johnny can hook me up with free lap dances, I thought sarcastically.

It was also my turn to rub my temples as I had a massive headache coming on. A public venue like this would be a security nightmare. I also couldn't use my full team for protection as I couldn't bring Stella. Johnny might be willing to help out, but there was no way he was letting a girl who looked only ten years old anywhere near his club. I doubted he would let Stella in her Hyde form stroll through his place either.

It got worse as Max added, "Their largest table only seats eight. The Sheikh and his party are five, so Kurt and I make seven, so there is only one seat left for your team."

"How about I just fry you right now and collect on the contract on your head? You're making it very difficult in this scenario to keep you alive."

Max shrugged. "The way I'm feeling right now, you'd probably be doing me a favor. Speaking of which, is there anything else you need from me? I'm going to pop two more painkillers and go back to bed..."

I shook my head but then said, "Just Johnny's number."

He gave me the phone number and I entered it into my phone and then he left me to my thoughts.

I probably wouldn't be able to wear my armor tonight, as it would attract too much attention in a place like that. Also, as Bree and Liv were both female, they would stick out like sore thumbs and would keep being mistaken for strippers or staff. My eyes widened as I realized that was the solution. I grinned to myself as I kicked around the idea of adding them both to Johnny's lineup for the night but dismissed that. Liv was crazy enough that she might enjoy dancing around naked on stage, but Bree would lose her shit. After this morning, if I mentioned something like that, she would kill me. They could work as staff. I was sure there'd be shooter girls buzzing around the place, and they'd both done that before being turned. They'd blend in better and be able to keep an eye on everyone in place.

I called Johnny and introduced myself and asked about adding Liv and Bree to his staff for the night.

"Sure, but I ain't adding them to the payroll."

"Not a problem," I said.

"Have them here at nine. I'll have Cassandra give them a crash course on the job and they should be fine."

"What do they need to wear?"

"They just need to bring high heels. We've plenty of spare uniforms—you'd be amazed at the turnover we have with shooter girls."

I didn't comment on that and ended the call.

Stella and Blue had wandered over in the meantime and asked who I was talking to. I explained about Johnny, our ten o'clock meeting, and my idea for inserting Liv and Bree into the place.

"They aren't going to be happy with you," warned Stella.

"Better than my first plan. I originally was thinking about adding them in as strippers," I said with a grin.

Stella shook her head at me but giggled. She frowned and asked, "How am I going to get in there?"

"You're not. I was going to have you on standby either here or back at the lab in case things go south."

Blue floored me when she said, "I'll work as a stripper."

I didn't know what to say to that. Blue had mentioned a few times that humans were too hung up on nudity, so I knew she didn't have a problem with it. Her form was attractive and a naked blue alien on stage would certainly put the 'exotic' in exotic dancing. Add in her warrior training and her superb conditioning and reflexes and I had no doubt she'd put on a heck of a show. I instantly pictured her doing a dance with her flaming sword and knew the patrons would be mesmerized. Up on stage, she'd also have an eagle's view of the place. I was tempted but decided against it. I had no idea how far the stage was from the table Max had booked and it might take too much time for her to get Max to safety.

I shook my head and her tail stopped moving around happily and went straight down, meaning she was upset. "I'm sure you would be amazing, and I'd have loved to have seen that, but it would put you too far away from Max to get him to safety in time. I want you with Stella, monitoring the whole place from the shadows. That way if things go wrong, you can open a portal, yank Max through, and send in Stella to rescue us."

Blue starred at me with her purple eyes and slowly nodded her head. "That is a more tactically wise arrangement; I concur with your reasons."

I was relieved when her tail resumed its usual random motions and she was contented once again.

"Okay, let's go over the meetings for this afternoon and tonight and see if we are missing anything…"

Chapter 17

Wednesday, July 31

Kurt, Bree, Blue, Alteea, and I made it down to the boardroom just after noon. The Aloha staff had already set up the main table with glasses of water and there was coffee brewed in the side kitchen and trays of pastries set out there as well.

We secured the doors and began our sweep of the room. Well, my team started the sweep while I grabbed a coffee. I was still tired from last night and Marion's healing was also catching up to me. It probably wasn't a good sign that I was so wiped, and the day had barely begun.

As I came out of the side kitchen, Bree and Kurt intercepted me and pulled me back into it.

I raised an eyebrow at Bree; she looked concerned.

She moved closer to me and said in a low voice, "Something's wrong. Kurt and I can hear seven extra heartbeats in the room out there. By their scent, all of them are male."

Kurt gave a nod of agreement with Bree's statement.

I frowned at that as that made no sense. If there were seven invisible Enhanced Individuals out there, then I should have seen their auras. I racked my brain trying to figure out what was going on. I didn't doubt Bree and Kurt's Were senses, and if they said there were seven men out there, then there were. By the lack of auras, I had to assume that our mystery guests were human. The invisibility must be from a spell or some sort of Mad Scientist tech. Whatever they were, I also figured that we had to deal with them before Max arrived. I sighed to myself as I thought about the warning from the hotel that even the slightest incident would get us kicked out. Not only did we have to take care of the invisible owners of the seven heartbeats but we also had to do it as discretely as possible. "Where are they in the room?"

Bree quietly said, "Three are standing along the wall farthest from us. Two are up against the wall behind the main screen. The last two are standing along the near wall."

I visualized the room in my head while I tried to casually drink my coffee. The only empty wall was the one at the front of the room with the main doors, which worked in our favor as that meant we were out of sight here in the kitchen.

Alteea buzzed into the kitchen and said, "There are no clocks under the tables."

I called on my Air power to pull her closer to me and quietly explained about our hidden guests. Once I was done, I gave her a mission to start the plan I was developing.

Alteea nodded and flew up to the ceiling. She pushed one of the cream-colored ceiling tiles up and disappeared behind it.

Bree and Kurt both looked at me and I went over my plan. Once Bree and Kurt were on board, I left them in the kitchen and went to find Blue.

Blue was near the main screen, so I walked up to her and said, "Walk with me. I want to do one last sweep of the room before Max arrives."

Blue frowned at that but shrugged and followed me as I tried to casually walk to the front of the room to get us out of earshot of our uninvited guests.

I pointed at the main doors. I hoped our guests assumed I was just discussing the security of the meeting and not get alarmed. I leaned closer to Blue and explained what was happening. Blue didn't react and just nodded as if we were discussing something mundane.

After I described what I wanted her to do, we separated and took up positions on opposite sides of the room.

Now we were just waiting for the signal that would put my plan into motion. I called on my powers, so I'd be ready when the time came.

Human or not, these invisible intruders had me seriously concerned. I hated not knowing exactly what we were dealing with. Besides being invisible, I had no idea what other surprises they might have for us. I worried about what weapons or spells they might attack us with. They might be armored. They might also have spells or tech that made them faster or stronger than normal humans.

I also wondered what was taking Alteea so long. I sent her into the ceiling to find the cabling to the video camera that was monitoring this room. Her job was to burn through the cables and disable the camera so we could hopefully take out the intruders without the Aloha being any the wiser.

I smiled as my phone vibrated and played, *Pour Some Sugar on Me*, which was my custom ringtone for Alteea. Her text told me that her task was complete. I looked over at Blue and she gave me a slight nod to show she was ready.

Showtime! I raised my hand towards the wall and let out a blast of chain lightning powerful enough to fry an elephant.

I winced as the row of fluorescent lights in the ceiling along the wall I'd hit exploded and went out. Three males wrapped from head to toe in black appeared. They shook as the electricity coursed through them and then collapsed to the floor and went still. They had swords sheathed behind their backs. The hilts and guards were also wrapped in black cloth. By the curve and shape of the sheath, I could tell the swords were katanas.

Upon seeing the three dead ninjas, I knew what we were dealing with. These were members of the Hidden Hand. The Hidden Hand was a group of Japanese assassins whose infamous history went back centuries. Ancient human assassin guilds weren't something I paid much attention to or followed. The only reason I knew about the Hidden Hand was their initials were the same as my Hamilton Hurricane alias. I found out about them when I was just starting my hero career. I'd done an Internet search on the initials *H.H.* to see who else was using them.

Besides launching lightning, I'd also taken the precaution of thickening the air around me. That extra protection saved my life, as two katana blades suddenly appeared out of nowhere and hung suspended in the Air shield I'd put up. The blades were slowly moving towards me as their unseen owners continued driving them forward.

I extended my hands and released a bolt of lightning from each, aiming towards the bottom of the blades. Two more black-clad males were revealed as the electricity struck home. They both dropped like puppets with their strings cut.

Five down, two more to go, I thought with satisfaction.

A sharp ringing of steel on steel echoed across the room and my attention was pulled to Blue who was currently sword fighting with two katana blades that were slicing through the air around her. Blue nimbly avoided one blade while parrying the other with her flaming magic sword.

A familiar angry growl erupted from the side kitchen and Bree in her standing Werepanther form came charging out. Kurt was right behind her but still in his human form.

I called on my Electrical powers but held my strike due to the two invisible assassins being too close to Blue. I gasped as Blue just managed to parry a blow that would have separated her head from her shoulders. The swords swung through the air so fast, they were almost too quick to see. Even with my concern for Blue's safety, a part of me couldn't help but admire her grace and skill as she continued her deadly dance.

Blue smiled as her sword cut through some invisible cloth, leaving a gash of blood that seemed to hang suspended in the air. She jumped over the blade from one opponent and intercepted with her sword the blade coming in high from the other.

I kicked around the idea of using a low-powered strike of lightning so I'd only knock them all out. I dismissed that for three reasons: one, Blue wouldn't be happy at me for zapping her, and there was also a risk that if I mistimed it, the momentum from one of the blades would strike Blue while all three were being stunned. Lastly, Bree was rapidly closing in on Blue's attackers with Kurt right on her heels.

Blue swung her sword at the assassin closest to Bree to keep him engaged with her. Bree pounced on him from behind and drove him to the floor. The assassin screamed briefly as Bree's fangs and claws struck home.

Blue turned to her remaining opponent and launched a flurry of blows at him almost faster than the eye could see. A second later, the flaming tip of her Keetiyatomi appeared to be floating in the air as she ran her opponent through. She yanked the sword up and free, leaving a fatal cauterized wound in its wake. The opponent and his sword tumbled to the floor and remained there.

Bree stood up and let out a low growl of triumph at her victory.

I counted seven downed bodies but dealing with invisible opponents had my paranoia running over time. I kept the air thickened around me as a precaution and said, "Kurt, Bree, do a lap of the room and make sure we have no other guests."

Bree went counterclockwise around the quiet room while Kurt went the opposite way. They met on the other side of the room and Kurt simply said, "Clear!" and Bree nodded her furry head.

I released my power and took a deep breath. I glanced around the room at the five exposed bodies and the two partially visible ones. One of the exposed bodies had a medallion around his neck. I moved closer and examined it. A clenched fist in the center of the pendant confirmed for me that that these were indeed Hidden Hand assassins. Knowing they were ruthless murderers made me feel instantly better about our use of lethal force.

I realized that we weren't done yet. I checked my phone and we had twenty-five minutes before the meeting started and now needed to get rid of the bodies and clean up the room. "Blue, open a portal to the lab. Everyone start grabbing bodies and let's get this place cleared."

Thankfully, my kills and Blue's didn't leave any stains, but Bree's kill had spilled blood on the carpet. I grabbed some carpet cleaner from the lab and went to work while the rest of the team disposed of the bodies.

Alteea returned, and after a quick look around disappeared into the kitchen. I had no doubt that she was sampling one of the sugary pastries, but she earned that for taking out the camera.

I had barely finished scrubbing the blood out of the carpet when I heard banging on the door. An Aloha employee was asking if everything was okay. I tossed the cleaning supplies through the still open portal and went to answer the door.

I thickened the air around me and unlocked the door. A concerned middle-aged man in an Aloha uniform looked at me and around me into the room. "You must be here about the lights that went out, thank you for your quick response."

"Lights?" he asked as I stepped back to let him in.

I pointed out the row of burnt-out ceiling lights and he blinked in surprise. I told him that we had a meeting starting in ten minutes but that it should be done by two o'clock and they could fix them then before our four o'clock meeting started. He nodded, took one last look around, and then left. I secured the door behind him and exhaled in relief that we'd gotten away with it.

The seminar started on time, though we had to make do with only Kurt, Blue, Alteea, and me as Max's protection. Stella and Bree were both back at the lab. Bree was stuffing down food to make up for the calories she burned by changing forms. Stella was stripping and getting rid of the bodies. Blue had made her promise that Stella would keep any swords or other weapons for her collection. Stella also wanted to recover any of the invisible cloth on the two assassins that I hadn't fried. I assumed she either wanted to study the cloth or had an idea for a new invention.

The Scots at the meeting were all ex-military, but I was surprised that none of them were armed. Or at least they weren't carrying guns, as I suspected that there was probably a knife or two tucked away here or there.

As Max droned on about superior supply chains and logistics, my thoughts turned back to our encounter with the Hidden Hand. When I'd learned about them back when I was starting out as a hero, I got the impression that they were a relatively large organization. Taking out seven of their members certainly didn't end the Hidden Hand. The question was, would they send more, or would they just write this off as a loss and move on?

Time was on our side. As they were based out of Japan, and it was roughly a twenty-four-hour flight from Japan to Vegas, the earliest they could get another team here was tomorrow afternoon. And that was if they sent the next team right away. They'd probably wait a few hours at least for the first team to report in. So, it was more likely that if they did send another team, it would arrive tomorrow night. That meant they'd have to strike on Friday. Due to the limited timeline, my inclination was that they wouldn't bother sending another team. Either way, I couldn't control if they did or not, so the best we could do was be alert for another strike on Friday and deal with it if it happened.

I was impressed that the moment the meeting ended and we showed our guests the door, there were Aloha staff waiting with ladders and a box of new fluorescent bulbs. They entered the room and started replacing the fixtures. We left them to it and used the shadows to return to Max's suite.

Chapter 18

Wednesday, July 31

Our next sweep of the boardroom was clear of invisible assassins or things that go boom. The lights along the left side of the room were working again, and I wondered if the camera was up and running again too. I sent Alteea up into the ceiling to check if her handiwork was still intact.

She returned five minutes later and informed me that the cables were still disconnected. I had mixed feelings about the camera being down. On the upside, if we were attacked and kept things low profile, we probably wouldn't be out on the street. On the flipside, it also meant that we were on our own as hotel security wouldn't be aware of any disturbances unless things really got out of hand. I was leaning towards the camera being off as a benefit.

Five minutes before the meeting was to start, Max and I were seated at the main table and discussing tonight's security as we waited. The security arrangements reminded me that I still hadn't told Bree about her shooter girl roll. I was going to mention it when we were sweeping the room earlier, but she'd made a couple of shots at me about this morning and didn't seem to be in the best of moods. I chickened out and figured I'd tell her after we got through this meeting instead.

A group of Taiwanese men in business suits showed up at the main entrance. Kurt greeted them and led them to their table. I was doubly relieved as I looked them over. They had no auras which meant they were all human. I also didn't spot any telltale bulges in their jackets, so they weren't armed either, or at least not carrying anything large enough to show. I hoped this meant my luck was changing because between my near-death experience with Bree this morning, the Hidden Hand, and the dread I was feeling about tonight's meeting, I really wanted this meeting to be uneventful and boring.

Max got up and I followed him as he greeted each of the men. I kept the air thickened between him and each of the men as a precaution. Thankfully, it wasn't needed.

Once they were seated, Max grabbed the remote and started his presentation. Stella and Bree took up stations on either side of the room. Kurt was sitting with me, and Max stayed within a few feet of us as he stood there droning on about superior supply chains.

About thirty minutes into it, I was starting to relax as things were going well. The clients were enraptured with Max and his presentation, and not once had they done anything suspicious or made any sudden movements.

A small fireball flared across the room and Alteea let loose a high pitched "Lincoln!" I wondered what had gotten into her when I spotted a stream of tiny rainbow auras pouring out of an air conditioning vent in the ceiling at the far end of the room.

I pointed at the ceiling and yelled, "Pixie swarm! Blue, get Max and everyone but Stella out of here. Stella, change now!"

The cloud of fae dove towards us and I called on my Air power and sent a large gust of wind towards them to push them back.

Out of the corner of my eye, I saw Kurt almost toss Max at Blue and was relieved when he disappeared into the shadows.

Screams and yells erupted from the Taiwanese men as they looked in horror at Stella's hideous alter ego. Thankfully, Bree herded them towards the shadows and Kurt started manhandling them through.

As Bree ran by me, she yelled, "Damn it! I left my pixie cookbook at home..."

I smiled at that. Bree brought up these imaginary recipes every time Alteea tried to take or sneak one of Bree's desserts or sugary snacks. I knew Bree was kidding as she would no more eat a pixie than I would.

Speaking of our beloved pixie, she had dropped her glamor and was floating just over my left shoulder. Her hands were aflame, and she had a determined look on her face.

"Go with Bree!" I ordered.

She shook her pretty little head and said, "No, Master, my place is here!"

Stella grunted as she took up station on my right.

Kurt and Bree followed the last of the clients into the shadows and disappeared. Blue raised a questioning eyebrow at me and gestured towards the portal. I was tempted to flee with them but figured that if the pixies were here to kill Max then we'd have to deal with them sooner rather than later anyways. I shook my head, "Go. Close the portal behind you."

I turned my attention back to the swarm. The cloud was pinned against the far wall. I could increase the pressure until I flattened them against the wall and that would take out the entire swarm. The problem was letting loose hurricane-type winds in here would do a ton of damage and Max would be out his damage deposit and we'd be out of the streets. I also didn't want the deaths of an entire swarm on my hands.

We were at a stalemate. I wondered if we could negotiate with the queen. I frantically searched the tiny auras and realized their queen wasn't among them. That was odd; there were close to a hundred pixies here, which was about the upper limit for a swarm. There was no way a swarm would leave the queen behind and unprotected. The outlines of the auras were all about six inches high, which probably meant the prince wasn't here either. Something was wrong here.

"Any thoughts?" I asked.

To my surprise, Alteea bobbed her head and said, "Drop the wind, Master. I have a plan!"

I wasn't sure about stopping my attack, but I couldn't keep it up forever and figured I'd give Alteea a chance.

The moment I cut off the flow of air, Alteea yelled, "I'm Alteea Brightmoon of the Forestrunners Clan and I demand parley!"

An angry buzz of wings was the swarm's reply as the entire cloud surged towards us. I thickened the air between us and them, expecting mini fireballs, poison darts, frost arrows, and tiny lightning blasts to rain down on us. I also began building up a massive electrical attack which would takeout three-quarters of their number. However, it would unfortunately give a boost to the ones that had an Air affinity.

As the cloud got closer, I started to raise my hand but Alteea said, "Don't! They will parley, but if you attack then they will show no mercy as we violated the peace."

My gut churned as the deadly cloud approached, but I lowered my hand. I prayed to Odin that Alteea was right or things were going to really suck in the next few seconds. Images of tiny claws and fangs stripping the flesh off my bones popped vividly into my mind.

To my relief, the entire swarm stopped about twenty feet from us and, as one, dropped their glamour. A pixie with unkept green hair, wearing a dirty and worn-looking emerald green sash, a rusty beer cap as a helmet, and holding a sharpened six-inch Popsicle stick continued towards us. The condition of the pixie had me taking a closer look at her and the rest of them. I was puzzled at the poor state of the swarm. They were all disheveled, grimy, and gaunt. The members of Alteea's old swarm all looked like mini supermodels except for the wings, claws, and fangs. I wondered why they were in such poor condition.

The lead pixie stopped about ten feet from us and announced, "I am Peata Coyotesbane, head guard for Queen Deepatra of the Silverstream Clan, and I accept your parley!"

Alteea's face went red and her whole body shook with rage, "Why does your queen not appear—is she a coward?"

By Odin's beard, Alteea, are you trying to get us killed? I thought as the swarm behind Peata beat their wings rapidly and an angry chorus erupted briefly from them.

Unbowed, Alteea added, "I was assigned to my master, the Hamilton Hurricane, by my queen due to his heroic deeds. He has slain a true demon and dispatched a master vampire in her own lair. He commands a beast, a vampire, an alien who moves with the shadows, and this indestructible monster, all of which bend knee to him. You pay him insult by not bringing your rightful queen here to parley."

To my surprise, Peata bowed her head and apologized, "No disrespect intended, oh great warrior. Our queen and prince have been taken and we are forced to serve humans…"

Sparks of rage dripped from my hand at the last part. The cruelty at keeping the swarm in this state was inexcusable. A pixie's diet consisted of two things—sugar and blood. A five-pound bag of sugar would feed the entire swarm for a day or two and would cost less than a couple of bucks.

Murmurs erupted from the swarm and I realized it was because of the show I was unintentionally putting on and I forced down my anger to stop it from happening.

Humans controlling the swarm also explained why they were trying to kill Max for a $4 million hit contract. Pixies, in general, had no use for money, and I'm not even sure they understood the concept of it. The people behind this swarm, though, were playing a dangerous game. If they harmed or lost possession of the queen and the prince, their lifespans would be measured in seconds.

Alteea's high-pitched voice pulled me from my thoughts. "If we free your queen and prince, will you end this attack?"

I wasn't overjoyed about Alteea volunteering our services, but I'd much prefer to nail the people responsible for this than a group of innocent pixies. I also wondered why people kept using proxies to strike at Max rather than doing it themselves. Maybe Max's Merchant of Death reputation was darker then I realized? On the other hand, I was talking about people who killed for money, which wasn't a group known for their honor and courage.

My heart almost broke at the expression of hope that flashed across Peata's face for a brief moment before being replaced by sadness. "I don't think it is possible to free them. The humans have them in a glass container. They have a gas canister attached that will go off if the container is tampered with or if any of the humans die. We'd have freed them ourselves if it wasn't for this."

An idea popped into my head and I said, "I think we can get around that..."

Chapter 19

Wednesday, July 31

Ten minutes later, we had roughed out a plan. Blue had joined us and used the shadows to locate the room the two assassins were staying in. I'd also had Blue pop back home and grab the almost full ten-pound bag of sugar that was there and gave that to the swarm. They devoured it like a plague of locusts on a farmer's crop.

Once we had the plan figured out, I had Blue take Stella to the lab where Max, Kurt, Bree, and the businessmen were hiding out. I asked her to transport them all to Max's suite and to bring back Bree in her standing Werepanther form. Stella and Kurt would stay to protect Max. Bree was more suited to the mission than Stella was since speed was of the essence.

A few minutes later, Bree's dark and dangerous form emerged from the shadows. Screams and cries of "Beast" erupted from the swarm. My concern grew as flames, electricity, poison, and frost began rapidly forming in all the pixies' hands.

"Calm yourselves!" yelled Alteea and she quickly added, "The beast is with us. You are in no danger!"

She darted off to Bree and landed right on the bridge of Bree's snout. Alteea bent over and rubbed the short fur at her feet and said, "Who's a good kitty?"

I was floored at Alteea for doing this as I knew she was absolutely terrified of Bree when she was in either of her Were forms. Other than a slight tremble to her hands, Alteea had managed to control her fear admirably.

Bree almost went cross-eyed as her ice blue cat's eyes stared at the crazy pixie petting her, and she gave a confused growl. The growl roughly translated to 'what the heck?' though she might actually have used a much stronger four-letter word—Growl was a tricky language with its nuances.

Thankfully, Alteea's actions had calmed the swarm and they called off the attack.

I smiled to myself as the moment the swarm relaxed, Alteea hopped off Bree and darted back into the air. The entire group of pixies eyed Alteea with newfound respect.

Bree wandered over to where Blue and I were standing, and we briefed her on the plan. Peata had sworn that the two would-be assassins were human which meant the rescue should be pretty straightforward. Blue had also spied on the room for a few minutes after she found it and didn't see anything that concerned her. Our targets were a man and woman and I assumed they were a couple.

I wondered how they'd managed to capture an entire swarm; that wouldn't have been easy. I didn't want to underestimate them, so I asked Peata about it. "How did they manage to capture you?"

Peata popped the last of her sugar granules into her tiny mouth and shrugged. "We went to sleep one night and the next morning we awoke in glass containers with nasty headaches."

There was no way humans could be quiet enough to move sleeping pixies into containers without waking them. It hit me that they must have used some sort of knockout or sleeping gas. The headaches were probably a side effect. Using gas in an urban environment would have been tricky but they might not have been in one. "Where was your swarm located?"

Peata scratched her head and then said, "In the trees."

I mentally facepalmed myself for my phrasing of the question and tried again. "What was the human name for the area you were in?"

Peata shrugged. "We don't pay attention to human names. There were very few of them around our home."

The lack of humans meant they hadn't been in an urban environment but that still left a lot of possible places, so I tried another track, "What were the biggest threats to your swarm?"

"Alligators and snakes," said Peata with a shudder.

Alligators were only in the southeastern United States which narrowed things down.

I was going to try to narrow it down further, but Blue said, "Zack, if we wait much longer, the targets are going to figure something went wrong and become more alert."

I quickly weighed whether it was worth getting more information or getting on with the plan and decided Blue was right. "Okay, Blue, open a portal. Bree, get ready to go when Blue gives the nod. Remember you need to take them down without killing them."

I found out from Peata that the couple each wore a device on their wrists that sounded like heartrate monitors. This was how they kept the swarm from attacking them. If either of them died, the gas would be released and would kill the queen and the prince.

I started calling on my Air powers as Blue made a small gesture with her hand.

A few seconds later, Blue gave the green light. "Go!"

Bree dove into the portal and I was right behind her. I popped out into a standard room at the Aloha. The room reeked of tobacco smoke and shit. The man had a long beard and a big gut. He wore a trucker hat, flannel shirt, and jeans and looked like a reject from *Duck Dynasty*. He cried out as Bree pounced on him and drove him into a wall. His eyes rolled up into his head and he collapsed. The tall scarecrow-like woman dropped the lit cigarette that was in her hand and scrambled towards the bed. I knew Bree would take her down shortly and focused on my part of the mission.

I frantically looked over the feces-stained glass containers against the wall for the one holding the queen and the prince. It was the farthest one from me and had a large green metal cylindrical tank attached to it. The nozzle of the gas canister was connected to a hole at the bottom of the tank. I moved over to it and used my Air power to create a protective barrier around the two pixies trapped inside it.

A brief scream came from the woman, followed by a large crash behind me. I assumed Bree had tackled her.

Blue came out of the shadows and raised a purple eyebrow at me. I nodded to indicate that the barrier was up, and Blue ignited her sword. The thickened air around the two pixies served two purposes. The first was to protect them in case the gas was released. The second was to keep them in place so they wouldn't be hurt by what Blue was about to do.

Blue made a precise horizontal swing with her blade and it sliced through the top of the container just about an inch below the top of it. She immediately extinguished the blade and used the tip of the sword to push the top of the tank off it. To my relief, the air around the nozzle remained normal so we hadn't set off the tank.

Peata darted in and hovered above the tank, "This way, my Queen, I will take you to safety."

I released the air around the two pixies so they could follow Peata. Blue was already opening another portal. My anger grew as the redheaded queen and prince weakly flew out of the tank. I could clearly see the prince's ribs outlined in his gaunt form. The queen's skin hung loosely from her frame in places due to her extreme weight loss.

Pixies lived to do two things—eat and fornicate. Most pixies were born female and only about one in a hundred was male. When a male was born, he and the mother were sent away with ten other pixies to start another swarm. The mother became the queen of this new swarm. Since the queen no longer got to mate, she was given the first taste of any food the swarm acquired, and after she'd had her fill, the rest was shared among the swarm. As a result, the queen was usually what I'd kindly describe as plump.

Seeing the queen in such a sad state had me pissed. Once they disappeared into the shadows, I turned my full attention to the woman Bree had pinned against the wall. The woman was whimpering in fear as Bree had her clawed paw around her throat. The low, enraged growls coming from Bree's fanged maw probably added to the woman's terror.

Before I could even start verbally laying into the woman, an angry loud buzzing suddenly erupted from the shadows. I gulped as a cloud of rainbow auras descended into the room. It hit me what was about to happen, and all I could do was yell, "Bree, duck!"

Bree dove away from the woman. The woman barely had time to scream before they began tearing her apart. My stomach lurched, as it looked like she was being attacked by fifty mini chainsaws and she exploded in a cloud of gore. The unconscious man suffered the same fate a moment later as the other half of the swarm descended on his prone form. This time I looked away.

A hiss started in the corner of the room and I remembered the gas canister. I called my powers to me and created a small cyclone to suck up the gas. Now I just had to figure out what to do with it.

Thankfully, Blue stepped out of the shadows a moment later.

"Blue, open another portal to some place with no people around!"

Blue made a motion with her hands and gave me a nod. Now for the tricky part. I kept the vortex going but also redirected my Air power to lift the tank towards the open portal. I started to sweat from the effort and focus needed to do both these things at the same time.

I managed to get the tank and the twister through the portal and let out a sigh of relief.

By the time that was done, all that was left of the man was a pile of shredded flannel, a gleaming skeleton with bad teeth, and a Confederate flag belt buckle. The woman was in the same state, minus the flannel and the belt buckle. The walls and carpet around the corpses were splattered in blood and looked like a bad Jackson Pollock painting.

The queen, with her guards and her son in tow, took to the air and approached me. The rest of the swarm followed behind them. Seeing their blood-covered faces had me instantly thickening the air around us as a precaution.

The queen stopped about five feet from me and hovered in the air. "You have provided us our freedom, and I, Queen Deepatra, am in your debt, Elemental."

I struggled with what to do here. The swarm had just murdered two humans and, therefore, we should take them down and turn any survivors over to the authorities, but I couldn't find it in myself to do that. There was a certain justice in what happened—a dark justice I'll admit, but justice nevertheless. If we weren't going to turn them in, that meant we needed to make sure the crime never happened, or at least make sure that there was no evidence of the crime.

Blue and Bree both looked at me, wondering what I was going to do. I shook my head and sighed before replying to the queen. "We'll deal with the debt later, your Majesty, for now we need to make all of this disappear or your swarm will be hunted to the ends of the Earth. Will you allow me to direct you and your swarm to accomplish this?"

She nodded and I turned to Blue. "Open a portal to the hangar in the lab. We need to move everything out of here and destroy it."

Blue made a gesture and the shadow portal was opened.

"Bree, go through the portal and get the roll of plastic from the supply room."

I didn't wait for her before turning back to Queen Deepatra. "I need every drop of blood cleaned from the floor and the walls, your Majesty."

"Consider it done."

The swarm darted off. I blinked as pixies began licking the blood off the wall and sucking it from the carpet. It made a disturbing image that I'd never be able to purge from my mind.

Thankfully, Bree returned from the shadows with the large roll of plastic in her paws and distracted me.

I pointed at the bed and said, "Roll it out over the bed. Once that is done, put the remains on it."

I call on my Air powers and used them to lift all the remaining filthy glass containers from the floor and floated them in the air. I walked them to the portal and stepped through. The stench of pixie waste coming off them almost made me gag. My anger returned at the thought of those poor creatures being held in them. It did, however, make me feel a little better about covering up the murders.

Twenty minutes later, the hotel room was empty and cleaned. The pixies had scoured the room and dumped random hairs, bugs, flakes of skin, ash, and just about any little thing that shouldn't be there on the plastic roll. I was willing to bet that the last time the room had been this clean was when it was new. Even if police were alerted and searched this room, I doubted they'd find anything.

I gave the room one last look over and Bree hauled the plastic tarp through the shadows. Satisfied that we were good, I stepped into the shadows.

The swarm stood around on the floor of the hangar and looked exhausted and worn. Whatever energy they had gained from their vengeance meal had passed and the effects of their long captivity had caught up to them.

"Bree, change back and use the Food-O-Tron to get some more food into them, okay?"

Bree nodded and her body began trembling as she changed back to her human form.

I spotted Alteea fluttering nearby and told her to go with Bree. I turned my back so when Bree returned to her naked human form, I wouldn't see it. She had gotten pretty cool with me seeing her nude after changing, but with how this morning went, I didn't want to push my luck. Especially as I still hadn't told her about her role at the strip club this evening.

I pointed at the tarp on the floor and said to Blue, "You take one end; I'll take the other. Let's get rid of this stuff."

Fifteen minutes later, everything from the room had been turned into atoms or whatever the disintegrator ray in the garbage disposal did. The only thing that didn't get vaporized was a handgun that had been tucked into a drawer by the bed. That was what the woman had been going for when Bree jumped her. Blue took the gun and added it to her growing collection of firearms and things that go boom. By the way her collection was growing recently, I wondered if we should start calling her bedroom 'the Armory.'

We joined Bree, Alteea, and the swarm in the main room, which had a party-like atmosphere going on, as each time Bree dropped off another pint glass of blood or a tray of cinnamon buns, a chorus of cheers went up from the pixies.

I stopped dead and blinked stupidly when I spotted Alteea. The prince was showing Alteea his appreciation vigorously on top of a cinnamon roll. She was smiling, moaning, and covered in icing—at least I hoped it was icing. That was another image I'd have trouble purging from my mind. I forced my eyes away from the spectacle and decided to help Bree at the Food-O-Tron.

Bree was wearing a comfy-looking set of gray sweats. She shook her head as she passed me carrying another glass of blood, "Make a single remark about wishing you were a pixie, and I will deck you…"

I held up my hands in surrender. "Nope. I fled over here to get away from that scene."

Bree had already pulled the lever on the Food-O-Tron, so I just stood there alone with my thoughts. Another cheer went up from the pixies as Bree made her latest delivery. The swarm was happy at being fed and being free, but they couldn't stay here. One pixie in my life was enough. Now I just had to figure out what to do with them.

Chapter 20

Wednesday, July 31

It was almost six by the time we made it back to Max's suite. Blue had managed to locate an uninhabited island in Northern Ontario for the swarm. We'd done the same for Alteea's former swarm. We got them settled there and left them with a hundred pounds of sugar to get them started. There was plenty of game and fish around the island, so blood supply wouldn't be an issue for them.

Speaking of pixies, after Alteea's sticky tryst with Prince Moog, Bree had picked her up and unceremoniously dumped our tiny winged companion in the shower to get clean. Our now freshly washed pixie was currently sound asleep on a couch cushion with a contented grin on her face.

Max had ordered room service and we were waiting for it to arrive. Bree took that time to ask what was on the schedule for this evening and I realized I couldn't put off telling her any longer. "Max has a ten o'clock meeting at the Silver Tassel Gentlemen's Club."

Bree just nodded casually and started walking back to the dining table.

She took that remarkably well.

Not a second after that though, she stopped dead in her tracks. "We are going to a strip club?"

"Yup," I said as she turned and faced me.

She glared at me. "This was your perverted idea, wasn't it?"

Before I could defend myself, Max jumped to my rescue. "Zack had nothing to do with this. It was all my doing. I think he is as unhappy about it as you are."

Her expression towards me softened and she turned her attention to Max. "I thought you had more class than this."

Max shrugged. "Client satisfaction is the key to my business, and the client likes looking at naked women."

Bree growled in frustration but didn't say anything more to Max. I watched the wheels turning in her head as she stood there. After a pause, she asked, "How the heck is Stella going to get into a strip club?"

I shook my head. "She's not. She and Blue will be here watching from the shadows, and if things go badly, they'll jump in."

She frowned a bit at that but seemed to be okay with that part of the plan. "Um, aren't Liv and I going to stand out in there?"

I took a deep breath and said, "Funny you should mention that..."

Bree groaned and then glared at me. "I'm not going to like what you're about to say, am I?"

"The owner of the club is letting you and Liv work as shooter girls for the night." To my surprise, Bree just blinked at this. After a long silence, I asked, "You okay?"

"Yeah, sorry. You took me off guard. Knowing what a perv you are, I figured you'd suggest we be strippers for the night. Shooter girl isn't that bad—at least I'll make a little money doing it and get to keep my clothes on."

I winced at the first part. "Yeah, about that. Johnny said he isn't paying you two for this."

"Do we get to keep our tips?"

"I'd assume so."

"Good. Shooter girls get crap pay; it's the tips that make the job worthwhile."

And with that she joined Stella and Blue at the table. That went much smoother than I dared hoped; maybe Liv's influence on her was a good thing after all.

***

Just before ten, Blue opened a shadow portal and Max, Kurt, and I emerged in a dimly lit hallway in the club. The bass of the music was loud enough that I could feel it throbbing through the floor. I seriously wondered how Max was going to get any business done in this environment but that was his problem not mine. My problem was keeping him alive.

Kurt led the way out with Max directly behind him and I followed both of them. The hallway came out near the main bar area. A large bouncer had spotted us and began making his way over to us. He probably wondered how three strangers had suddenly appeared. Kurt headed for an older man who was sitting at the bar in a suit. Kurt nodded at the man and then stepped aside as Max came forward and shook the guy's hand. The moment Max did this, the bouncer shrugged and turned to return to his original spot. It hit me that this man must be Johnny.

Max and he exchanged greetings and said a few things that I didn't catch over the blaring music. Max pointed at me and Johnny yelled, "Those ladies you sent me are stunning—if they want to make some real money on the stage just let me know…"

I smiled at that. He was still alive and in one piece, which meant he hadn't made that offer to Bree. I simply said, "I'll let them know."

Max and Johnny chatted for a bit longer. I took the opportunity to scan the club for threats. There were two Werewolves in human form in perverts' row in front of the main stage. They were in leather and looked to be part of a biker gang. To the left of the stage, there was another group that looked like a couple of professional athletes with their entourages. The one athlete had an aura that was an orange core with a red and white checker pattern around the outside, which meant he was a Tank. The aura wasn't even an inch in size, so he wasn't that powerful. Power was relative though; he'd still be able to take a hit that would level most men, and he would probably be able to knock me out cold with a single well-placed punch.

The Werewolves made me glad Alteea had stayed home, as their sensitive noses would be able to track her even if she had her glamor up. When I asked Alteea if she was coming, she gave me a lazy grin and said, "It has been a long day, Master. Can I stay here?" The moment I said that was fine, she rolled over and went back to sleep on the cushion.

To my surprise, there was a group of women hanging out in a booth at the far side of the club watching the show who were neither strippers nor employees. They weren't the only ones, as there were a few women walking around the club too. I realized that my understanding of strip clubs being men-only establishments was outdated. Bree and Liv didn't have to work as shooter girls as they could've blended in here with no issues. In my defense, I'd only been to a strip club once in my life and that was fourteen years ago for a buddy's nineteenth birthday; back then, it had been men only.

Having Liv and Bree work as shooter girls wasn't the worst thing though. Potential assassins wouldn't pay as much attention to employees as they would customers. It also gave Liv and Bree a reason to get close to the patrons and keep a closer eye on them as possible threats to Max.

On the right side of the main stage, there were a few older men sitting apart from each other getting drunk and watching the show. The topless blonde on the main stage caught my attention. The way she was swinging around and moving on the pole had me betting she'd had some gymnastics or acrobat training in her past.

I tore my eyes away from her as I spotted Bree approaching a table filled with what looked like college frat buddies. I groaned at her uniform as I knew she'd make me pay for it. The top was a white form-fitting, low-cut crop top which her ample chest was trying its very best to pop out of. I swear if she sneezed, she'd be flashing nipples at the entire place. The black shorts were tightly clad around her ass and the bottom curves of her cheeks were exposed.

I'll give her credit though; she was taking it all in stride as I watched her smile, flirt, and angle 'the girls' strategically at the frat boys. They were all rapidly pulling money from their pockets in their haste to buy shots.

I didn't see Liv anywhere and wondered where my favorite crazy vampire was. I continued my scan, but the rest of the crowd was a mix of guys in business suits and tourists.

Johnny pointed to a table back from the center stage with a reserved sign on it and Max nodded. Kurt took the lead again and we followed him on the long walk to the table. The place was massive. Besides the mainstage in the center, there were two smaller ones on either side of it. The stage between the bar and the main one was currently unlit, but the one on the far side of the room had a dancer strutting her stuff.

The closer we got to the table, the more I hated it. It was against the back wall which was good but directly above us was the open DJ booth, which was another possible attack vector. The table was actually a large booth that was shaped as a three-quarter circle with the top of the circle against the wall. The height of the booth wouldn't be high enough to cover our heads and left them exposed. There were matching booths on both sides of our table. The one to the right was currently open, and the one to the left had a group of businessmen around it.

The front of the table was open and facing the main stage. This pretty much meant we could be attacked from any direction.

Max got in the booth first, Kurt went next, and I sat beside Kurt on the far right of the booth.

I spotted Liv enter the room with a tray full of shots in her left hand. She winked at me as she walked by and approached the row of bikers to offer them drinks. One of the bikers grabbed her ass, and before anyone could blink, Liv used her free hand to drive his head hard into the side of the stage. His limp hand dropped away from Liv as he was out cold. I tensed, expecting the bikers to lose it, but they just laughed and pointed at their unconscious buddy. They practically started throwing money at Liv after that.

I couldn't help but admire how good Liv looked in those cheeky short shorts, and part of me hoped she'd keep them after this job was done.

A server came by and dropped off an ice bucket with a bottle of champagne to our table. I mentally shook my head at the server's outfit, as it was much more modest than the shooter girl uniform and I just knew Bree would be pointing that out at the end of the night.

"Johnny sends his compliments. Can I get anyone something else to drink?"

"Champagne is good. When we finish that bottle, bring another," said Max.

I asked for a Coke and Kurt didn't say anything, so I assumed he was drinking champagne too. I envied his Were metabolism as he could chug that entire bottle and wouldn't even get the faintest buzz from it.

The waitress left to get my Coke and glasses for the champagne, and I went back to scanning the club. The inner entrance doors opened, and a group of tourists came in. Behind them, at the doors, I spotted a bouncer in a Silver Tassel uniform who had a Werebear aura. The bouncer's size was intimidating; he was a mountain of a man and wasn't someone any sane person would want to mess with. I checked out the other three bouncers positioned inside the club again and none of them had auras.

A smattering of applause and cheers filled the room as the spry blonde on the main stage finished up her routine and exited. She had barely left when the lights around the main stage went down and a spotlight on the stage entrance came up.

The DJ's voice boomed over the loudspeakers, *"Okay, gentlemen, give it up for the feisty and lovely CASSANDRA!!!"*

An edgy guitar riff and heavy bass drumbeat began to play as the curtain parted and a jaw-dropping redhead strutted out on to the stage. She had hair that cascaded down in ringlets over her shoulders, back, and chest. My heart melted at the emerald green eyes that popped against her auburn hair and pale complexion. She wore a sheer green teddy with matching green satin bra and panties. The outfit was finished off with a bright red pair of four-inch heels. I'd always had a weakness for redheads, and this certainly wasn't helping me keep an eye on the place.

Her large chest and short height had me drawing comparisons to Bree. I wondered if Bree would ever consider dying her hair red. I quickly dismissed that for two reasons. One, if I brought it up anytime soon, she would know where I got the idea and slug me for it. The other reason was that Bree dying her hair was a waste of time—the moment she changed back and forth from her Were form, it would be gone.

I was mesmerized as I watched Cassandra dance and twirl around on the stage and couldn't pull my eyes away.

A minute or so later, my enthrallment was rudely shattered as Bree walked by and smacked the back of my head hard with her empty drink tray.

Oh sure! Now she wants to be mission-focused, I thought to myself as I rubbed my head.

I sighed as I knew she was right and got back to checking for threats, doing my best to ignore the sheer teddy that the angel on the stage had just whimsically removed. The club was quickly filling up. I didn't spot any new Enhanceds, but that didn't do much to calm my nerves—a human with a knife or a gun would kill Max just as dead.

I checked my watch, and saw that it was already quarter after ten and I wondered where the sheikh and his party were. I half yelled over to Max to ask about this.

He shrugged. "The sheikh works on his own clock. It's not unusual for him to be late."

I cursed under my breath at this. The sooner he arrived, the sooner we could finish and get Max safely tucked away again.

The song changed to something slower and I caught Cassandra out of the corner of my eye, teasing her fingers around the front clasp of her bra. I really wanted to keep watching but the growing bump on the back of my head throbbed and reminded me that I had other things I should be doing.

Liv and Bree were blending in nicely and were keeping a close eye on everything around them. I was proud that they were so focused and staying on mission. It made me being distracted by Cassandra that much worse.

I continued scanning for threats. The biggest ones were the two Werewolf bikers and the athletic Tank, but neither they, nor any of their party, had so much as glanced towards us. There was a group of subdued businessmen at a table across the stage from us that were pinging my radar. Something was off with the group. The four of them weren't drinking enough and seemed to be spending as much time checking us out as they were the eye candy.

I leaned closer to Kurt and said, "Don't look now. The table at your eleven o'clock might be a problem."

Kurt drained his flute and then said, "*Ja*, I saw them."

I went back to searching the club and tried my best to ignore Cassandra's spectacular naked breasts as she danced away on stage.

***

The Silver Tassel was full by the time the sheikh and his party arrived. It was now a quarter to eleven. The three of us awkwardly got to our feet as they approached, the table preventing us from standing straight. The sheikh introduced his party but between his accent and the blaring music I barely caught a word of it.

He was younger than I expected, and I put him in his mid-thirties which made him a year or two older than I was. He was a good-looking man, especially when he smiled which seemed to be most of the time. Between his looks and wealth, I couldn't imagine his love life was hurting and wondered why he'd be interested in hanging out at a strip club. It might be that it was a culture thing and places like this didn't exist where he was from. Or maybe he just wanted to blend in and felt this was a very American thing to do.

He slid in the opposite side of the booth and moved around until he was beside Max. A tall, thick bodyguard got in next. His suit jacket opened enough that I spotted the holstered 9mm and I immediately

140

shifted the thickened air I had around Max to block any shots coming from his direction.

The next man, who was short, wore glasses, and carried a briefcase, got in next. I pegged him as an accountant or advisor. I didn't like not knowing the contents of that briefcase but there wasn't much I could do about. I doubted it was a bomb, as that would put the sheikh in danger, and if his guards were even half-competent, they would have searched it thoroughly. I was more worried it contained a submachine gun or something along those lines. I made a note to keep an eye on him.

Another large bodyguard, who looked like he could be the brother of the first one, got in next. The bulge in the chest of his suit meant he was armed too.

The last guy in the party barely looked old enough to even get in here. He shared the sheikh's good looks and I guessed he was a younger brother or cousin.

Our server returned and brought a fresh bottle of champagne to replace the one Max and Kurt had almost emptied during our wait. She cracked it open and filled the glasses for the sheikh and his party. The second guard though covered his and asked for water.

Max and the sheikh were chatting until the house lights changed and a new stripper came on to the stage. I blinked as a petite Asian woman strolled on stage in a schoolgirl uniform, her long dark hair in pigtails. This made her look younger than she already was and I wondered if she was legally old enough to be up on stage. I reasoned with myself that she must be old enough as I couldn't see Johnny risking his club and license by putting a minor on stage. Her youthful appearance made me uncomfortable, which made it much easier for me to focus on everything around us like I was supposed to be doing.

I kept scanning for threats but with each passing minute the itch between my shoulder blades was growing. The four businessmen across the stage kept checking us out. They were trying not to be overt about it, but I had caught them doing it too many times for it to be coincidence. They hadn't done anything directly but part of me kept waiting for the hammer to fall.

After three songs, the schoolgirl stripper left the stage and was replaced by a silicone blonde Barbie who looked like she belonged up there. At least she looked old enough to be doing this.

I waved Bree over as she passed by and she offered me a shot.

I fished out a twenty-dollar bill, leaned into her and said, "Keep an eye on the four businessmen across the stage from us. They're paying too much attention to us."

I took the shot from her and gave her the twenty to keep up appearances.

She nodded and walked away. I was going to pour the shot out under the table but gave it to Kurt instead. He just shrugged and downed it.

The sheikh and his party seemed to be having a good time. Our server was replacing the bottle of champagne every couple of songs like clockwork. I had no idea what the cost per bottle was but had no doubt that Max was running up an eyepopping tab. I hoped the sheikh's business was worth it.

The main act changed a few more times and then the lights went down and lasers and strobe lights flashed across the club. A smoke machine started up around the main stage.

The DJ's voice came blasting out of the speakers around the club, *"And now for our feature presentation of the night... give it up for the FEMME FATALES!"*

The crowd erupted as the sultry-sounding theme to *Mike Hammer* started playing. The curtains parted and out of the smoke walked three of the most beautiful women I'd ever seen. The brunette woman in the center was carrying a Thompson machine gun like a twenties gangster would. The gangster theme was this woman's shtick, as she was wearing a wide-brimmed black hat pulled low, a dark pinstriped suit which just covered her waist, a matching vest and white dress shirt under the jacket, a striped red tie, black stockings and garters came out from under the suit and ended with thigh-high black heeled boots.

The ladies on other side of her were almost identical except that one was a blonde and the other was a raven-haired beauty. They were carrying silenced pistols and had their hair slicked back. They were going for more of a James Bond type of look. They were wearing black tuxes with red bowties, matching red cummerbunds, and white dress shirts. They too went with the black stockings, garter, and thigh-high boots.

The crowd roared as they stood there and posed. The two outside girls had their guns pointed straight up, while the girl in the center slowly panned the crowd with the Thompson. The smoke curled and silhouetted around them as they stayed motionless. The lights changed and the entire stage was spotlighted.

As one, the long-legged women sauntered down the runway. I hoped Liv and Bree were paying attention for the next fifteen minutes or so as the ladies had my full attention.

Just before the women reached the end of the stage, Liv's voice boomed over the music and the crowd noise.

She yelled just one word: "Washington!"

Her voice snapped me out of the spell I'd been under and I somehow instinctively knew she'd meant 'Lincoln.' I increased the power to thicken the air around us for protection.

A moment after that, the ladies on stage pointed their three guns directly at our table and opened fire.

Chapter 21

Thursday, August 1

A wall of lead hung suspended in the air over our table as bullet after bullet rained down on us. The blonde on the end had fired maybe two shots before she was beaned savagely off the head by a spinning drink tray. She was knocked out and fell back off the stage and into the lap of one of the old men that was drinking close to the stage. The old guy beamed like it was his birthday, Christmas, and his first kiss all rolled into one as he cradled her limp form.

Not two seconds later, the other two female assassins went tumbling off the stage as they were tackled by a familiar scantily clad dark-haired vampire. The three of them crashed into perverts' row. One of the Werewolf bikers, who had been sitting at the end of the row beside the pro athlete's party, got knocked back into that group and spilled all their drinks. The Tank, without a second's hesitation, tossed him away. The unfortunate biker then slammed into the table of drunken frat boys and pitchers of beer went flying. All three groups jumped to their feet and a melee ensued.

Across the stage, the businessmen I'd been concerned about all night pulled pistols from their jackets and continued where the strippers had left off. More rounds joined my growing collection in the air.

A pair of blue hands emerged from the shadows under the table and gripped Max's legs. A moment later he was pulled under the table and disappeared. The sheikh's bodyguard pushed his charge down into the empty spot Max had just occupied and shielded him from the gunfire.

The gunfire fire stopped as Bree bounded over the side of the businessmen's booth and tackled them.

Screams and yells filled the entire place as the club descended into pure pandemonium. The bouncers had joined the fray between the bikers, frat boys, and the pro athletes. Stools and bottles were being broken over heads as the brawl continued. The smart ones were fleeing for the exits as fast as their legs would carry them.

The music changed and *Saturday Night's Alright for Fighting* came blaring out of the speakers.

At least the DJ has a sense of humor, I thought. I did, however, mentally deduct him points for it being a Wednesday night.

With Max gone and safe, I was no longer confined to the table and used my Air power to lift myself into the air and above the fray. I flew over to where Bree was taking on the businessmen assassins. One of them was out cold and lying on the floor in front of the booth. Bree was exchanging blows with two of them. The fourth was pointing his gun at Bree, trying to line up a shot.

I sent a bolt of lightning at him and he screamed as it slammed into him. The white electricity was stupid bright in the confines of the darkened club and temporarily blinded me. I took myself up higher to the ceiling and waited for my vision to get back to normal. I also kept the air thickened beneath me in case anyone took a shot at me.

I frantically kept blinking and urging the spots in my eyes to clear. Between the music and the spots, I was practically deaf and blind and hated how vulnerable I felt. I reassured myself that Bree could handle the two men she was fighting with and Liv should have no issues taking down the two women she'd been grappling with. Max was safe and with him gone, there wasn't a target here for anyone to take a shot at.

My vision came back into focus and I spotted one of the Werewolf bikers shaking violently and beginning to change forms—Bree would have to wait. I flew towards him and sent another blast of lightning out. This time I closed my eyes before releasing it, like I should have done the first time.

I opened my eyes and was relieved to find the biker out cold on the floor. I spotted one of the female assassins lying face down over a table in pervert row. She was out of the fight. I didn't see the other one but did spot Liv dropping a right hook on a frat boy that had gotten near her. If she was fighting with anyone now, that probably meant she'd dealt with the other woman too.

Not a second later, I spotted two feet clad in black leather high-heeled boots sticking out from under one of the booths. The legs weren't moving, and I realized that was the missing member of the Femme Fatales.

I pivoted around in the air and went to check on Bree. I smiled as she drove the head of the last man into the top of the booth and he went down. I was concerned when I spotted the blood splashed over her white top. I landed in front of the booth. I pointed at her shirt and yelled, "You okay?"

She looked down and smiled. "Not mine!"

A loud shotgun blast filled the air and the music instantly stopped. I glanced over to see Johnny holding a sawed-off shotgun.

He yelled, "Cut this shit out or the next one goes into whoever doesn't stop!"

The brawl, after a few more punches and kicks, ceased. A brief silence filled the club before what sounded like every police siren in Las Vegas came to life and was headed in our direction. Each group hastily grabbed up their fallen comrades and shuffled to the door, no doubt hoping to avoid being detained by the local PD.

I had one concern nagging me—there had been a ton of shots fired in the club and I was worried someone got tagged. "Liv, Bree, do a search of the place and make sure no one has been shot."

They both nodded and began doing a search of the club.

I glanced over to the booth where Kurt and the sheikh and his party had been to find it completely empty. I was worried at this and was about to add that to Bree and Liv's search when my phone buzzed. I pulled it out of my pocket and saw there was a text from Stella that read, "*Max, Kurt, sheikh and party all safe and back at suite.*"

I was relieved and with each passing second the sirens were getting louder. I texted Stella back and asked her to get Blue to open a portal and grab Bree and Liv.

Just before the cops stormed the place, Liv and Bree finished their search and had found no one had been shot. Frankly, that had been a small miracle considering how many rounds were fired and the number of people in the club.

"Tell Blue not to wait up; I'll fly back to the hotel once I'm done here."

Bree and Liv nodded at that and then disappeared into the shadows.

Johnny, the bouncers, and I gathered up the Femme Fatales and businessmen/hitmen and dumped them on the center of the stage.

After zip-tying their wrists together, I sat on the edge of the stage with my hero ID out and held it and both my hands up and waited. I'd been tempted to disappear with my team, but I wanted to make sure all seven of the would-be assassins were taken into custody.

It was going to be a long night.

Chapter 22

Thursday, August 1

It was almost three in the morning by the time the LVPD detectives were done with me. I would have been stuck at the Silver Tassel much longer if it wasn't for two things: The first was Johnny had security cameras throughout the club and they had gotten everything on video. The other thing that helped was that the detectives assigned to the case were the same ones that had investigated the murder of Peter, Max's body double, so they knew all our details and I didn't have to go over them again.

As I walked out into the Tassel's mostly empty parking lot, I decided tonight had gone reasonably well. There were seven would-be assassins in custody, charged with attempted murder and various lesser charges. No one had died tonight. I shuddered to myself thinking about all the rounds fired inside the packed club and at how bad things could have gone. Max wasn't hurt and we were another day closer to completing our protection assignment. As a bonus, none of this had gone down at the Aloha, so we still had a place to sleep tonight.

I called on my Air power and used it to lift myself in the air. For a moment, as Blue had shadow travelled us to the club, I worried about finding my way back to the hotel. The Silver Tassel was in an industrial area and I had no clue where I was. My fears disappeared as I gained more altitude and spotted the lights of the Las Vegas strip gleaming like stars in the distance. Even better, I soon picked out the Aloha's sign and giant electronic billboard that cycled through the various acts performing there this week.

Flying over the strip at night was amazing. Each massive hotel was its own spectacle. The fountains, the lights, a pirate ship, the miniature Eiffel tower, rollercoasters, canals, and Odin-only-knew what else I flew over had me swiveling my head all over the place to take it all in. I made a mental note to take Liv up for flight over all of this once things were done, as I knew she'd love it.

To avoid attention, I landed on top of the multistory parking lot attached at the back of the hotel.

Ten minutes later, I quietly crept into the suite and got ready for bed. As I brushed my teeth, I argued with myself about where I would sleep. I was wiped and needed a good night's rest, and the idea of sleeping on the couch didn't appeal. In the end, I decided to risk my life and crawled into bed with Bree.

***

I was disoriented the next morning when I awoke. Something warm was pressed up behind me. I felt hot breath on the back of my neck. An arm was wrapped around me and a hand was against my chest. A huge smile came to my lips as I realized it was Bree spooning me for a change.

"Bree! Wake up," I whispered loudly.

A sleepy "Huh?" was her response.

"Bree!"

"What?"

"You're taking advantage of me. To think I trusted you with my virtue…" I added in a falsetto voice.

She pulled her hand back like it was on fire and rolled away from me. I flipped over and said, "I knew you couldn't resist my manly body." Bree rolled her eyes at me and I continued, "Now, I believe the price for keeping molestation a secret from a certain crazy vampire was breakfast. I'll take a ham and cheese omelet, home fries, and a tall glass of orange juice…"

Bree groaned. "You can't be serious."

"That breakfast isn't going to cook itself, missy. Or maybe you think Liv will react well to me telling her about her best friend groping me and spending the entire night pressing her feminine charms up again me, trying to seduce me."

"That wasn't what happened…" she started to argue, but then Bree just sighed and nodded in defeat. She threw back the blankets and got out of bed.

With a grin, I added, "I'm going to take a nice hot shower to recover from this ordeal. I will be locking the bathroom door to prevent you from gawking at my naked form."

Bree just growled under her breath and flipped me the bird as she left the room.

After a nice long shower, I got dressed and joined Bree in the dining area of the suite.

Bree shook her head at the smug grin I had splashed across my face. "You're such a dick…"

"What? Is it wrong I'm enjoying being on the other side of the pervert equation for a change?"

Bree sighed and got up.

"Where are you going?" I asked.

"To put on a bra, as you are back on your normal side of the 'pervert equation' as you aptly put it."

Well, that had to be the shortest moral victory in history, I thought to myself as Bree disappeared back into the bedroom.

***

I arrived at Max's suite just past noon. He was on the couch by himself working away on a laptop. Stella, Blue, and Alteea were at the dining table and looked to be enjoying lunch together.

I headed over to Max. I fished out the bill I had in my pocket and handed it to him before I sat down.

"What's this?"

"Your tab from the Silver Tassel. Johnny asked me to give it to you."

He opened it and studied it for a brief second before folding it and placing it on the table.

"Where's Kurt?" I asked, as it was uncommon to find the big German not attached to Max's hip.

"Making the rounds of the security team."

"Do you have a minute to go over today's schedule?" I smiled and added, "Hopefully no strip clubs, brothels, or anything of that nature on it today…"

Max shook his head. "Fortunately, no. The only thing on today's menu is a seminar with some European buyers in the boardroom at three. After that, we'll be back here as I want to check over the numbers for tomorrow's big proposal and give everything one last look over."

This was the easiest day we'd had yet; maybe this morning's victory over Bree really was a good omen.

One day I would learn not to jinx myself with thoughts like that as not ten seconds after thinking that, Kurt stumbled in from the main suite entrance bloody and pale.

He was clutching his stomach and blood was seeping out from under his hand. He was also bleeding badly from what looked like a knife wound that started on the right side of his neck and went to his right shoulder. I was puzzled by the wounds—he was a Were, and even in human form, his healing should be better than this.

Max and I leapt to our feet and rushed over to him.

"Stella, get Marion on the phone and tell her to expect incoming," I yelled as I ran.

"Kurt, what happened?" asked Max as he reached the big guy.

"Rick attacked me. Sensed it coming because of the silver knife he used."

Silver would explain why the wounds weren't healing right. Rick was one of the guards and I wondered why he would attack Kurt.

The answer hit me like a hammer—it wasn't Rick; it could have been the Rose making their attempt for the contract. The Rose taking out Kurt so they could impersonate him made sense. In all the attacks the Rose made, they always took the form of someone the victim trusted. Max trusted no one more than Kurt. The more I thought about it the more it made sense. "It wasn't Rick; it was the Rose,"

Blue and Stella both perked up at that and I added, "Where did the Rose go after they attacked you?"

"It was Rick. His scent was a perfect match—the nose doesn't lie..." argued Kurt.

I shook my head. "The Rose is a shapechanger; they can mimic every physical trait of a person exactly, including scent."

Kurt winced and gave me a look of disbelief but said, "After he got me twice with the knife, I lashed out with a kick and knocked him back. He fled down the hall. I was down one level and took the stairs up here, worried this was the start of another attack on Max."

Stella appeared beside me, "Marion's waiting."

I nodded at her. "Blue, open a portal to Marion. Stella, take Kurt and Max there. Blue stay here."

I dashed for the door and crossed the hall to the suite we were using. After fumbling with my keycard to get the door open, I entered and yelled, "Bree!"

She popped her head out of the bedroom, a white bathrobe and towel around her head and asked, "What's up?"

I passed by her and started putting on my armor. While I did that, I brought her up to speed with what happened and added, "I need you to grab some towels. Go down where Kurt was attacked and clean up the mess and get rid of any evidence."

"Why?"

"Because if the hotel finds blood or a knife in the hallway, we are all out on our asses. Once you are done, join Blue in Max's suite," I said as I slipped my helmet on.

She nodded and I ran back to Max's suite. I was pleased that Blue already had her communication glasses on.

"Open a portal to outside the building, and I will fly around and try and spot the Rose's aura. Once Bree gets here, send her to Marion's and use the shadows to try and locate the Rose."

Blue made a small motion with her hand. She pointed at the shadows and said, "Portal's open, go!"

I stepped through the shadows and suddenly found myself in a freefall. Blue had opened the portal high up on the shady side of the Aloha. I called on my Air power and used it to put some wind under me to stop my rapid descent.

It would have been nice if Blue had mentioned the surprise drop to me before I stepped through, I thought, shaking my head. I kicked around giving her a lecture about it when this was done but realized she'd probably counter with something like 'A warrior going into battle should be prepared for any contingencies' or some other warrior-Zen type of crap.

I let it go and focused on finding the Rose. I knew their aura so if I saw an orange one with an alternating black and white pattern around it, I had them. The bad news was the Aloha was huge and there was a fair amount of people coming and going.

I did a lap around the hotel and confirmed there were three main ways out—the front entrance to the strip, the main drive-up entrance at the side, and the multistory parking lot at the back. I turned around and flew to the hotel beside the Aloha and landed on its roof. From there I had a direct view of the main entrance and a decent one of both the strip entrance and the parking lot exit.

I tried to recall what Rick looked like but realized it probably didn't matter as the Rose probably would take on another identity as soon as their attack on Kurt failed. It also dawned on me that Blue looking for the Rose via the shadows would be a waste of time if the Rose had changed their identity.

I activated the comms on the helmet. *"Blue?"*

"Here."

I told her my theory about the Rose being in a new identity while I continued scanning the crowds.

"I concur with your assessment. What should I do instead?"

"Use the shadows to monitor all exits from the hotel. Focus on anyone by themselves and contact me if you see someone acting suspicious."

"Roger that."

I doubted the Rose would do anything to draw attention to themselves. They hadn't remained free for all this time because they were an amateur. The reputation of the Rose also had me worrying I was missing something. The attack on Kurt seemed a bit sloppy. Though by the gash running from his neck to his shoulder, they'd only missed slitting his throat open and killing him by a split second. My paranoia was running into overdrive and I kicked around that maybe the attack on Kurt was a ruse.

I opened the comms again. *"Blue, if anyone shows up at the door to the suite, assume they are hostile and might be the Rose. When Bree gets there, draw your sword and keep her back. Make her change her hand to her panther claw to prove it is her. If I show up at the door, I will use my powers to prove it is me."*

"I fail to see how the panther claw proves it is Bree. A shapechanger would be able to change their hand to a panther claw."

"No. A shapechanger can take on someone's appearance but not their powers. They might be able to change their hand into a panther claw, but the process will look different from how Bree would do it," I said.

"Understood."

I realized that I would probably make Blue open a shadow portal as well to prove Blue was Blue. For a moment, I worried that Kurt might not have been Kurt and the wounds were a ruse but then remembered the aura around him was his and not the Rose's. This shapechanger stuff really made you do some crazy paranoid thinking.

I was worried about Kurt. Silver did nasty things to Weres and I hoped he wasn't too badly poisoned by it. I reassured myself that he was in Marion's care and she knew her stuff. At least Max was safe at Marion's, which was also one less thing to worry about. We had hours before his next meeting, so that wasn't an issue either.

I started doing some quick math in my head as I kept checking out the crowds below. It would probably take the Rose a couple of minutes to get to an elevator, another couple of minutes to ride it down, and probably five minutes to get out through the crowds in the casino. It probably took Kurt a couple of minutes to get to us, and in the time we'd got him to Marion's and I put on my armor and got out here was probably another five minutes. That meant that there was no way they'd already gotten out before I was here. That too was presuming that the Rose immediately left the Aloha with no delays. It was more likely they stopped and took on someone else's identity first and that had to add a few minutes at least.

It was another brutally hot day again in Vegas. Stella's cooling system for the suit was doing its job but it barely seemed to be keeping ahead of the heat. The unit was probably also going at full bore so it would be draining the batteries rapidly. If the batteries died, I'd be done in a couple of minutes as I'd be roasted alive in this suit. Stella mentioned that under optimum conditions, the batteries should hold out for four hours. That meant I probably had less than two under this intense heat. That should be more than enough time. If I didn't spot the Rose in the next fifteen minutes, they were probably gone.

My excitement grew as I spotted an aura coming out the main exit, but it quickly faded when I saw the purple core, which meant Were.

Minutes went by and I still hadn't gotten the slightest whiff of the Rose. With each passing second, I feared that the Rose had slipped by me and I debated whether I should start flying in widening circles from the Aloha in hopes of locating them.

I spotted a tan sedan that screamed rental car by its plain looks pulling out from the parking lot. A large group of people exiting the main entrance pulled my attention back there. Just as I turned my head back to the entrance, I swore I spotted a brief flash of orange aura out of the corner of my eye. I looked back to the sedan. It was driving away from me and heading towards the main strip. The angle completely blocked my view of the driver.

I started calling my Air power to me so I could fly after the car that was receding into the distance, but I hesitated. I questioned whether I had actually seen that flash of orange or not. If I left this position and went after it and was wrong, I'd be leaving both entrances unguarded and the Rose could get away.

As I stood there struggling whether to pursue the vehicle or not, my deceased mother's voice came rushing back to me, *No decision is worse than a bad decision.* I smiled at that. In the hero game, like bounty hunting, every second mattered. Mom always drove home that I needed to be decisive or people would die.

I leapt off the building and streaked after the car. This was the right play. I could catch the car in no time, confirm whether it was the Rose or not, and go from there. If it wasn't the Rose, I'd return to my post. The window for the Rose to slip out one of the entrances while I was gone was slim.

I arced my flight to the left of the car, as I wanted to get a side view of the driver without tipping them off to my presence. I smiled as the traffic lights ahead of them changed and the brake lights on the plain sedan lit up. I got closer but the sun was glaring off the driver's side window making it difficult to get a good view inside.

I went higher, hoping that the higher angle would cut down on the glare. My heartrate sped up as I spotted the Rose's aura. They were in the form of a middle-aged woman in a business outfit, which wasn't a bad choice as it would allow them to blend in easily with other businesspeople in town for conventions. But how would I get them out of the car? My lightning attack was useless as the rubber tires would ground the car. I could use my Air power under one side of the car to flip it once it was moving. The problem was the traffic was heavy down there and I'd risk injuring an innocent doing that. I decided that my best play was to tail the car and then pounce on the Rose once they got out of it.

I hovered at a forty-five degree angle above and behind the car. They wouldn't be able to spot me in their rearview at this angle and would be lucky to spot me in their side mirror. I planned on maintaining this height and distance as I pursued.

I opened the comms to Blue, "*I found the Rose. They are in a tan Ford sedan, disguised as a businesswoman. I plan on tailing it from the air and taking the Rose when they exit the vehicle.*"

"Roger that. Bree's back and we are at Marion's now."

"How's Kurt?"

"Marion's healed the wounds, but he is weak and delusional."

I cursed under my breath as that sounded like the silver poisoning was bad. The light changed and the Rose made a right onto Las Vegas Boulevard. I flew after the car and continued updating Blue on where we were heading.

Their current heading had them traveling south, which puzzled me. I figured they'd be trying to get out of town as quick as possible and that would mean McCarron airport, but that was north, and they were going in the opposite direction. I mentioned this to Blue.

"Hold on, we have a Google map of Las Vegas up now. If they turn right on Tropicana, they might be heading for the freeway which would be the quickest way to the airport."

"You're probably right. They are in the right-hand lane and have made no attempt to get over."

A minute later they were on Tropicana heading west. *"You were right."*

They didn't get over which also made it look like the airport via the freeway was the plan. Things were going great until about a hundred yards from the on-ramp when the car suddenly swung out to get past the traffic they were stuck behind and lurched forward. The Rose, once past the cars, threw the car right and gunned it onto the on-ramp.

I'd been spotted. I banked in the air and chased after my prey.

Chapter 23

Thursday, August 1

The Rose rocketed off the ramp onto the freeway doing Odin-only-knew what speed. They skipped over two lanes and barely missed taking out a minivan full of kids. The mom locked up her brakes and honked her displeasure.

I had no worries about losing the Rose as there was no way the sedan could get enough speed to ditch me. I also didn't have to contend with traffic either. The Rose though was trying their best to shake me. They continued accelerating as they weaved dangerously in and out of traffic. My biggest fear was them losing control and crashing into someone.

"Blue, I've been spotted. The Rose is on the freeway heading north at speed."

"Roger that."

The Rose went under a bridge and I lost sight of them for a couple of seconds, but once I cleared the bridge they were back in view.

Blue's voice came over the comms, *"I just spotted a tan car from the shadows when it passed under the Flamingo Road bridge."*

"I have no idea what the road is, but they did just pass under a bridge."

An SUV honked angrily as the Rose swerved by them, missing them by inches.

"Any idea on how you are going to stop them?"

With the speed they were doing, it would be super easy to use my Air power to flip them but that wasn't an option in this traffic. *"No clue. I guess it will be a race to see which one of us runs out of gas first…"*

"Okay, stay with them. We have a plan on how to stop them."

My gut churned at those words and I screamed, *"NO ANTI-TANK MISSILES!!!"*

"Roger that."

"Blue what is your plan?" I asked but got no response. I tried calling her name a few more times but she wasn't answering.

A police cruiser that was sitting at the side of the highway fired up its lights and siren and chased after the Rose. It hit me that this was the perfect solution. When the Rose failed to pull over, the LVPD officer would call in support and they would stop the car. Law Enforcement couldn't collect bounties, so all I had to do was wait until they stopped the car, then swoop in and tell them who it was behind the wheel and the bounty was ours.

I was ticked that I didn't think of this myself. On the other hand, at home I was usually the one bailing out local law enforcement due to some Enhanced on a rampage that they couldn't handle, so I wasn't used to the situation being reversed.

The only problem was I had a slightly bloodthirsty and way too aggressive blue alien who had a plan. I frantically tried the comms again but didn't get any response.

Way behind us another police car joined the chase.

A minute later, an LVPD helicopter came screaming in and got above the fleeing car. Thankfully, I was low enough that I was out of its flight path. I decided to be proactive and get in a claim before this chase came to an end.

"911—what's your emergency?"

I gave them my name, hero alias, and hero ID number and informed them that the tan Ford the officers and I were currently pursuing was being driven by the Rose who was wanted for multiple murders by the FBI, Interpol, and just about every law enforcement agency on the planet.

The operator had me stand by while she confirmed my details but did say she would pass the information along to the responding officers.

That relieved my one greatest worry—if the car hadn't been reported stolen and the chase got too dangerous, they'd call it off. If they knew a wanted murder was behind the wheel, there was no way they were stopping the pursuit. They would also commit more resources to it.

I groaned as I spotted Stella's Hyde form leaping from the shadows of one of the many huge billboards lining the sides of the freeway. Her jump was on target and she crashed down directly in the path of the oncoming tan sedan. On Stella's right was a semi and to her left, the center median. The Rose was trapped. I wanted to look away, as I had no idea if Stella's Hyde form could take the blow from a two-ton car traveling at that speed.

The Rose jerked the steering wheel hard left, probably trying to use the shoulder to get around Stella but they lost control of the vehicle. It caught air as it crashed into the barrier. I watched in horror as it flipped over the barrier and plowed into the side of an eighteen-wheeler hauling a fuel trailer in the southbound lane. It was like a giant fist had punched the side of the cylindrical trailer. The semi locked up its brakes and made a huge cloud of smoke as it laid thick dark lines of rubber along the tarmac.

Gallons of gas streamed out of the punctured trailer and I thickened the air around me as I dove for the cab of the truck. The second the truck came to a stop, the driver yanked open the door and leaped out of the cab. I pushed a cushion of air under him and scooped him up as I flew by.

We'd barely cleared the truck when an earth-shaking boom went off behind us. I redirected the thickened air to our tails and the concussion of the blast almost knocked me off course. It passed and I gained some altitude to avoid the bridge that was fast approaching. The driver was surprisingly calm, but I did catch a few lines of the Lord's Prayer hastily being mumbled beneath me.

I looped us back around and landed about 200 feet from the burning rig. The truck and car were both totally engulfed in flames and thick black smoke. I spotted a slightly disheveled and charred Hyde getting to her feet. She shook her head and grunted loudly but seemed to be alright.

After checking that the trucker was okay, I made my way over to her. Police cruisers screeched to a halt near us. I popped the panel on the armor to reveal my hero ID and said, "Change back and look cute and cuddly for the nice officers..."

A moment later, Stella asked in her crisp English accent, "Do you think there will be enough DNA left to make a bounty claim?"

By the intensity of the blaze, the authorities would be lucky to find a piece of the car, never mind a body. I shook my head and sighed as I realized I was probably watching $5 million going up in smoke.

"Look at the bright side..." said Stella with a small grin. I cocked an eyebrow, and she added, "At least there were no anti-tank missiles..."

Chapter 24

Thursday, August 1

The LVPD had plenty of questions for me due to the flaming crater in middle of the Las Vegas Expressway. Thankfully, my call to 911 made me a witness rather than a suspect. I went over what had happened from Kurt getting stabbed right up to the crash. They took Stella aside while I was doing this and had her go over everything that happened this afternoon.

While I was giving my statement off to the side of the highway, I occasionally glanced over to where the Las Vegas Fire Department battled the intense blaze. Each time I looked at the fire, it reminded me that there was $5 million worth of bounty going up in smoke. I was ticked that we missed out on the bounty, but at least the Rose's decade-plus career of murder-for-hire was finished. This also meant there was one less person out there gunning for Max.

Once they'd gotten our statements, they asked us to wait around while they compared our stories.

Stella tried to be optimistic about all of it. "We may get the bounty in time. If the Rose doesn't strike in the next year or so, they will have to conclude that this was the Rose that was killed here today."

I shook my head. "It doesn't work that way. The UN Bounty Commission will argue that maybe the Rose just retired or was keeping a low profile. The only way we get paid is with proof, and by the intensity of that fire, there is no way they are pulling any DNA from that."

Stella went quiet for a moment. "It is bloody hot out here."

I laughed. "You should have built a cooling system for yourself as I'm feeling quite comfortable at this moment." It also helped that we were in the shade from one the billboards at the side of the highway and not standing in the brutal sun. "At least you aren't one of those firefighters…"

I didn't even want to imagine how badly those poor bastards were suffering in full gear, standing near a raging inferno and out in the desert sun. The raging inferno was a bit of an exaggeration now, as they had gotten the fire under control and now it was more a smoldering wreck.

One of the officers came back and said, "The young lady is free to go, but we ask that you remain here in case we have more questions. Does she require one of us to give her a lift back to your hotel?"

I shook my head. "One of my teammates will be here shortly and will take her to the Aloha."

He nodded and went back to his patrol car, probably to get back in the AC.

I opened a channel to Blue and asked her to come get Stella. I didn't get a response and jumped out of my skin when Blue appeared out of thin air beside us.

"How's Kurt doing now?"

Blue's tail lowered a bit and she said, "He is still in rough shape, but he is now resting, and Marion feels his condition is improving."

I checked the time on my phone, and it was coming up on two o'clock. "Is Max still planning on having that meeting at three?" Blue nodded. "Stella can leave, but they want me to stay here, so it will be just you, Stella, Bree, and Alteea."

Blue shrugged, "We'll be able to handle anything that pops up. With the Rose dead, we've eliminated the only threat I was deeply concerned about."

"Okay, good luck."

Blue opened a portal and said, "Call us when you require a lift back."

I nodded and they left.

Five minutes later, two black SUVs with tinted windows and flashing lights in their grilles approached at high speed on the shoulder. They slid to a halt about fifty feet away and a bunch of suits got out— the FBI had arrived. One of the six agents had an aura around her that marked her as a mage. The presence of the mage meant that this was an FBI EIRT team.

The officer who had taken my statement approached them. The Feds held out their badges and then exchanged words with the cop. After a minute, he pointed to me and the four agents, including the mage, approached us. The two other agents continued questioning the cop.

I studied the guy leading the EIRT team as the four of them walked over. By the number of gray hairs around his temples, I guessed he was probably in his mid-forties. That seemed a bit old to be leading an EIRT team, but he was in good shape, and by the confident way he carried himself, I was willing to bet that the younger members of his team had to work to keep up with him.

The lead agent introduced himself as Agent Danvers and held out his ID. I glanced at it just long enough to see his first name was Gerry.

"How sure are you that it was the Rose in that crash, Mr. Stevens?" he asked with a wary look in his eyes.

His eyes also betrayed that he'd seen a lot of bad stuff in his life, which wasn't a total surprise if he'd been on an EIRT for as long as I suspected he'd been. By his alert demeanor and posture, I suspected that there might have been some military service in his background too.

"Call me Zack, and I'm one hundred percent sure."

A look of disbelief rolled across his face. "You do know the Rose is a shapeshifter?"

No shit was the first answer that came to my mind. I took a deep breath and decided to play this another way. "I am very much aware of that."

"So how can you be sure that was the Rose?"

I didn't like revealing my aura ability, but as I had to give it away to the FBI agent in Chicago, I had no doubt that it was in a file somewhere.

"The same way I know that the lady on your right is a mage. Her primary focus is Water and Ice magic, she is competent in Earth and Nature magic, might have enough Fire magic to maybe light a candle and just enough Air magic to blow out that same candle. Also, while she looks to be in her twenties, I'm guessing her real age is late thirties or early forties."

I smiled to myself at the surprised reactions on the agents' faces.

The mage commented first, "Almost dead-on but you were under on the age estimate. I turned forty-five last week. I'm Agent Maggie Cross, but everyone calls me Mags."

I gave her a smile and wink. "I'm not foolish enough to risk overestimating a lady's age."

The mage nodded and asked, "How did you know that?"

I explained about my ability to see auras. "If you check your records, you will see I tangled with the Rose in Chicago a month or so ago when they killed a federal judge. The Rose had a unique aura. The person in the car I was chasing with the assistance of the LVPD had that same aura."

Mags was about to ask another question when Stella suddenly appeared beside us out of the shadows. I jumped at her surprise appearance and a couple of the agents reached for their weapons but stopped when they saw what looked to be a ten-year-old girl. It always amused me that people took Stella's appearance at face value. I knew their reactions would be completely different if she'd popped out in her other form.

Stella had a huge grin on her face and carried a bloody towel. Before she could say anything, I said, "This is Stella. She is one of my teammates and is much older than her youthful appearance indicates. One of my other teammates is a shadow traveler and that is how she suddenly appeared here."

With the introduction out of way, I turned to Stella and asked, "Why are you back here and what's with the towel?"

"The towel isn't important, but what is inside is…" she paused as if to draw out the moment and then added, "A silver knife that was used by the Rose to attack Kurt. Bree recovered it and as it was silver, she didn't touch it and used the towel to pick it up."

My mind raced and I realized that the Rose's DNA might be on that knife. If the DNA was there, that proved that the Rose was here, and we had a bounty claim. Stella was about to open the towel to show the knife, so I hastily added, "Don't expose the knife." I turned to the FBI agents and asked, "Do you have an evidence bag?"

One of the agents ran back to the lead SUV and pulled out a large plastic bag from it and put on a pair of latex gloves. He returned and carefully took the towel from Stella and put it and the hidden knife in the bag and sealed it. He labeled the bag and returned it to the SUV.

Agent Danvers and Mags then had a bunch of questions for us. I tried to get them to let Stella go so she could return to the hotel to protect Max during his upcoming meeting with the European buyers, but they wouldn't go for it. I cursed to myself as this meant it was just Blue, Bree, and Alteea protecting Max and prayed the meeting went incident free. I tried to think positive thoughts, as Blue and Bree weren't pushovers and any assassin running into them was in for an unpleasant surprise.

At least Agent Danvers took us back to one of the SUVs and finished the interviews in the comfort of the vehicle's air conditioning.

It was after five when the agents were done questioning us. By that time, Blue had contacted me and said the meeting went fine and nothing happened with Max. The FBI also gave me a bounty claim number for the Rose. The claim was conditional on with the outcome of the testing that would be conducted on the knife. They did indicate that they'd run the tests as quickly as possible as they too wanted to confirm that the Rose was no longer a threat.

Chapter 25

Thursday, August 1

We were all in good spirits while we had a small celebration dinner in Max's suite that night. To everyone's relief, Marion had reported that the worst of Kurt's silver poisoning had passed, and he was resting comfortably. She wanted to keep him for a few more hours just to be sure. We planned on picking him up when Blue went back to the house to fetch Liv when the sun went down here.

The entire team, including me, were optimistic that the test on the knife for the Rose's DNA would come back positive. The $5 million bounty, plus the $2 million we'd get in less than twenty-four hours for protecting Max and the quarter million we'd already made for rescuing the families from the Binoa Cartel meant this was turning out to be a record earnings week for us.

It dawned on me that between the money I'd already earned, and my share of this latest windfall, I could invest the money and live quite comfortably for the rest of my days. That meant I had the financial resources to go back to being a hero full-time. I liked bounty hunting and loved being a part of this team, but there was a part of me that missed my old hero days. Knowing I had the financial means to do this gave me pause. I knew my departed mother would say I had a responsibility to use my powers to help people and nothing was more important than that.

As I sat there pondering the future, I glanced around the table at my teammates. Alteea was smiling and covered in icing sugar as she attacked the pastry in front of her. Bree was making happy noises as she devoured her three meals. Stella and Blue were engaged in conversation as they ate. Blue's tail made lazy circles behind her and Stella's young-looking face was carefree and beautiful. Could I leave them and go back to being a hero? I wasn't even considering Liv here, which made things even more difficult due to our on again/off again romantic relationship. I also knew they'd all continue bounty hunting without me. Due to their extended lifespans, all of them needed to make a lot more money to be able to live comfortably for the rest of their long lives. What if one of them got killed because I wasn't there with them, could I live with that? The answer to that question made me realize that I wasn't going anywhere anytime soon.

I smiled as a solution to my dilemma came to me. The hardest part about being a hero was supporting myself financially. I could use some of the money I made going forward to set up a foundation which would help heroes that were in that same situation. I could probably get a list of active heroes from EIRT and check them out. I could add those who were struggling financially to the fund. This would keep more heroes out on patrol and make the world a safer place. I made a mental note to do just that once this case was done.

I focused back on the next twenty-four hours and decided to be proactive. "Max, what is on the schedule for tomorrow?"

Max swallowed the mouthful of steak he was eating and said, "I have a one o'clock meeting in the boardroom tomorrow with a new group of clients. That's it, other than the six o'clock meeting with the Iraqi defense minister at his suite at the Flying Dutchman."

The Flying Dutchman was a nautical themed resort hotel down the street from us. While the name sounded cheesy, the hotel was one the highest rated and expensive hotels on the strip.

The hairs on the back of my neck went up at the mention of new clients. My first thought was these were assassins posing as clients to get a shot at Max. "I don't like the idea of you meeting with unfamiliar clients right now."

Max paused in lifting another piece of steak to his lips and said, "They are a newly formed PMC. All of them are former Black Horse employees. Dan referred them to me."

Dan was the CEO of Black Horse and he and Max had a long history. Max trusted Dan and if he referred them, and that they were ex-employees of his company, things must have ended on good terms. I still didn't like it. "How newly formed?"

Max shrugged, "Last month or so."

I felt better at that answer as the hit contract had been posted less than a week ago, so that meant it wasn't formed as a ruse to get a shot at Max. That didn't mean four million in cash wasn't something a newly formed PMC might be tempted by though.

We were so close to finishing this that I was probably just being overly paranoid. I wondered if this was what a beat cop who had one week to go before getting in his twenty-five years or a soldier who had one last patrol to go before his tour was done felt like.

I forced myself to relax, as we had things covered. For the big meeting at six tomorrow, Max had rented a room that was two doors down from the Minister's suite. We'd be able to shadow travel there, then walk not even a hundred feet, and Max could submit his proposal. At that point, the contract was over, and Max would be still alive, and we'd get paid and could go home. For tonight, Max was safe and secure in this suite. We'd have Kurt back in a couple of hours. The Rose was off the board. We could thoroughly sweep the boardroom beforehand, and Blue, Stella, Bree, Alteea, and I should be able to handle anything that came up during the meeting. I stopped worrying and just enjoyed my food.

***

Just after sunset, Blue was about to retrieve Liv and Kurt when Bree asked to go with her as she wanted to pick up another change of clothes from the house and Alteea wanted to go as well. Blue shrugged and opened a portal and the three of them disappeared.

That left Stella, Max, and I alone in the suite. The three of us were on the two couches. Max was pecking away at his laptop, and Stella was reading a murder mystery and yawning, and I was studying a lore manual on my phone.

Moments later, I was alerted by an odd sensation that got stronger with each passing second. There was a Fire elemental nearby and by how powerful the sensation was, the elemental was either one of the most powerful I'd ever run into or there was more than one.

I yelled, "Lincoln!" and grabbed Max and tossed him to the floor and thickened the air around us for protection.

Stella instantly transformed into her massive Hyde form. The couch groaned under the strain of the new weight.

The front door to the suite opened and the guard from outside entered. "Sir, we have reports of—"

A large *boom* cut off the rest and floor-to-ceiling windows exploded inwards as a huge fireball whooshed over our heads. An immense wave of heat passed over top of us, followed by a brief scream of pain and terror as the guard took the full brunt of the fireball and was engulfed. I was about to go help him, but one glance over towards him and it was obvious he was already dead.

Glass rained down all around us and flames erupted from the two adjoining bedrooms. I blinked in shock as I realized they'd hit all three rooms of the suite with fireballs at the same time. Screams came from below us, which meant they'd also attacked the suite under us. I wondered if they hit all nine suites. I prayed that wasn't the case, as nine suites being hit at once by three fireballs each meant there were twenty-seven Fire elementals out there—those weren't good odds. I doubted there were that many, but we were clearly outnumbered.

I kept the air thickened around us and readied my Electrical power to defend us. I lifted my head and looked out towards the strip. Streaks of flame lit up the night sky as Fire elemental after Fire elemental flew by.

"Max, we can't stay here. We need to go," I said as I shifted off him.

He had a dazed look on his face but nodded and started getting to his feet.

Stella's Hyde form was slightly charred, and the tip of her longer left braid was on fire. I pointed at it and asked, "You okay?"

She grunted, which I took to mean 'yes,' and she patted out the flames with her big misshapen hand.

A bright flare to my left caught my attention. A male surrounded by flames flew in and landed just in front of the missing window. Without hesitation, I sent a blast of lightning at him. A cry of agony came from within the flames and they instantly went out. He spasmed as the electricity coursed through his nude form. The man collapsed, fell back, and disappeared out into the night sky.

That was the one downside to Fire elementals—they needed to surround themselves with flame to heat the air around them to fly, and their clothing didn't survive the heat. I wondered what people would make of the naked corpse, but figured as this was Vegas it probably wasn't the weirdest thing the locals had seen this week.

"Time to go," I said as I grabbed Max.

We hadn't gone two steps when another Fire elemental popped out of the burning bedroom near us. I shot another blast of lightning and got a higher-pitched brief scream as the woman shook and collapsed.

Two down. Odin only knows how many more to go. I hustled Max towards the front door. Max stumbled as he caught sight of the burning corpse of his former guard, but I yanked him forward. He could grieve later if we survived. I too was upset at the loss, and it bugged me even more that I couldn't even remember the poor guard's name.

Alarms started going off all through the hotel and I smiled as sprinklers in the suite came to life. Water was good. The more of it the better, as that would put them at a disadvantage.

Another Fire elemental came out of the other bedroom and I tossed lightning his way. I cursed as he dove back into the bedroom and the light blue bolt arced over his head and missed. It did, however, give us enough time to reach the doors to the suite.

"Stella, block the door and don't let anyone through!" I yelled as we came out into the main hallway.

I spied the stairwell to our right and dashed for it. Max was about to charge through, but I jerked him back. I held up my hand to indicate he should wait and then carefully pulled the door open with my gauntleted hand.

"…they killed cousin Johnny," said a gruff voice with a Southern twang to it from the floor below.

"Let's get up there and burn them all!" replied an angry female voice with a similar accent.

The cousin part had me guessing that all these elementals were related. I realized that this must be a Fire elemental clan. I knew there were elemental clans out there from my mother's lectures, but I'd yet to run into one. The idea behind them was to create stronger elementals; if two people with the same power bred, there was a greater chance of their offspring gaining those powers. It also made learning to deal with your powers easier, as there were a ton of people who could help.

I quietly pulled the door closed and said, "New plan—Stella, delay them as much as you can. Max, run!"

Stella grunted and moved into the spot in front of the doorway to the stairs.

I pointed down the hallway and we started running. I hated leaving Stella behind but didn't have much choice. I had no doubt that she'd be able to take whoever was coming up the stairs. The problem was this put her back at Max's suite and that elemental I missed earlier would get at least one free shot at her.

The door to the next suite down the hall from Max's opened and another elemental in all his flaming glory appeared. I raised my hand and blasted him with lightning. He didn't even make a sound as he was blown off his feet and tumbled lifelessly back into the room. The dead elemental crashed back into another elemental who was right behind him and they both went down.

I cursed myself for using a bit too much juice there. With the number of elementals attacking us, I needed to use my power sparingly. From the lightning I'd already been tossing around, I was going to be on reserves soon if I wasn't careful.

An "*Oh sh—*" came from the end of the hall where we'd left Stella. An angry grunt cut off the rest of it. I glanced back and saw that Stella had lifted one of the men and tossed him hard back into the staircase and then charged in.

That was a smart plan on her part as now her back wouldn't be exposed. In the tight confines of the stairwell, all the advantages were Stella's.

A moment later, the elemental I'd missed came out of Max's suite. He turned towards me and raised his hands.

It was my turn for an 'Oh Shit' moment as I knew what was coming. I had two options: stay and fight or run. The problem with fighting is I had no one to watch my back. I could deflect the fireballs in front of me, but if another Fire elemental popped out behind me, we'd be dead.

Max had gotten ahead of me by a good six feet now, due to me dealing with the elemental and being in armor which was slowing me down. I jumped and called my Air power to me so I could fly. I shot forward and snatched up Max as I went by. Once I had him, I poured on the speed.

Thankfully, the hallway was clear, and I prayed it stayed that way; at this speed, if someone stepped out of their room at the wrong time, we'd all be in for a world of hurt.

I heard a loud *whoosh*, and things got much brighter behind us as the elemental tossed the fireball I'd been expecting. In the confines of the hallway, we had nowhere to hide. It would be a race between us and the fireball to the end of the hall.

Doors blurred by us as I kept pouring on the speed. I'd flown faster in my life, but in the tight confines of the hallway, it felt faster.

I didn't dare look back but started to sweat as I sensed it getting closer. The hallway junction was coming up which meant I needed to decide which way to go. A left took me to the elevators and beyond that another wing of this floor. A slight right took me to the opposite wing of this one. A hard right put us at the viewing balcony for the giant waterfall in the center of the hotel.

I ruled out the slight right, as I worried the fireball might deflect and continue after us. Or it might explode and the blast might engulf us. The elevators were out, as they'd be off due to the fire alarms, but I could head down that left wing to the end of it to reach another set of stairs. But that put us in another long hallway. I was betting that the Fire elemental was flying behind his fireball which meant I only had one option.

I tossed out a massive blast of air to my left as we reached the junction and gritted my teeth at the high force that racked us as we went sharply right. Max grunted and I felt every extra pound of it in my stomach, arms, and leg muscles. We just barely cleared the balcony to the viewing area and emerged over the open falls area. The air behind us lit up as the fireball streaked past not even a second later.

*That was too **damn** close.*

Max screamed as I dove. Due to our speed, I couldn't dive us sharply enough and we hit the main falls. The water pounded us like a sledgehammer, and I lost control of the flight. We split apart and began tumbling down to the watery abyss below.

Chapter 26

Thursday, August 1

Floors flashed by me as I desperately tried to figure out which way was up. I used my Air power to stop my spin and get my bearings.

Max screamed as he tumbled towards the pool of water beneath us and I pushed a blast of wind behind me to catch up to him. I grabbed him and then sent out a massive blast of air in front of us to slow us down.

I felt an odd tingle across my skin just before we hit the water. I found out later that was from going through a spell the hotel had installed to keep the mist and splash impacts of the waterfall contained to the pool area.

I'd slowed our descent enough that we only made a small splash as we entered the clear water. I let go of Max and he swam away from me. I went to swim after him, but the weight of my armor rapidly filling up with water was pulling me down.

Fear gripped me as with each stroke sideways, I was going farther down. Thankfully, oxygen was one of the two elements of water which meant I still could use my Air powers even under water. I stopped swimming and pointed my hands straight down and released a huge torrent of air from both hands. My descent slowed, then stopped and then I gradually started surfacing. I yanked open the face plate and sucked in air as I breached the surface of the pool.

I hovered just above the water but had to use a ton of air power to do it due to the extreme weight of my waterlogged suit. I took a deep breath and flipped myself upside down. Water streamed out of the opening around my face. Once it slowed to a trickle, I righted myself.

Max was at the side of the pool near the falls and was starting to climb out. I glanced up and streaking down towards Max was another fireball with the Fire elemental just behind it.

"Max, take a deep breath!" I yelled and sent a blast of air towards him.

He glanced up and his eyes became saucers as he spotted the fireball coming at him. The wall of air hit first and tossed him into the falls.

I smiled as Max rolled into the cavity behind the falls. He'd be safe there for now.

A moment later, the fireball impacted the area Max had been moments before. A huge cloud of steam obscured my view of Max, but I'd worry about him later.

The Fire elemental was closing in and tossed a string of small fireballs at me. I poured on the speed to go up and meet him. In aerial combat, altitude was life.

I went to thicken the air above me to protect myself from the strings of small fireballs raining down on me, but the moment I started to do that, my speed began dropping off dramatically—I was running out of juice.

I spiraled around the incoming fireballs as I continued rising to meet the Fire elemental. I frantically popped the small hatch on my left arm. I was relieved that no water came out of the compartment, which meant the Taser should still be good. That was confirmed when I slammed the red button and electricity from the built-in Taser coursed through my body. I moaned as the sweet juice rapidly recharged my dwindling power. The boost ended too soon for my liking, but it had been enough, and my speed increased.

The elemental stopped tossing fireballs just after I blew by him. He'd made a mistake by giving up the high ground, and by the way he abruptly stopped his descent, he must have realized this. That was the opening I needed. I looped back head-over-heels and extended my hand towards his prone almost-hovering form. A jagged light blue arc of lightning shot out from my hand and streaked towards him. He managed to dodge enough to avoid the full blast in the chest, but I'd clipped his leg and that was enough. The flames around him went out and he shook for a brief second before his eyes rolled up in his head and he passed out. His unconscious form began falling towards the pool of water below.

I watched him awkwardly hit the surface of the water less than five seconds later in a big splash. I winced in sympathy as that water would feel like concrete from the height he fell from. I expected him to float back up to the surface, but his body just stayed prone and lifeless at the bottom of the pool. The impact must have driven all the air from his lungs.

I took a second to assess things. The suit was noticeably warmer, and I realized that my untended swim in the pool must have shorted out Stella's cooling system. It also hit me that I needed to call for reinforcements. I tried my suit's comm system to call Blue to bring the cavalry and get Max out of here, but nothing happened. Whether the water shorted it too or it had been damaged sometime during the fight, it was now toast.

Max and I were on our own for now. There were still alarms going off throughout the hotel, and anytime now it should be swarming with law enforcement and rescue personnel, so hopefully this was just about over. I prayed it was as I'd used up some of the boost I got from the Taser and my powers were back to running dangerously low again.

I decreased the air under me and that allowed me to slowly descend to ground level. I was going to grab Max and get the heck out of here. If we could find a phone, I could call Blue and we'd be out of here and in the safety of the underground lab in London in seconds.

I stopped a few feet above the pool of water and faced towards Max. I gestured for him to come out, but he tilted his head up, and with a look of fear on his usually composed face, he pointed his arm almost vertically. My gut tightened as I looked up to see what had Max so worked up and mentally groaned at the sight of three more Fire elementals flying down towards us.

They were in a V formation with what I assumed was a male in the lead with another male back and to his left and a female mirroring him on the right. All three were encompassed in flame so it was hard to tell their true forms.

The leader stopped about twenty floors up and the two others followed his lead and hovered in a triangle beside him.

"DIE!" screamed the leader as he extended his hands and launched a fireball the size of a small sun at me.

This isn't good, I thought as I flew to the edge of the pool to avoid the attack. The three-on-one situation sucked and, worse, these ones knew what they were doing. They didn't surrender the high ground like the last guy did. I also didn't have a lot left in the tank to deal with them which meant I needed to make all my shots count. I still had the second Taser boost in my right arm but decided to keep that in reserve for now.

The two followers began raining down a stream of mini fireballs at me. I cursed to myself as these two had obviously worked together as he sent his stream left and she sent hers right. The leader, seeing that I'd avoided his first fireball, sent a larger one at me between the stream of minis. I couldn't afford using energy to shield the air above me to deflect them, so I just concentrated on flying around them.

I needed to get closer, and the leader was my first target as his bright red aura was easily double the size of his lackeys.

The first massive fireball hit the water below, and a huge cloud of steam rose from beneath me. Between that and the heat from the smaller ones I was dodging, it was starting to get quite toasty inside my suit. I was sweating buckets, and with every passing second, I pined over the loss of Stella's cooling system.

I barely managed to avoid a stream of mini fireballs that flashed by me and realized I needed to do something. The higher I got the shorter the range they had to hit me. I spied the downpour of water from the falls and I realized that was my ticket to solving all my problems—I could use the cavity behind it to stay safe.

I dodged around another fireball attack. I stopped trying to gain altitude and made a beeline for the water. A wall of fire rained down in front of me as the Fire elementals must have realized what I was trying to do. I turned slightly to the right and the moment they angled their shots in that direction, jerked hard left. They corrected but I had a window and poured on the speed.

I hit the water a split second before the flames would have had me. I instantly lost a good ten feet of altitude as the force of the waterfall slammed into me. I also had to push a blast of air in front of me to stop from plowing into the wall behind it. I glanced down. Max was looking up at me but seemed okay.

Fireballs hit the front of the falls but instantly disappeared into clouds of steam. The fog was so thick that the three Fire elementals were just bright blurs above me.

I hovered there, debating what to do. I could float down and hide with Max. Any Fire elemental coming through the falls would be vulnerable, as the water would extinguish their flames. It would also take them a few precious seconds to heat the air around them to dry off, at which point I could drop them with lightning. The problem was we'd be trapped. If they had other weapons on them, we'd be like fish in a barrel. I could thicken the air to protect us from that until my power gave out. The other problem was I didn't know how many more elementals were out there. Once they had us pinned down, they could all show up and rush us. Even if just the three of them came through at once, I'd drop one for sure, two maybe, but I probably wouldn't be able to take out the third in time.

I decided to take the fight to them. I pushed air under me and flew up behind the falls. The two lackeys kept trying to shoot fireballs at me, but the shield of water kept me safe. The leader must have said something, as they stopped firing a few seconds later. I needed to take down that lead elemental; he was just too competent an adversary.

As I reached the same height as they were, the leader began matching my altitude and his two groupies followed.

I climbed higher but they stayed with me. I only had eight more floors to go and I'd reach the crest of the falls. I needed to get out from behind the water to use my lightning attack, but the second I popped out of here the three of them would burn me to a crisp.

With four floors to go, inspiration struck me. I began building up most of my remaining power and prayed this worked.

One floor before I would have hit the top of the falls, I lashed out with a quick blast of hurricane force winds at the falls. The water pushed out like a wave in front of me and collided with all three elementals. Steam erupted all around them as the water extinguished them instantly. They screamed as their nude forms began to fall to the ground.

I flew out from behind the water and chased them down. I was betting they wouldn't be able to dry themselves off fast enough before they hit the water but if they did, I'd finish them off with lightning.

With five floors to go before impact, the leader flamed back to life. I didn't hesitate and lashed out with an arc of electricity. Unfortunately, he was just as quick and shot a fireball at me. He cried out as the electricity hit him but I didn't see the result as I jinked left to avoid his attack. It was my turn to scream as the fireball clipped my right arm. The instantly super-heated material of the suit melted into my flesh.

The agonizing pain caused me to lose control of my Air power and I dropped like a stone. Somehow in all of this I remembered that water was death. If I fell into the pool in this armor with a bad arm I would drown.

I lashed out and sent a blast of air out from my left arm. It pushed me back into the falls and I slammed into the back wall behind it. Stars flashed in my head and I was pretty sure I cracked a rib or two on impact. I dropped the last six feet to the ground and landed hard enough on my ass that it knocked the wind out of me, and I may have blacked out for a moment.

I came to with Max yelling my name.

I coughed and then let out a short yelp of pain as I tried to use my right arm to lift my helmet visor. The mangled arm felt like someone was running a cheese grater up and down it while pouring vinegar over it. I glanced down at it and wished I hadn't. The arm was a mix of melted armor and blackened, bloodied flesh.

"Zack, you okay?" asked Max as he hovered in front of me.

I gave him a weak nod and this time used my left arm to pop the front of my visor. I winced as the motion caused the messed-up ribs on that side of me to flare up.

"You sure?"

I was about to shrug, but with my injured ribs thought better of it. "Yeah… gimme a minute."

I wiggled my toes and was relieved that I was able to do that. I slowly moved my legs side to side, and they worked. I bent my knees a bit and they worked to, so everything from the waist down was okay. My entire right arm was toast and flared up every other second to let me know that. My left arm was functional, but moving it caused the ribs to be unhappy. I seemed to be breathing okay which was a plus. I doubted I'd be able to stand up without help, but I was alive, which was better than the three elementals I'd just dealt with could say.

Max held out his hand to help me to my feet. I really didn't want to even try to move but was worried there were more threats coming or that one of the three survived. I clenched my teeth and grabbed his hand with my left. I shifted my legs under me and gave him a nod.

He pulled and I screamed as I rose to my feet. Between the ribs and the arm, the pain was almost bad enough that I came close to blacking out again. Thankfully, between Max and the nice solid wall behind me I managed to stay on my feet.

I looked out from the falls and all three of the Fire elementals were floating face down and lifeless in the pool. I breathed a deep sigh of relief at that.

However, that relief disappeared as two more flaming Elementals flew out from above the falls.

Chapter 27

Thursday, August 1

"How many of these guys are there?" I asked in disbelief as the two newcomers streaked towards us.

I tried calling on my powers and there was barely enough there for me to blow a candle. I perked up as I remembered the other Taser, but a glance at my right arm where it was stored shattered that hope. The whole hatch was fused into one large blob and there was no way I would be able to access it.

Max looked up and asked, "What are we going to do?"

"Hope that law enforcement shows up in a timely manner?"

Max shot me a skeptical look. He was probably right. Their main priority would be evacuating the hotel and getting the mass of innocent people to safety. An EIRT team was probably on its way but it was anyone's guess how long it would be until they arrived.

Two large fireballs came towards us, but I almost ignored them—I knew they wouldn't make it through the falls.

"I have nothing left power-wise, so this is going to come down to a fist fight. If they come through the falls, they won't be able to access their powers for a few seconds, so that's when we hit them. You take the bigger one. Try and pushed him back into the falls and the pool; if they are in or under the water, they are just human..."

Max nodded and we both kept watching the Fire elementals get closer. The two fireballs hit, and a cloud of steam came up, blocking our view for a few moments.

My little speech to Max sounded better than reality. I was in no shape to fight—I was only standing because of the wall behind me. If they came in to get us, we were probably dead. I took solace in the fact that I had taken seven of the bastards down and if these two came for us, I would do my best to drown another one with me. I also felt better knowing none of my teammates were going down with me. Stella was probably fine, and the rest were safe at home.

When the steam cleared, I blinked in shock at the sight of a familiar crazy vampire with a sword and a Werepanther freefalling towards the pool. I spied a small rainbow aura hovering behind Liv's form. My gut churned in fear for them. Liv shouldn't be anywhere near a Fire elemental, as vampires and fire are a bad mix and yet she was diving right at them.

It probably only took them seconds to reach the hovering elementals, but it seemed like hours. I just kept praying that the Fire elementals didn't look up because if they did, Liv and Bree were dead.

Bree struck first and roared in pain as she drove her clawed feet hard into the back of the first elemental. By the way his head snapped back, I was pretty sure she'd broken his neck, which was confirmed a moment later when the flames around him went out. To my horror though, Bree's furry feet and legs were on fire from the contact.

Liv struck the other elemental and he erupted in a cloud of gore as her sword cut him in half vertically. Liv screamed and let go of her sword as the flames jumped to her, but then the weirdest thing happened; all the fire was sucked behind her.

I blinked in a stupor, trying to figure out what just happened and then spied the small rainbow aura behind her. Alteea's element was fire. She'd used her power to pull the flames to her and save Liv. That wonderful little pixie was getting every donut, candy, pie, or whatever sugary snack she wanted tonight.

Whatever joy I had at Liv being saved vanished as I turned my attention back to Bree. The fur on her upper body was now alight too. She hit the water with a huge splash which put out the flames, but I had no idea whether the impact had killed her or not. Liv hit the water a split second behind her.

I stepped closer to the waterfall and frantically watched the surface of the pool.

C'mon, c'mon, surface, please Odin let them surface! I thought as I kept waiting for them to breach the top of the water. Seconds ticked by and they still hadn't appeared.

Alteea's rainbow aura circled above the water, no doubt waiting for Liv and Bree.

I started worrying that they had drowned but then remembered Liv couldn't drown as vampires didn't need to breathe. That didn't soothe my fears about Bree though.

Max and I cheered as a black soggy furred head popped out of the water and roared in triumph. I winced as my cheering had aggravated my injured ribs but barely cared as Liv's smiling face also came to the surface. She said something to Bree, but I couldn't hear them over the rush of the waterfall. Bree shook her head and they both started swimming for the side of the pool.

"Should we join them?" asked Max.

I nodded but then frowned. I wanted to, but I didn't relish the thought of stepping under the falls again as my ribs and arm wouldn't be happy at the force of the water hitting them. If I slipped and fell into the pool, I was done for if my teammates didn't save me in time.

I jumped and yelped in pain as a familiar voice said, "I'd suggest you come this way…"

I gritted my teeth to deal with the pain but smiled as Blue pointed to the open shadow portal.

"What took you so long?" I asked with a grin.

"I sent Bree, Liv, and Alteea to assist you while I went to find Stella. Was their help not sufficient?"

"They did great. Is Stella okay?"

Blue nodded, "She is back at the lab with Kurt. He wanted to come fight, but I judged him not healthy enough to be useful. He didn't want to take my advice, so I had Stella detain him…"

Kurt would be seriously pissed at not being able to help Max. I worried that he might get mad enough to lose control of his beast. Stella's Hyde form would be impervious to any of his attacks, but the poor guy had been silver poisoned and changing would weaken him even more. "Max, go and see Kurt."

Without hesitation, Max entered the portal. I followed him and Blue was right behind me.

We arrived at the lab to find Kurt yelling what I guessed were obscenities in harsh German at Stella's Hyde form, which currently had him in a bearhug.

"Kurt!" yelled Max and the German Were instantly cut off his tirade.

Stella, sensing Kurt's sudden calmness, bent over and put him back on the floor and released her hold.

He rushed over to Max and started to say, "Max, I tried—"

Max held up a hand and said, "It's fine. I'm okay and you need to take it easy, my friend."

Seeing that everything was okay here, I turned to Blue and said, "Let's go get our Olympic diving team…"

By her puzzled look, I realized she had no idea what I was talking about and explained about Liv and Bree's recent dive off a forty-story balcony. I was hoping that Blue would have thought their little plan was risky and foolhardy, but as I continued to explain, her smile grew and her tail made big happy circular motions behind her, and I knew she approved. "Oh c'mon, you actually think their plan was a good one?"

"It worked. They weighed the risks and came up with a tactically sound plan."

"TACTICALLY SOUND? You are as insane as they are…" I stopped as my arm flared up in pain again and my cracked ribs also tried their best to compete with the arm. I realized we could debate this later. "Open a portal and let's go get them."

She nodded and studied the shadows for a moment, probably searching for Bree, Liv, and Alteea. After a few seconds, she made a gesture and opened a portal. I stepped through into an unfamiliar darkened hallway. I heard the hotel's alarms going off, so I knew we were back at the Aloha, but I wasn't sure where.

Blue popped out of the shadows and took the lead. I followed and we came out of the hallway into a deserted casino floor. The waterfall was about a hundred feet to our left. Blue and I got to it just as Liv and Bree were getting out of the tank of water.

Liv got out awkwardly, her right foot at an odd angle, and I assumed she must have busted it on impact with the water. Bree's usually thick furred form looked terrible as it was mostly bald and patchy and there were areas that looked painfully burned. I was mesmerized as I watched the surface of her skin shimmer and move as she healed right before my eyes—Were healing for the win!

Between the changing forms and extra healing, Bree would be hungry enough to eat a horse. Liv's ankle and any other damage would be healed when we got some blood into her. Marion should be able to fix my arm and ribs, though I wasn't looking forward to separating the fused armor from my flesh—that was going to truly suck. We were all alive and the bad guys were dead, so I'd take the win. "Let's go home."

"FBI! NOBODY MOVE!"

So much for going home, I thought as I spied the heavily armed EIRT team pointing more guns at us than I was comfortable with.

Chapter 28

Thursday, August 1

At least I had some luck as it was the same EIRT team that responded to the Rose incident. Agent Danvers recognized me too and asked, "Hostiles down?"

"I think so. Any of the ones we ran into we took down, but there were a lot of them, so there might be one or two around somewhere. Give me a minute and I can confirm if there are any left."

He lowered his pistol and said to his team, "Form up around them and stay alert for new threats."

Four of the agents took up positions in a square around us. They kept their guns out and up, constantly scanning for threats. I did note that they kept their fingers off the triggers—it was always nice dealing with professionals. Agent Danvers and Mags the mage both moved closer to us.

I turned to Blue and said, "Blue, use the shadows and search the hotel for more elementals or people that need assistance.

She cupped her hands in front of her to create a small shadow and went into a trance-like state as she gazed into the void.

Agent Danvers cocked an eyebrow at me, and I explained Blue's shadow abilities were useful for more than just transportation.

By the time I'd finished my explanation, Blue snapped out of her trance and said, "We are clear. There are some management and a couple of security guys in the hotel's main vault area. A couple of Aloha maintenance employees are smoking in the sub-basement unconcerned about the alarms. I didn't see a single Fire elemental. There are also many law enforcement personnel and firefighters entering the building. I only scanned the suites that were attacked and some of the nearby ones, but the majority of the rooms I didn't scan. I can do those too, but it will take some time."

Agent Danvers said, "Impressive, and I doubt they are hiding out in any of the rooms. We spotted a group of Fire elementals flying away from the building on the way in." He turned his attention to the four agents guarding our perimeter and ordered them to secure the suites that had been attacked.

They lowered their weapons and headed off.

Mags cocked a sly smile at me and said, "Between this and the tanker explosion, it seems if we need to find you, we just need to follow the smoke..."

I laughed and immediately regretted it as both my arm and ribs flared up.

"Sorry," she added, "You obviously need medical attention. We can call in a healer we have on retainer."

I was tempted to take her up on her offer but spotted Liv standing awkwardly on one leg due to her busted ankle, and Bree was pacing and growling softly which meant she was hungry, so I went with another plan. I also remembered Max and Kurt were back at the lab waiting for us.

I shook my head and turned to Stella, "Call Marion and see if she's available. If she is, ask if we can pick her up and take her to the lab."

A team of firefighters came up to us and asked Agent Danvers if the place was clear of hostiles and he nodded, and they headed for the stairs. I didn't envy them having to climb almost forty floors of stairs in full gear. It was also a waste of their time, as the hotel's own fire suppression systems had probably dealt with the fires.

Stella spoke up, interrupting my musings, "Marion is home and waiting for us to pick her up."

I asked Blue to open a portal, but Agent Danvers said, "I can't let you all go as we need a statement."

"Our client Max, who was a witness too, is back at our base with his bodyguard. If we go there, you can get his statement too."

Mags perked up at this and said, "I can go with them and get the statement."

Agent Danvers frowned. "How safe is this shadow travelling?"

"Safer than flying. Honestly, I can't count how many times my team and I have used the shadows and we've never had an issue. Blue also shadow-travels the English Vampire Court—if there was any risk, do you think Elizabeth would use them?"

He looked at Mags and asked, "You sure?"

She smiled and said, "I've always wanted to shadow travel and it is better than sifting through incinerated rooms looking for evidence."

Agent Danvers shook his head in resignation and waved us off. Blue led us back to the hallway we arrived in and opened a portal. Bree helped Liv through first and I spied a small rainbow aura dart in with them. Mags paused for a brief moment and then stepped into the shadows ahead of me. Stella and Blue came through behind us.

We came out into the underground lab and Mags just stood there gazing around in wonder. I'd been here so many times that I also forgot what an impressive piece of nineteenth-century engineering it really was. Just the shear amount of polished wood and brass alone made it amazing to look at, but add in the Tesla coils, the Food-O-Tron, the two tables filled with Stella's inventing stuff and that it was Odin-only-knew how far underground, and it was truly awe inspiring.

Kurt and Max were at a table with cast iron pans in front of them from the Food-O-Tron. Kurt's gaze instantly locked onto Mags as a possible threat.

"Max, Kurt, this is Agent Cross of the FBI. She needs to ask us some questions about our recent adventure."

Kurt's intensity level instantly lowered, and he went back to his food.

Bree and Liv had already made a beeline for the Food-O-Tron.

"We'll get Marion and be right back," said Stella and she and Blue disappeared into the shadows again.

I wandered over to the two arcing Tesla coils and pressed up against one. I sighed as I got some current running through me and began recharging my powers, but I longed to fly up between them and get some real juice flowing through me. Thankfully, in less than a minute, I had built up enough power to push some air under me and get me there. I moaned loudly as the bolts of electricity surged through me. It felt so good, I almost forgot about my messed-up arm and cracked ribs.

I got less than a couple of minutes in there before Marion called my name. I sighed and flew down to them. Marion's eyes locked on my arm.

I was about to shrug but remembered my messed-up arm and ribs. "Fire elemental got a piece of me…he got it worse than I did."

She shook her head at me and led me over to an empty table beside Max and Kurt. Blue and Stella followed us. Mags left us to it and joined Max and Kurt. She pulled out a small notepad and started asking Max questions.

Bree stomped by us still in her Were form growling under her breath. I spotted Liv happily draining the last of her pint mug of blood and was relieved to see her standing comfortably on both feet. Liv must have gotten first dibs on the Food-O-Tron, hence the angry Were. I assumed Bree waited until Liv was done, then set the machine to replicate some food and was going to her room to change back in private.

I almost screamed when Marion grabbed my arm to examine it but managed to tone it down to a short yelp.

"Zack, I have no idea how we are going to get this arm piece off," she said shaking her head at me.

Blue gave me a pointy-toothed filled grin and I knew I wasn't going to like what she was about to say.

"I believe I can be of assistance with that..." she said, pulling her Keetiyatomi blade from its sheath.

I realized she was planning to use her magically enhanced blade to cut it off from me. I truly hated that option, but it was probably the best one we had. Blue's skill with that sword was unmatched, and I knew she'd strike true and not go any deeper than she had to but that didn't mean I wasn't anxious for her to do this. I decided to stall. "How about we get the rest of the armor off me and Marion can start with my ribs first?"

Blue shrugged and tucked her sword away for the moment. Marion and I started taking off the armor. Stella wandered off.

In short order, and with only a bit of discomfort in the process, I was standing there in my shorts and T-shirt with only the mangled right arm piece of my armor still on. Marion went to work on healing my ribs.

Stella returned carrying what looked like an eight-inch piece of broom handle. I asked her about it and she just gave me a small smile and said, "You'll see."

Ten minutes later, my ribs tingled but no longer hurt as Marion had done her usual magic, which meant it was time to deal with the arm.

"Grab the edge of the table," said Blue as she pulled out her sword again.

I used my left arm to move my messed up right arm up and over. I was able to sort of grip the table with my right hand.

Marion waited until I was in position and moved closer. "I can numb the shoulder area and that should lessen the pain but that is the best I can do with the armor in the way."

She placed her hands on the exposed skin near the top of the armor and after a brief tingling sensation most of the arm went numb which was awesome, except I couldn't feel if I was gripping the table or not. I could see that it was but worried that on contact, it would slip off. "Marion, can you hold my hand in place?"

She moved over and placed her hands over mine.

"Do not move," stated Blue as I heard her sword ignite behind me.

"Wait!" yelled Stella. "Zack, open your mouth."

I gave her a puzzled look but did as she asked. Stella put the piece of broomstick along the corners of my mouth and said, "Bite down. It will stop you from accidentally biting off your tongue."

I was going to argue that it wasn't necessary, but the stern look on Stella's face ended that, and I bit down.

Liv blurred up and with an amused look on her face said, "Wow, Zack, we change out Blue's sword for a riding crop and you have some real *Fifty Shades of Grey* shit going on right now..."

Stella shushed her but Liv continued to giggle at my predicament.

A slight rush of air was followed by a quick *whoosh*, and I blinked in astonishment, as Blue had made her strike. It was clean and painless.

I was about to spit out the stick, but Marion shook her head at me and said, "That was the easy part, leave it in."

She took my arm and I looked away as I realized what she was about to do. Marion began peeling the armor back and then the pain came. The broom handle stuffed in my mouth was the only reason people back in Canada didn't hear my scream. Sweat broke out across my whole body as I tensed and tried not to move. I read about Dark Elves flaying their victims alive, but I never truly appreciated how barbaric and cruel that act truly was until that moment.

The mangled armor dropped to the floor with a wet clunk. I tried not to think about the more organic part of that noise, as that was from my flesh being around it.

I sighed in relief as a moment later Marion numbed my whole arm and then went about fixing it. I pointedly faced away from her—I didn't want to see how bad it was. I also took out the piece of wood from my mouth, which now had a definite set of teeth marks driven into it.

Bree came out of the hallway from her room in a pair of grey sweats. She blanched as she looked at me. "Damn, dude, that is gross."

Liv piped up and added, "Yeah, I've seen zombies with better looking arms."

It's the sympathy and kindness from my teammates that really keeps me going...not! I flipped them both the bird with my good hand. I probably should have been more annoyed with them, but if the situation were reversed, my humor would have kicked in and I probably would have made an inappropriate comment or two. Also, the fact that both of them leapt off a forty-story viewing balcony to save my ass drove home the fact they cared.

"You two, go away," Stella said firmly. "You're not helping."

They both mumbled apologies and wandered off to the Food-O-Tron. Out of the corner of my eye, I spied blood on the floor and my flesh-infused armor and wished I hadn't. My stomach lurched and I forced down the bile that rose from it.

I needed to think of something else and decided to review the whole encounter with the Fire elementals and whether there'd been anything we could have done better. I thought about the guard who'd been killed earlier.

"Max?" I asked without looking over at him.

"Yes?"

"What's the guard's name who was protecting the suite?"

"Doug. Doug Baker."

I nodded and repeated his name in my head to make sure I'd remember it. I had no doubt that Doug's flaming corpse would be another recurring cast member in my bad dreams. I recalled the screams below our suite and added the rest of Max's protection team to that list.

I staggered like I'd been hit, and my eyes welled up as I suddenly remembered the families we'd rescued from the cartel were staying in two of the suites. We saved them from being tortured by the Binoa Cartel and instead they all burned to death. Maybe they were worse off having been rescued by us.

"Zack? What is the matter?" asked Stella with concern.

I tried to speak but it took me a couple of tries before I could spit out, "The families from South America..."

Stella smiled and shook her head, which wasn't the reaction I'd been expecting. "They were moved to New York this morning. They're fine."

I exhaled deeply. "Thank Odin for that."

Stella nodded. "Max's New York branch was slammed with orders and begged Max to send them the guys from South America as soon as possible. The branch moved heaven and earth to secure them lodging out there and get them new identities. Sorry, we forgot to tell you that they'd been moved."

My right arm suddenly came back to life as pins and needles ran down its entire length.

"You're good to go but take it easy on that arm and get plenty of food and rest, okay?" said Marion.

I examined the arm which was now swathed in baby pink skin with not a single hair to be found. I knew from experience that my skin tone would return to its normal color in a few weeks. I moved it around and was pleased it was pain-free and functional.

I looked up to thank Marion for her healing and was caught off guard by how old she looked. Marion was in her early seventies but normally looked younger than that. The only time that wasn't true was times like now where she'd spent a ton of energy healing someone. Her age being reflected at me like this bothered me. We weren't related, but since my mother died, Marion was the closest thing I had to family. I shook those thoughts away and suggested we both visit the Food-O-Tron and get some nourishment.

She paused as if about to argue, probably due to eating at such a late hour, but gave me a small nod and we wandered over there together.

A few minutes later, we joined everyone at the table. Marion opted for tea and scones whereas I went with a heaping Philly cheesesteak and fries. I'd probably regret going with something so heavy this late at night but between the healing, the fight, and draining my powers, I was starving.

Max had covered most of what happened, but Mags peppered me with questions between bites to confirm his story. By the time I'd finished my meal, she had wrapped up her questions.

Stella asked, "As those elementals were taken down in the process of committing a crime, I'm assuming they are bounty applicable?"

Mags nodded. "Yes. As we don't yet know who they were, I don't know if they already had outstanding bounties on them, but between the murders, attempted murders, and arson, they will be assessed at a minimum of $25,000 each. According to my notes, your team took down twelve of them, so the initial claim will be for $300,000."

Marion smiled as she put down her tea and said, "If you made that much money tonight, I don't feel so bad about the bill I'm going to send you for the healing."

Mags' phone rang just after that. She answered it and didn't say much on her end of the conversation other than, "I'm fine… yes… interesting…I'm just wrapping up," and ended the call.

She turned her attention back to the table and said, "We have intel that the people involved in tonight's attack were a Fire elemental clan out of Arkansas. We've had interest in them for a while as there were rumors that they'd done contract hits like this in Mexico and Central America, but we were never able to pin it on them. We've had them under surveillance, and a large group of them were observed leaving their compound yesterday. The group managed to give the agent trailing them the slip and those who made it out alive haven't returned yet."

If the FBI hadn't moved on them, then that meant there wasn't an active bounty on them. Still, we made $300,000 which was good money. Another thought occurred to me and I asked, "How big is this clan?"

"Around thirty to thirty-five members."

Shit! That wasn't good. We'd killed twelve of them which meant there were still eighteen to twenty-three left. I doubted that they'd be stupid enough to hit us in Vegas again as the FBI, LVPD, and probably a whole bunch of other three letter agencies would be turning over every cactus in town to find them. This clan was probably made up of two or three families and they wouldn't appreciate the fact that we'd taken down twelve of their kin. I'd lay money that sometime in the future we'd have to deal with the rest of them. I didn't have Arkansas on my bucket list, so maybe if we just avoided that state, we'd be okay. That was a problem though for another day.

Mags turned to Max, "The Aloha wanted Agent Danvers to pass along that you are barred from their establishment and they won't be returning your security deposit."

Max shrugged, pulled out his phone and started making calls.

I had Blue take Mags back to the hotel and Marion back home. Stella left down the far hallway and came back with a plastic bag and started pitching the remains of my armor into it. I asked her what she was going to do with it, and she said she was going to put it in the disintegrator. I shook my head. "I need to send it to Grundy's to get it replaced under warranty."

"That armor smells terrible… please get rid of it!" moaned Bree, and Liv nodded firmly in agreement.

I sighed at sensitive Were and vampire noses and took the bag from Stella. I walked to the back of the room and opened the sealed walk-in freezer and put it in there for now which made them happy.

When I returned to the table, Max said, "I have booked us two suites at the Lucky 8 Casino and Resort. I also reserved one of their conference rooms for our one o'clock meeting tomorrow."

"Great, we can check in tomorrow morning. Tonight, you and Kurt are staying here."

Max looked like he wanted to argue but he glanced at Kurt's still-pale form and nodded. None of us were in any shape to have any more excitement this evening.

Max wasn't done though. "I also need to go home and get another laptop and some more clothes."

I shook my head. "Not happening. You have a price on your head. Your house is probably wired to explode the moment you step foot in it. There are probably snipers perched all around it and, with my luck, a whole host of drow or something equally unpleasant camped out in your basement, just waiting for you. Call your IT guy and have him ship a new laptop to the Lucky 8. Call Pierre and have him buy you a few new suits and ship them as well. For tonight, we have spare toothbrushes and whatever else you need."

Max started to argue that it'd be a quick trip, but Kurt cut him off with a sharp, "*Nein!*" and went back to his food.

Max sighed and dialed his phone. Blue returned and Stella got up from the table and announced she was off to bed, and Blue followed her. We wished them a good night.

I overheard part of Max's latest call and realized he was making sure the families of all the guards he'd lost tonight would be taken care of. Tonight's attack had been way too close and way too costly. We'd survived by the skin of our teeth, but unfortunately all seven of Max's bodyguards didn't. It hit me that the only guard besides Kurt who had survived the entire week was Brian, the guard Blue drove a steak-knife though to stop him from shooting Max. Due to his shooting hand being out of commission, Kurt had sent him back to New York and replaced him.

I was a bit surprised at how well Max was holding up. He took the deaths of his body double and the two guards the other night hard but tonight he barely seemed fazed by all that had happened. I wondered if he was purposely throwing himself into his work as a way of dealing with it. That might explain why he'd been so stubborn about going to the Lucky 8 and home to get another laptop and clothes. On the other hand, arms dealing was a dangerous business and he knew that. He'd only inherited his company once his uncle was murdered. He made a lot of money dealing arms but part of me wondered if down the road he'd feel it was all worth it. Thankfully, that was his problem and not mine. Mine was keeping him alive and we just had to do that for less than twenty-four hours and then we'd be done with all of this. I prayed tomorrow would be less eventful.

Chapter 29

Friday, August 2

I was up just after nine the next morning, which meant we just had to keep Max alive for nine more hours. I groaned to myself as I thought about all the things we had to do during that time.

On the upside, being at my room in the secret lab meant I didn't wake up with my hands on inappropriate places on a grumpy Were for a change, which made a nice change of pace.

After a quick shower, I joined everyone at the table. Bree and Alteea were both still sleeping and Liv was in her daytime death trance, so those three were the exception. I was pleased to see that Kurt looked much better and his normal color and vigor had returned.

We went over the day's itinerary during breakfast and soon were focused on the first hurdle of the day which was checking in.

"Stella, Blue, and I will visit the Lucky 8 first before you do, so we can scope out the place."

Kurt nodded. "I will join you too."

Max shrugged at that. "Should be pretty simple. The two suites I booked will allow us to check-in at VIP services and not the main desk."

Not being in the crowded main lobby would be a plus. Hopefully, the VIP check-in was in its own little room off from everything else. This trip had certainly been educational on how the other half lived. I always thought that the high-end suites at hotels were just bigger rooms that cost a crap ton of money. I wasn't wrong about that, but they also came with a ton of other perks like having their own check-in area, transportation to and from the airport, concierge services that could get you tickets or reservations to just about anywhere you want to see or go, private pool access, and a bunch of other nice amenities. I wasn't sure if those perks justified the extra cost or not, but they were handy.

It also dawned on me that we were probably part of that other half now with the money we'd already made this year. Heck, on this trip alone, if everything panned out, we would make north of seven million, though the money we got from Max wasn't tax-free like the bounties were, so maybe after tax it would be just under seven million. Either way, that was still a crap ton of money. I still planned on starting a foundation to support struggling heroes, but even doing that, I'd have a good chunk of money left over. After my hero days of living in a tiny roach-infested apartment and surviving off raman noodles most of the time, I wasn't sure if I could start staying in suites that cost the same for a night as I would have been lucky to make in a month back then.

Another part of me was tempted to live it up. If the fireball that messed up my arm had been another six inches over, I wouldn't have been around to collect a single penny of the money for this job. The job wasn't exactly low risk, and the chances that I'd live to a ripe old age where I'd die peacefully in my bed weren't good. So maybe living a bit for the now wouldn't be such a bad idea.

Stella pulled me from my musings by asking if I was ready to go. I nodded and five minutes later we were inside the Lucky 8.

As we came out of the darkened hallway and into the main lobby I was overwhelmed by the amount of people. The Aloha had been busy but not like this. To be fair, it was Friday and the start of the weekend, so it made sense that things were busier.

The Lucky 8 was impressive. It was obvious that red, black, and white were its main color theme. Something about this hotel called to me as it was elegant, airy, and well laid-out. Every fixture, decoration, and piece of furniture had been precisely placed. It was like someone had gone over every inch of the place and studied it thoroughly to maximize each item's impact. The hotel's Chinese-inspired décor was immaculate. China was never a place I'd had much interest in, but if this place was an accurate representation of the culture, then I seriously needed to change my opinion.

"Zack?" asked Stella, pulling me from my tourist routine.

"Sorry," I said, "Let's find the VIP check-in and do a quick run through of the place."

There were brochures in the main lobby, and we grabbed a couple for the hotel as they had a map of the place. The hotel was designed in a figure eight formation with two connected round towers. The main lobby where we were was dead center between the two towers. In the center of each of the towers were the casinos with restaurants, theaters, and shops around the outside. The second floor was more restaurants and shops. The VIP check-in was inside of the left tower.

The VIP check-in was much quieter than the rest of the place. It was divided up into two areas—the check-in desk and a small lounge that had complimentary coffee and pastries. There was a well-dressed man checking in with one of the clerks while his equally decked out wife sat with their two children in the lounge.

This was perfect as I highly doubted the husband and wife were an assassin team that brought their kids along on jobs. "Blue, use one of the attached bathrooms to get Max and bring him here now."

Blue nodded and headed for the restrooms at the back of the lounge area. Her old man disguise would make her exit from the men's room less odd when she returned with Max. Kurt followed her but stopped and waited at the entrance between the lounge and bathrooms.

"I miss the floral aromas of the Aloha, but this place seems even more upscale than the Aloha. It will be interesting to see what the suites are like," said Stella beside me.

Stella had pretty much summed up my own thoughts about the place perfectly, so I just nodded in response.

It was a little odd to be out in public without my armor and just in jeans and a T-shirt again. Which reminded me that I needed to get it to Grundy's to get fixed and made a mental note to do just that.

A minute later, Max and Blue came out of the bathroom and Kurt took his position on Max's right as the three of them walked over to the counter. Max handed over his credit card and a passport to the clerk and she started checking him in.

"What's the plan after this?" asked Stella.

I didn't like the idea of walking through the hotel and exposing Max, so I came up with a better plan. "Blue will take him back to the lab. Once she returns, the four of us will head up and check out the two suites. Once they are secure, Blue can get Max."

Stella nodded and Max, Kurt, and Blue had finished and were walking towards us. Max was carrying a box and I assumed it contained his replacement laptop. I was puzzled at how it had gotten here so fast and asked Max about it.

Max shrugged and said, "I had a private jet fly it and the suits out from New York."

I didn't know what to say to that. The way he casually said it made it seem like he had a burger delivered. We may have become well off financially from all the bounties, but Max was on a different level.

Shortly after that, Blue and Max disappeared into the bathroom together. Kurt wandered over and grabbed a coffee and a couple of pastries. We'd only had breakfast thirty minutes ago, but if living with Bree had taught me anything, it was that a Were will never pass up free food.

I grinned when a new rogue Were hunting strategy popped into my head. Rather than trying to track the Were down, we'd just rent a food truck, change the name to All-you-can-Eat Street Meat and wait for the Were to come to us.

Blue returned and the four of us headed up to the rooms. The hotel was forty-five stories, and we were on the forty-fourth floor of the right tower. Both suites were adjacent to each other. Kurt used the swipe card to enter the first one. As we entered the luxurious suite, Stella let out a soft "Wow" and I couldn't have agreed more. It was even more upscale than the suites at the Aloha. I probably would have spent more time admiring the leather furniture, the marble floors, and the décor but we were on a mission. "Search the suite, and once it is secure, Blue can get Max, and Stella and I will check out the other suite."

A few minutes later, we'd completed our search. Blue used the shadows, and I got the keycard to the other suite from Kurt.

Stella and I didn't find anything, well, other than that each of the two master bathrooms in the suite each had an inviting-looking hot tub, but that wasn't a security issue.

Max was already at the other suite when we returned. He was sitting in the living area with his new laptop and didn't even look up from it when we entered.

A minute later there was a knock at the door. This time Max did look up. "Those are probably my new suits…"

I nodded and thickened the air as a precaution before opening the door. Sure enough, there was a Lucky 8 employee with a flat wheeled dolly that had three suits hanging off its rail. They were all wrapped in a plastic with store tags still attached. He pushed it into the suite. I signed for them as Max gave the guy a twenty and sent him on his way.

Kurt came over, took the suits, and disappeared into one of the two bedrooms.

With Max settled in, I pulled out my phone and called Grundy's. I went over what had happened, and they said to bring the armor by and that it would all be covered under warranty and would take about a week to fix.

Twenty minutes later, I'd gone from Vegas to our London lab to fetch the armor to Grundy's in Toronto and back to Vegas. I don't think a day went by where I wasn't grateful for Blue's shadow traveling powers.

We had less than three hours before the meeting and I wanted to scope out the Lucky 8 and pay a visit to the Flying Dutchman hotel where the Iraqi defense minister was staying.

After checking out where the conference room was and the access points to it and the nearest exits, I hit the main casino level of the Lucky 8 and did a full walk around. The sheer grandeur of the place quickly had me gawking like a tourist. I really liked the Aloha, but this place was just that much nicer.

In case we need to vacate the hotel quickly without Blue's help, I decided to take a quick flight around outside of the hotel. I came out the strip-side entrance in the center of the hotel. Between the Lucky 8's entrance and the main strip, there were eight massive Chinese dragon statues standing upright with their mouths open to the sky. I knew from seeing them on the Internet that at night all eight would shoot huge flames into the night sky every five minutes or so. Though by the insane heat I was standing in, it felt like they were all breathing flames down at me right now.

Max had booked both suites until tomorrow and one of those was for us. I looked forward to seeing the dragons in all their glory this evening after the job was done.

I called on my power and I'm sure I surprised a few people when I suddenly shot off into the sky. I kept going until I was above the Lucky 8. The hotel was sandwiched between two other resort hotels. There were roads on either side of it that led from the main strip to the drive-up entrance at the back of the hotel. There was a large tunnel above that entrance that led to the pools behind the casino.

I figured out our possible exit routes and then my attention was pulled to the pool area. I envied all the people hanging out there and having a good time. There were actually three pools back there. A main one on the left and two smaller ones on the right. I knew the big one was for hotel guests and figured one of the two smaller ones was probably a private one for guests in the suites but was curious about the third one.

I flew lower and spotted a sign that read – Private, VIP Club Members only. I wasn't sure what that meant but guessed it must be for the super high rollers.

With the heat out here, the pools certainly seemed inviting and a part of me longed to be able to spend the day by the pool. I smiled as an idea came to mind. I glanced at my phone and figured I had enough time to pull this off and check out the other hotel before I needed to join the team to sweep the conference room.

Chapter 30

Friday, August 2

We'd finished securing the conference room and were just waiting for the former Black Horse employees to arrive. The room came up clean which I was expecting as the change of venue should have made it harder for anyone trying to cash in on the hit contract to find us.

The four members of Pegasus PMC arrived promptly at three. I was relieved that none of them had auras but that calm feeling disappeared almost instantly. All of them were in their late twenties or early thirties and in prime shape. Their suits each had the telltale bump of a concealed pistol in a shoulder holster. I'd gotten better in my time here about people carrying guns, but this group had my threat meter pinging off the scale. They were way too keyed up and alert for a business meeting. Each one of them was scoping out the room and they looked like they were ready to go into action at a moment's notice.

They shook hands with Kurt at the door and he led them over to the main table where Max and I were seated. I called on my Air power and thickened the air around us as a precaution. I was pleased that Blue, Stella, and Bree were all watching them like hawks from their positions around the room.

Max greeted them and shook each of their hands before they sat down around the table. Kurt took a seat to Max's left which put Max between us.

Even once they were seated, they continued scanning the room.

Max took his seat and just before he started his presentation, I jumped in and said, "Before this meeting gets started. My team and I are here as Max's protection due to a contract on his head. It has been a long week because of this, so forgive me if I'm extra cautious about his safety. If you have any thoughts about trying to collect on that contract, I'd strongly suggest you rethink that plan..." I paused and let some showy blue sparks drip from my hands and added, "If you try anything, I will fry all of you until you are smoldering ashes piled up in your designer shoes, understand?"

I got few raised eyebrows eyes at that, and I was pleased a bit of nervousness showed on a couple of their faces.

"Zack! These are my clients, and you are overstepping your role!" said Max, shaking his head.

The leader of the group grinned and said, "No worries, we've done protection details before and understand the stress Zack is under. I appreciate his warning." The smile left his eyes and his tone flattened.

Max shot me a look that displayed how unhappy he was about my comments, but he turned his attention back to the leader and said, "Thank you for your understanding, Jake. How about we get down to business then?"

Jake nodded, and Max started his pitch. I still felt something was off here and I gave each of my team members a pointed look. I was grateful that all of them seemed to be on the same page as each returned a small curt nod at my glance.

Two of the Pegasus members over the next ten minutes kept glancing nervously at their phones as Max continued his pitch. I wondered if they had another meeting after this one. Then I realized that perhaps they were checking their phones because they were expecting something to happen at a certain time.

Five minutes later, my suspicions were confirmed. Bree cocked her head like she was listening to something. She suddenly went tense and she yelled, "Lincoln!"

In the split second that followed, multiple things happened at once. All four members of Pegasus rapidly lowered their heads to the table and covered their ears. Kurt grabbed Max out of his chair and pulled him to the ground. Stella morphed into her Hyde form.

A loud sound pulled my attention to the main conference door, which collapsed inwards and fell off its hinges in a cloud of smoke. I cursed as a bright flash and the deafening boom of a flashbang grenade followed not even a second later, leaving me blind and my ears ringing. I dropped out of my chair and extended my Air shield around what I hoped was the three of us.

I frantically blinked my eyes, trying to clear the spots that impaired them. My hearing was messed up and I struggled to understand what the series of staccato pops were. My dazed mind finally figured out it was gunfire.

Being blind and mostly deaf while people were shooting at my team had my guts churning. I was tempted to lash out with a lightning attack but dismissed that as I was just as likely to fry Max or Blue by mistake. Ditto for a massive blast of air.

C'mon, c'mon, just let me see again! I thought as I continued to try and blink away the stars in my eyes.

A cry of pain echoed in the room over the continuing gunshots. The cry sounded male which at least meant it wasn't one of my teammates, but I worried that it might be Max.

An enraged growl came from nearby and I realized that Kurt had changed. I had mixed feelings about this. On the one side I was glad he was in Were form as it was stronger, faster, and able to soak up more damage than his human one. On the other hand, having a pissed off Werewolf inside the protective bubble of my Air shield made me more than a touch nervous as I had no idea of how in control Kurt was of his alter ego. If he attacked me, I was screwed as he was too close for me to defend myself.

The one piece of good news was my Air shield only prevented things from coming in and not out, so if he could focus his rage, it wouldn't stop him from going after the bad guys.

Another angry growl filled the room, and I smiled as I recognized it as Bree. My hearing was also getting better.

Warm fur brushed by me as Kurt shot off to deal with this attack. I felt around and found what I thought was a leg. I moved my hand around and found a smooth dress shoe which confirmed my leg theory.

"Max?" I asked.

"Yeah," he replied in a dazed tone.

"You okay?"

Another scream of pain filled the room before Max answered, "Think so."

Max's leg and shoe started showing up as a blurry dark outline in my vision and I took that as a good sign that my vision was returning. I crawled closer to Max which allowed me to shrink the size of the Air shield I had around us.

The next ten seconds or so was filled with more gunshots and cries of pain. So far, all the cries seemed to be masculine sounding, which as Max and I were hiding here, meant it was the attackers on the receiving end.

With every passing second, Max's prone form was becoming clearer and clearer and I smiled as I finally was able to mostly see again. I turned and noticed the plethora of bullets suspended in the air a few feet away that my Air shield had caught.

I blinked as a gore-covered arm suddenly joined the bullets floating in my Air shield. The arm wasn't attached to anyone. A nearby scream pulled my attention over to the side of the table where Bree and Kurt were tearing into the four members of Pegasus.

A body in tactical gear flew over them and I traced back its flight to Stella's Hyde form that was currently lumbering to the last attacker standing. He turned his assault rifle towards her and opened up. Stella roared and charged at him.

Before she reached him, an expression of shock and surprise flashed across his features as a flaming blade erupted from his chest and the rifle dropped from his lifeless hands. The sword disappeared back inside his chest and the attacker collapsed to the floor, revealing a grinning blue alien that had been standing behind him.

The room suddenly went quiet other than an alarm blaring off out in the hall. I got up and helped Max to his feet. I looked around at the carnage in the room with awe. There were bullet holes everywhere. Max's laptop now only had half a screen. The remaining half of the screen was splashed in blood.

Bree and Kurt faced each other and growled menacingly at one another. Kurt, though, lowered his brown furred head and Bree stopped growling. Both of them were covered in gore and the remains of the four Pegasus members around them looked like some sort of bloody modern art display. I tore my eyes from that as my stomach lurched.

I exhaled in relief that all my team members were in one piece and the threat to Max was over.

Chapter 31

Friday, August 2

I was grateful that I'd scoped out the hotel that the Iraqi defense minister was staying at beforehand, as we didn't wrap up with the LVPD until ten minutes before six which left us no time to recon the Flying Dutchman.

It would have taken longer, and we'd have missed the deadline to submit the proposal if it wasn't for the security at the Lucky 8. The conference room had a CCTV camera that had recorded most of the attack before it was hit by a stray round. That footage clearly showed that we were attacked and were just defending ourselves. Even with that, there were still eight bodies, and detectives had a ton of questions and paperwork for us.

The biggest surprise of the day was the attitude of the Lucky 8's management. I figured after the mess we'd made of their boardroom that we'd be out on our asses just like the Aloha. That also meant that the large sum of money I plunked down to secure a venue here for my after-mission surprise celebration was probably gone too. Rather than toss us out, they apologized and promised to comp the rooms we were staying in. They seemed to be distraught that their lax security had allowed four heavily armed individuals get on to the property and attack us. I was floored at this. Their attitude made much more sense when they asked Max and all of us to sign legal forms waiving them of all liability in this matter.

I was tempted to see if they'd waive the charges for my surprise celebration, but decided not to push our luck and just signed their forms without mentioning it.

Once we were finished with the police and hotel management, we used the shadows to return to Max's suite. We had just enough time to grab his printed proposal and our pixie, who had passed on attending our last meeting in favor of getting some more sleep. Blue opened a portal to the room Max had rented at the Flying Dutchman in advance for this purpose.

The room was just a standard room, but I was impressed that it still had plenty of open space and was tastefully decorated. I stopped admiring the room and focused back on the mission. "Alright people, we are in the home stretch now, let's finish this thing. Bree, take point, Max, Kurt, and I will follow you. Blue, Stella, Alteea, you three cover the rear. Stella, don't change unless something goes wrong or you spot a threat. Any questions?"

Bree nodded. "Yeah, where am I going?"

"Out the door and to your right. The Iraqi defense minister's suite is two doors down at the end of the hall."

I was almost giddy at the idea of this whole thing being over. Five more minutes and our job with Max was done. We'd have another two million in our account, and then it was time for my surprise party for the team. I could practically taste the cold beer I was going to have.

Bree reached for the door and I concentrated back on the mission. I called on my Air power and thickened the Air in front of her. We followed her out into the hall.

The two guards at the end of the hall wore suits and carried submachine guns and became alert at our appearance. The far one from us shifted his position so that he was beside the other guard but now facing towards us.

Max said, "We are here to see Minister—"

The guards, without warning, raised the guns and opened fire. Bullets hung suspended in front of Bree and Max as they were caught in my Air shield.

Bree and Kurt grabbed Max and yanked him behind me. The deep grunt behind me meant that Stella had changed forms, but I smiled as I knew that wouldn't be needed.

I extended my right hand towards the guards and let out a blast of chain lightning. The gunfire stopped as the two guards spasmed for a moment, then their eyes rolled up in their heads and they collapsed to the floor.

They were both still breathing as I'd purposely kept the power low enough just to knock them out. That had been a last second decision. I'd worried that the Minister wouldn't take it well that we'd killed two of his guards and Max's proposal would have been rejected. I assumed the guards had fired on us, hoping to collect the contract on Max. I doubted the Minister had anything to do with this.

I sensed Stella's massive Hyde presence behind me and said, "It's all over. Stella, change back."

A second later, Stella's crisp English accent asked, "Why would they be so bloody stupid as to attack us?"

I was about to remind her that money made people do stupid things when the door to the suite opened. A man in a tailored dark grey suit stepped out, and my knees instantly began to tremble. The aura around him had a silver core and the outer ring was four equal sections of red, yellow, blue, and brown. Silver core meant a member of the God class and four colors represented the four elements: fire, air, water, and earth. The aura also radiated out from his body by a good foot and half which meant this was one exceptionally powerful being.

Though I'd never seen this aura before, I knew from my lore reading what the creature was—a djinn, or as it was called in the west, a genie. Unlike what books and Hollywood portrayed, genies didn't grant three wishes and live in a lamp. They were demi-gods that had absolute control over the four elements. Basically, I was looking at a creature that was like the four most powerful elementals ever rolled into one body.

Normally, I loved meeting an Enhanced that I'd never seen before, but this was not one of those times. I had a few simple rules that have kept me alive through my hero and bounty hunter career and the number one rule on that list was to never mess with any member of the God class.

I swallowed in fear as he looked down and frowned at the sight of the two unconscious guards lying on the floor. His head shot up and turned in our direction. His eyes glowed red and he lifted his hand and sent massive blast of air towards us.

My Air shield disappeared almost instantly due the power of the assault. We were all picked up like ragdolls and tossed down the hall.

I crashed down and slid along the carpet which simultaneously knocked the wind out of me and gave me a matching set of carpet burns on both elbows. I heard groans behind me and took that as a good sign that at least some my team was still conscious.

A bright flare from the end of the hall caused me to lift my head and glance that way. The djinn was currently conjuring fire to his hands, and I was starting to measure my lifespan in seconds.

A high shrill familiar voice behind me cried, "FOR THE QUEEN!" and I blinked as Alteea darted over me and towards the djinn. A rapid sequence of thoughts poured into my mind. My first thought was if the djinn launched a fireball at her, Alteea wouldn't be hurt by it; in fact, she would probably get a boost from it. If the djinn switched to another element though, Alteea was dead. Which led to my final thought. If Alteea died, Liv would kill me, assuming of course the djinn didn't do it first.

A cry of pure fear came from the end of the hall. The djinn said one word in a language I wasn't familiar with, and the fire in his hands instantly disappeared. The djinn then dashed back into the suite and slammed the door hard behind him.

Holy shit! The djinn was scared of pixies.

That fear did make a certain amount of sense. Pixies all had elemental affinities which meant if you attacked them with fire, as an example, then at least a quarter of them would get a boost from it. They also worked together in the swarm, so the pixies that had the fire affinity would take the lead in the attack and shield the ones that didn't. If you took the elemental powers out of the equation, then it came down to a physical contest. The djinn would probably be able to swat a few of them down, but then the swarm would descend on him like a school of piranhas and tear him to pieces. It was odd though that he fled at one pixie, but when I thought about it, that too made sense—where there was one pixie, there were usually a lot more around. Alteea being solo with us was probably the lone exception to that rule.

"Come back and fight, you coward!" yelled Alteea as she pounded her tiny fists against the door.

"Alteea, get back here!" I said loudly as I got to my feet.

She darted back towards us with a proud smile on her cute little face. Tonight, after this was done, I was going supply her with all the sugar she could possibly eat.

Splinters exploded outwards from the suite as someone on the other side of it poured rounds into it. I let out a sigh of relief that I'd pulled Alteea back.

Alarms started going off throughout the hotel.

I turned and was pleased to see that everyone was getting to their feet. Bree and Kurt were both stripping off their clothes to change into their Were forms.

I started to tell both of them to stop, but I had to yell to be heard over the alarms. They both looked up at me half-naked with questioning looks. "Get dressed, this has all been a misunderstanding!"

Stella was in her Hyde form already, which was what I needed, and I added, "Stella, go kick open the door to the suite and then go inside, but do not attack anyone, okay?"

She nodded her wonderful, ugly mug at me and lumbered down the hall. I trailed after her and hoped I'd guessed the situation correctly. I was betting the two guards were acting on their own and not on the Minister's orders. The guards were probably hoping to kill Max, flee, and hide here in the US, and then collect the money and live happily ever after. The Minister was here to get bids on a $500 million arms deal. If he was looking to make some money, it would be easy for him to arrange a kickback from one of the bidders, and that bribe would certainly be more than four million.

Stella reached the doors, which were riddled with bullet holes, and effortlessly kicked them in. There had been a lull in the firing until that point, but as Stella charged through, the gunfire started back up. I knew the bullets wouldn't hurt Stella, but I prayed she was disciplined enough not to engage the shooters. I thickened the air in front of me and followed her into the suite.

As I stepped around Stella, the gunfire stopped as the distinctive clicks of magazines running dry filled the room. There were two guards with MP5 submachine guns who were frantically removing the spent mags and trying to reload. They were both standing in front of a set of couches. On the couches there was a distinguished older man with silver hair sitting and calmly watching all of this unfold. I blinked at his composure. I glanced around nervously looking for the djinn, but he wasn't anywhere to be seen.

I took advantage of the quiet and said, "Honorable Minister, we mean no harm, this has all been a misunderstanding. Your guards out front fired on us without warning, and we simply defended ourselves. They are both alive but unconscious. We are here with Max Schnell to submit his proposal."

More clicks filled the room as the two guards jammed in fresh magazines and raised their weapons. I sighed and started calling on my Electrical powers.

A split second before they fired, the Minister said something sharply in what I assumed was Arabic and both guards lowered their weapons slightly but held their fire.

"Minister Fakhri, greetings!" said Max as he stepped out in front of me with his hands raised. In his right hand was the printed proposal.

I scrambled to extend my Air shield to cover him as the guards turned their guns towards Max.

"Max! Good to see you my friend!" said Minister Fakhri.

Max surprised me by saying something in a long string of Arabic. Fakhri frowned and the two of them went back and forth in Arabic for a bit. Between the Japanese that he had spoken earlier in the week, and now Arabic, I was impressed at Max's worldliness.

In the end, the Minister nodded and turned his attention to the guards. He pointed to the hall and issued sharp commands in his native language. The guards nodded and lowered their weapons. The guards took a wide route around Stella and disappeared into the hall. I assumed to check on their unconscious companions.

Max, with Kurt now at his side, continued chatting with the Minister who seemed much more relaxed. Stella switched back to her human form which caused the Minister to pause in his conversation with Max.

Alarms were still ringing out throughout the hotel and it would only be a matter of time before the LVPD showed up to investigate the shots. I mentally sighed to myself as I figured we'd be spending the next few hours giving statements. As we were at the Flying Dutchman, and not the Lucky 8, at least that meant we wouldn't be getting kicked out of our hotel, and my after-mission surprise party would be delayed but would still happen.

I checked my phone and smiled when I saw that it was 6:03 p.m. We'd done it; we'd kept Max alive and completed the job. The hit contract expired three minutes ago, which meant that Max no longer had a price on his head.

The guards dragged in their two unconscious companions and zip-tied their hands together. By the look the Minister was giving the two would-be assassins, I almost pitied them as I had a feeling their lives were going to truly suck in the near future.

Max handed over his proposal and he and the Minister shook hands.

Max turned to us and said, "The Minister has agreed to handle the authorities. He and his men have diplomatic immunity. I have a reservation for dinner at seven that I don't want to miss, so if I could trouble Blue to open a portal back to my suite, we can all be on our way. The Minister would also like us gone so he can coax his genie out from his hiding spot in the bathroom."

I blinked at that and then smiled.

Blue opened a door to a powder room that was beside us and used the shadows there to open a portal. We all stepped through and popped out in Max's suite.

Max shook my hand and said, "Thank you and your team for your efforts this week. I will transfer the money to your account in the next few minutes."

"It's been, um, interesting. I'm glad it all worked out."

Max grinned and said, "If I happen to get another contract on me, I'll be giving you a call. There is another convention here next year..."

I wasn't sure what to say to that. I couldn't deny that this week had been extremely profitable, but I wasn't that keen on doing the whole bodyguard thing again and preferred to stick to bounties. Bounties were much more straightforward. "You have our number if you need our services again."

Max nodded. "If you or your team needs any military-grade weapons or hardware, I'll hook you up at a steeply discounted price."

My gut knotted up as Blue suddenly got a gleam in her purple eyes and her tail began rapidly moving in happy circles behind her. A vision of Blue riding on top of a battle tank with a missile launcher on her shoulder and a grin that displayed her shark-like teeth popped into my head. I rapidly shifted to put myself between her and Max. "Thanks for that offer, Max; we'll keep it in mind. You have that dinner appointment, so we won't keep you. Bye."

I aggressively herded my team out as they waved goodbye to Max and Kurt and breathed a deep sigh of relief as the door to the suite closed behind us.

Blue was about to say something, but Bree said, "We did it! Let's celebrate by hitting the all-you-can eat buffet downstairs."

I silently thanked Odin for Bree's endless appetite as Blue slumped her shoulders, knowing it was pointless to delay a Were from her food.

We had a few hours until the sun went down when Liv would be able to join us, which meant watching Bree put the 'all' in all-you-can-eat sounded like a great idea.

Epilogue

"**O**H MY GOD! This is all for us?" asked Liv as she excitedly looked around the moonlit VIP pool area.

I nodded. "It's all ours until dawn."

"Damn, Zack, this must have cost a fortune," said Bree as she looked around in awe.

I shrugged. "The cost doesn't matter. It has been a long week and we made a ton of cash; let's just enjoy ourselves, okay?"

Stella shook her head. "It's not fair that you are paying for this yourself. At least put it through the company."

"No. This is my gift to all of you…" I paused as I spotted Thelma, our pool hostess, walking back towards us with a plastic cooler in one hand and a similar sized box cradled in the other and added, "I also got most of you gifts for this evening."

Thelma entered our cabana and handed off the goodies to me. "Can I get anyone something to eat or drink?"

I shook my head and asked, "Thelma, could you give us a few minutes to get settled in?"

She nodded and left. I'd requested that our host or hostess be Enhanced so that Blue could drop her disguise, Alteea wouldn't have to keep her glamor up, and our hostess wouldn't get freaked out at Liv's superhuman speed or Bree's unending appetite. I'd been disappointed at not seeing an aura around Thelma when she greeted us. Thelma almost immediately relieved those concerns and explained that while she wasn't Enhanced, she'd been dating a Wererat for five years, her brother was married to an Earth elemental, and her mother taught cryptozoology at the University of Las Vegas. On hearing that, I had Blue and Alteea drop their disguises.

Seeing Blue in her true form, Thelma got a look of awe on her face and had said, "Wow! My mother would give her right arm to talk with you."

I was still amused at Blue's response—"I have no use for a human appendage, but if you provide me her contact information, I will arrange to visit her." Thankfully, Blue had given Thelma a big grin and a wink to show she was joking about the human appendage part.

I put the gifts down on the coffee table. I was impressed at how nice the cabana was. Out front there were loungers with cushions and towels on them. Inside the cabana there was a couch and comfy looking chair with a coffee table between them, a large screen TV that was playing CNN with the sound off, and a small fridge. The fridge had been stocked with a fresh fruit tray, bottled water, and sodas. On top of the fridge was an ice bucket with a bottle of Cristal chilling in it and champagne glasses placed beside it.

Liv was practically bouncing with excitement and eying the cooler and the box that had my gifts in them, so I decided to start with her gift first and opened the cooler. I pulled out the wine bottle from the ice-filled cooler it was resting in and handed it to Liv.

She studied it for a moment and then grinned, "You trying to get me drunk or something?"

"I know you swore off drow blood after draining Lilith but I thought you might want to cut loose tonight."

That drow blood had been stupid expensive, but there were very few things that made a vampire tipsy and I wanted to make sure Liv had a good time tonight. To acquire it, I'd bugged Max for the name of his supplier and had to pay a premium for it to get here in time.

I opened the box and pulled out two bottles with light green liquid inside and handed them to Bree.

She frowned as she read the label and said, "Absinthe, why do I need this?"

"Those bottles are almost 90 percent pure alcohol. I figured we'd see if we could overcome your Were tolerance to alcohol."

A small grin appeared on Bree's face and she said, "I'm sensing a theme here."

I fished around in the box and pulled out a miniature bottle of ice wine and handed it off to my favorite pixie, but Liv intercepted it. "You are not getting my little darling drunk!"

"Alteea is sixty-two years old and saved our asses this afternoon..." I argued.

Liv looked at Alteea who just grinned, and she reluctantly handed off the tiny bottle. I grabbed another package from the box and said,

"I have another gift for Alteea," I paused and put the package down on the coffee table. I cracked it open and displayed its contents.

Liv asked, "What is that?"

"That is eleven types of sugar from all over the world."

Alteea let out an excited squeal and her wings buzzed loudly as she divebombed the offered sweetness. She let out a moan as she sampled a couple of the sugars.

I smiled and grabbed the last item from the box. I handed Blue a polished dark wood box and she cocked a purple eyebrow at me. "I know alcohol is poisonous to you, but I remembered that tobacco is something your alien system can handle and has the same effect as alcohol does for us. Inside that box are a dozen premium cigars."

"You can smoke those outside the cabana," said Bree in a firm tone.

Blue just grinned and nodded. I realized that Bree's sensitive Were nose wouldn't be happy at the scent of cigar smoke, but Blue would be mindful of that.

I turned to Stella and said, "I didn't get you anything, but we do have a very nice bottle of champagne here that the two of us can drink..."

Stella nodded and Liv said, "Hold on, before this party gets started, Blue needs to take Bree and I home so we can get our bathing suits."

Blue opened a portal in the shadows beside the cabana. Liv and Bree disappeared and Blue asked, "Stella, do you wish to change too?"

Stella shook her head and Blue left.

I cracked open the bottle of Cristal and poured Stella and I each a glass. We clinked our glasses together and said "Cheers!" before tasting it.

Stella smiled after her sip and said, "This is lovely. All of this is a wonderful surprise, thank you."

"We earned it. I can also see why you and Blue love this town. The food and accommodations are amazing."

We grabbed a seat on the couch after that and sat quietly drinking our bubbly while watching Alteea happily sampling all her sugars.

A minute later, Thelma returned and frowned at the sight of Stella drinking. "I can't allow a minor to be drinking on hotel grounds."

"She is 127 years old..."

Thelma gave me a look of disbelief at that and I just sighed and said, "Stella, show the nice lady your other form."

Stella put her champagne flute on the table and stood up. Thelma gave out a small gasp of surprise as Stella's small form was replaced by much larger alternate one.

"My God, a Hyde! My mother would love to talk to you as well. I thought they all went extinct over a hundred years ago."

Stella's image returned to her normal human one and said, "Not quite all extinct."

"Are you really 127 years old?" Stella nodded. "Amazing. Please enjoy your champagne."

Thelma asked about food and drink and I ordered a couple of appetizer sampler platters. I was still stuffed from the buffet but figured Bree would happily take more food.

Thelma left us and a minute later, Blue, Bree and Liv returned. My jaw dropped as I checked out Bree and Liv who were now in swimsuits. Well, Bree was in a one-piece black swimsuit, Liv was wearing some small black triangles that were held together with string. I honestly didn't think it was possible to use less material in a swimsuit than what Liv had on.

"Damn, I thought I was the only one handing out gifts tonight..." I said as I continued admiring both of them.

Liv smiled at this and did a pirouette to show off her tiny bikini. Bree just rolled her eyes and walked past me.

All of us except for Alteea, who was still enjoying her sugar buffet on the coffee table, got settled on the loungers out front. Blue took the far one at the front on the left which put her downwind from Bree. Stella settled down with her glass of champagne on the lounger beside Blue. Bree took the one nearest the cabana and farthest from Blue, I took the one beside her and Liv took the one beside me and across from Blue.

I watched Blue open her box of cigars and get one out. She drew her Keetiyatomi blade, which had me concerned for a moment, until she used it to skillfully cut the tip off the cigar and then ignite the blade to light her cigar.

Just as she got an ember on the end of it and took a puff of it, Stella said, "I'll take one of those..."

Blue's purple eyes widened a bit in surprise, but she shrugged and handed the one she'd just started off to Stella. Seeing a ten-year-old-looking girl happily puffing on a cigar and downing a flute of champagne was an odd sight, but the happy grin on Stella's face made it all worthwhile.

Blue was unwrapping another cigar when a loud cough and a wheeze to my left caught my attention. I turned to see Bree looking at the bottle of absinthe like it was the devil's own brew.

"Jesus, Zack, next time just get me freaking rocket fuel instead; it would be less harsh than this stuff!" said Bree.

Liv laughed and said, "Don't be such a wuss… I'll chug mine if you chug yours."

I turned as Liv held up her bottle of drow blood in challenge at Bree. Bree sighed but gave a small nod.

"Wait!" I said, "How about a toast before that?"

I got nods all round and held up my glass. "To a job well done, and to the best teammates a guy could ask for!"

A chorus of "Cheers!" echoed around the pool and we all drank.

"By the Summer Queen! What is this nectar called?" asked Alteea as her wings beat excitedly.

"Ice wine."

"This has to be the greatest human beverage ever," she said as she took another sip.

"Go easy on that," warned Liv.

Bree laughed, "Says the crazy lady who is about to down a whole bottle of drow blood…"

Liv shrugged and giggled. "Let's do this!"

Bree and Liv nodded at each other and lifted their bottles. I watched in awe as they both started chugging back their drinks.

"Oh, I want to play too!" announced Alteea who started shotgunning her small bottle as well.

When in Rome… I thought and downed the rest of my glass of champagne.

I finished mine before they did as I had much less to drink. To my surprise, Stella waved her empty glass at me and looked longingly towards the cabana where the rest of the bottle was chilling on ice. I took the hint and got up to get it.

I'd just picked up the bottle when Liv announced, "Done!" in a triumphant tone. A moment later, Alteea also yelled, "Done!" which was followed by an extremely loud burp from her tiny form and then giggles erupted.

Bree gasped and rasped out, "Done!" which was followed by a plea for water. I grabbed a bottle from the fridge and tossed it to her.

As I came out of the cabana with the champagne bottle, Thelma arrived carrying a tray of appetizers. She was going to put it on the coffee table in the cabana, but Bree stopped her and liberated one of the two platters.

I topped up my glass and poured the rest of the bottle in Stella's glass. Thelma took the empty bottle from me and asked if I'd like another. Stella gave me a smile and nod, so I ordered one more.

I started to get a small buzz and decided that before I got too drunk, I wanted to go swimming. I stripped off my T-shirt and wandered over to Liv to see if she wanted to join me.

She was now lying back on the lounger with her eyes closed. "Do you mind, you are blocking my moonlight!" she said without opening her eyes.

I rolled my eyes at her. "I was going to go swimming; did you want to join me?"

She shook her head, "Nope. I'm going to lie here and work on my tan."

"Do you really think you can tan from moonlight?"

"Sure, why not. It feels just like sunlight on my skin when I used to be human. Besides, isn't moonlight just reflected sunlight? I'm so pale that I'm like the walking dead."

Bree snorted and said, "You are the walking dead..."

Liv just flipped her the bird but didn't open her eyes. I really wasn't sure if she could tan or not, but I smiled as a thought occurred to me. "Aren't you worried about tan lines?"

Liv's eyes flashed open, "Oh my god! I hadn't even thought about that."

She sat up, reached behind herself and undid her bikini top. A second later, the top was on the lounger beside her.

"Liv!" exclaimed Bree who shook her head disapprovingly at her now topless friend.

"What? He's seen them before..."

Liv started to reach for the ties on the sides of her bikini bottoms and Bree said, "Don't you dare!" Liv paused and looked over to Bree who was glaring at her. Bree added, "He doesn't care about your tan lines—he is just trying to get you naked!"

Liv sighed, shrugged, and laid back down still wearing the bottoms to her suit.

I turned to Bree and said with a smile, "Since topless seems to be the theme for the night…" and eyed her magnificent chest in her one-piece.

She threw her towel at me and said, "In your dreams!"

I just smiled and nodded in full agreement with her statement. "Anyone want to go swimming with me?"

Bree shook her head and went back to finishing off her food. I looked over at Stella and Blue.

Stella said, "Maybe later," and Blue nodded at this.

"I will," chimed a shrill voice buzzing beside me.

Alteea and I hit the pool together. I noticed on the walk over that her flight was a touch unsteady and realized my little pixie was starting to feel the ice wine. I forgot about that as I got into the pool. The water was warmer than I expected it to be. I wasn't sure if the pool was heated or it was just from being under the hot Vegas sun all day, but it felt great.

Alteea just flew to the center of the pool and stopped flapping her translucent wings. She laughed as she plunged towards the water. She made a small splash as she entered the pool. I swam towards her to make she sure was okay.

Her head popped up and giggled as she spat out some water. She flew out and then dived right back into the water again.

In the next five minutes, Alteea went from "I feel all tingly," to "Whoa," and giggles to "I feel dizzy," to "I'm not feeling so good" At that last comment, I carried her from the pool, and we made it to a nearby bush where my drunken pixie proceeded to toss her cookies.

"ZACK!" yelled Liv from over by the cabana.

I cursed vamp hearing and knew I was in trouble.

A moment later, Liv blurred over, but instead of stopping in front of me, she fell into me and we both went back into the pool with a splash.

I surfaced and Liv's head popped out of the water a second later. "You naughty man," slurred Liv, "you got me and my baby drunk!"

I was about to answer, when Alteea flew up from the bush, wiped her hand across her mouth and said, "That sure tasted better going down," and giggled.

Liv turned to Alteea and asked, "Are you okay, little one?"

Alteea bobbed her head and then frowned, "I think so. I'm going to lie down."

We watched her fly in a mostly straight line back to the cabana. "Let's make sure she's okay," I suggested.

Liv nodded and I followed her out of the pool. I'd like to think that I let her lead because I was being a gentleman, but as my eyes almost never left her shapely bum in that tiny thong bikini on the way back, I may have had other motivations.

By the time we made it back, Alteea was curled up asleep on a cushion on the couch in the cabana.

Liv seemed satisfied that Alteea was alright and suggested that we might as well go swimming again.

"We'll join you," announced Stella as she and Blue both snubbed out the small stubs of their cigars in the ashtray.

To my amusement, both of them were a touch unsteady getting to their feet. Blue moved to a darkened area to the side of the cabana and opened a shadow portal. She tugged off her boots and then tossed them into the portal. She untied the sheath to her Keetiyatomi blade, and it too went into the portal. A few daggers, a wire garrote, two throwing stars, and various other instruments of death also went into the shadows.

I turned at the sound of Bree's voice. "If everyone else is going swimming, I'm in too."

Bree's ice blue eyes went wide, and I traced back to where she was staring and my jaw dropped at Blue's fully nude form sauntering towards the pool with her tail happily swaying behind her.

Liv slapped me on the back of my head and said, "Stop checking out the naked blue alien!"

I shook my head and said, "It's not the nudity. This is the first time I've ever seen her unarmed."

Liv laughed. "Look closely at her braid…"

I shifted my sight to Blue's purple ponytail and smiled at the sight of the two throwing daggers weaved into it.

Blue dove gracefully into the pool. Stella half ran and half stumbled towards the pool, laughing the whole way. She leapt up and cannonballed into the pool.

Bree and Liv thought this was hilarious and I decided it was time for me to have my own fun. I called on my Air power and Bree's laughter abruptly cut off as they rose into the air.

"Zack!" yelled Bree as I floated them towards the pool as I walked behind them.

Liv just laughed at my antics.

I moved them out to the center of the pool, about six feet above the water and cut off the flow of air under them.

Bree screamed as she plunged into the pool and Liv just giggled. They both made two good-sized splashes as they hit the water.

I dove in after them and the night just got wilder after that...

***

I groaned as I cracked open my eyes the next morning. My head was pounding, and for a moment, I had no idea where I was. I realized I was inside an empty bathtub. I finally recognized that I was in one of our suite's bathrooms. I was wearing a cream-colored lampshade on my head, a black garter around my waist and a catcher's mitt on my left hand and nothing else. Alteea was passed out inside the mitt.

I closed my eyes and parts of last night started coming back to me. I winced at a few of the memories. The emu especially was one of those memories I'd sooner forget, and I hoped we returned the poor bird to wherever we got it from.

I carefully slipped my hand out of the baseball glove as not to disturb the sleeping pixie, and slowly got out of the tub to find some pants.

As I placed the lampshade on the counter and wrapped a towel around myself for modesty, I smiled. *What happens in Vegas, stays in Vegas.*

The End

Author's Note

I hope you are enjoying reading the Bounty series as much as I have enjoyed writing it. I would greatly appreciate your honest review from wherever you purchased this book.

If you are a fan of the series and want to keep up to date with news about the Bounty series, please visit my website at http://www.markusmatthews.com or my Facebook page at https://www.facebook.com/TheBountySeries/ or on Instagram at https://www.instagram.com/authormarkusmatthews/.

Also, if you want to give feedback or have questions, you can e-mail me at me@markusmatthews.com. I'd love to hear your thoughts.

Lastly, thank you for reading and supporting the series. I can't express how much that means to me.

\- Markus Matthews (November 2020)